COWBOY IN A KILT

KILTED HEARTS
BOOK ONE

KAIT NOLAN

TAKE THE LEAP PUBLISHING

ONE

"It always rains the day a good man dies."

Raleigh Beaumont felt a smile tug the corner of his mouth, because the weather was bone dry. They'd been in a drought for the past few weeks. "Mama used to say that. She'd also say not to speak ill of the dead."

"Your daddy was probably the only thing your mama and I really disagreed on." Charlotte Vasquez came to lean beside him on the split-rail fence bordering the north pasture, propping one booted foot up as they both looked out over the rolling hills of the East Texas ranch that had been in his family for generations. "Luther Beaumont was a bastard, and we both know it."

"You're not wrong." One corner of his mouth quirking, Raleigh glanced down at the tiny Latina woman, who barely came to the top of his shoulder.

When Raleigh's mama, Lily, had been diagnosed with stage-four cancer, it had been Charlotte who'd taken a leave of absence from her job as a high-powered executive and moved in to care for her—and by extension, Raleigh. His daddy hadn't stuck around to watch Lily's decline as illness stole her vitality and vivacious-ness, leaving her only a shell of the woman she'd once been. Luther had thrown himself into keeping the ranch running smoothly. At the time, Raleigh had convinced himself his father was only outrunning the inevitable grief. That he was protecting the legacy he'd married into.

He'd learned better since.

"I mean, come on," Charlotte continued. "He moves that little hussy—" Said hussy being Twila, Luther's second wife, who was a bare seven years older than Raleigh himself. "—into the house when your mama's barely been six months in the ground? She only married him for his money, and he married her for the trophy." Her tone rang with bitter judgment, though it had been nearly fifteen years.

Raleigh stretched an arm across her shoulders, tugging her in for a hug. In the wake of Lily's death, Charlotte had convinced Luther to let her stay on as housekeeper, so she'd be around as a mother-figure to Raleigh because, God knew, Twila didn't have a maternal bone in her body. Back then, he hadn't understood what she'd given up for him, but at sixteen, that link to the mother he hadn't wanted to forget had saved Raleigh. And though he was well grown now, somehow, Charlotte had never left. He'd once asked her why, and she'd told him that losing his mother like that had shown her there were far more important things in life than breaking her back to climb a corporate ladder, and until she found another of them, she was staying planted near him.

"You didn't have to be here today. I'm a big boy. I can handle the reading of the will."

She squeezed him back, her head only coming to his shoulder. "Of course, I did. You need somebody here who's an ally."

They both turned to see a black Ford F-150 pulling up in the circular drive in front of the house.

"Looks like you weren't the only one with that idea," Raleigh murmured.

A familiar lanky figure climbed out of the truck and headed in their direction. Ezekiel Shaw was one of Raleigh's oldest and best friends. The one who'd as often been the instigator of mischief as the one to help him out of it.

Charlotte shot him a knowing smile. "Hey, Trouble."

Zeke grinned and pulled her in for a hug of his own. "Hey, Charlotte. When you gonna run away from this place and marry me?"

"I can't marry you. Who'd be around to keep this one on the straight and narrow once he takes over the ranch?"

He clutched his chest in dramatic fashion. "Breakin' my heart, woman."

"Somehow, I think you'll survive." But a twinkle in her rich chocolate eyes softened the dry retort.

Turning to Raleigh, Zeke hauled him in for a back-thumping hug. "You holding up?"

"Ready to get this show on the road. What're you doing out here?"

Zeke pulled a flask out of his pocket and offered it. "Figured I'd be around for moral support, just in case."

Raleigh waved away what he knew would be bourbon. "You think things won't go well with the reading of the will?"

He shrugged. "Got no reason to think one way or the other. I just know you and Twila don't exactly get on."

"She'll be out of my life soon enough." And thank God for it. Raleigh was itching to truly take over the reins and begin implementing the plans for diversification and modernization that his father had rejected.

"From your mouth to God's ear," Charlotte muttered.

A whistle sounded behind them.

Hamp Browning, the family attorney, waved from the front porch. "Come on! It's time."

They strode toward the house, where Zeke dropped into one of the rocking chairs on the porch. "We'll see you on the other side."

Charlotte squeezed his shoulder once. "We'll be right out here."

Raleigh followed Hamp back to Luther's study. Kitted out in lots of wood and leather, the room still smelled of his daddy and the cigar he habitually allowed himself at the end of the day. He could just imagine the old man leaned back in the chair behind the massive desk set in front of the picture window that framed their spread. But it wasn't his seat anymore. After today, it would be Raleigh's.

Twila sat in one of the two chairs in front of the desk, looking like she'd come dressed for a board meeting instead of the reading of a will at home. She'd never fit in around here, with her city airs and high-heeled shoes. He didn't think he'd ever even seen her on a horse, and the only time she'd come out to the barn was to track down her husband. God forbid she risk stepping in something in her Feragucci shoes. Raleigh figured she'd be lighting out of here almost as soon as the reading was over. Back to Dallas, to her high-society friends.

He lowered himself into the other chair as Hamp circled around to the opposite side of the desk. The old man sat with a creak of springs and leather, running a hand down the tie that fell to the paunch overhanging his belt, then back up to smooth his big walrus mustache. Not for the first time, Raleigh thought he wouldn't look out of place as an extra in a western. Maybe in a leather vest at a poker table or behind the bar in an old saloon. The thought of it had his lips twitching into a smile. His mama would've appreciated the image. She had loved her westerns.

On a sigh, Hamp opened the folder he'd placed on the blotter. "Let's get to it, shall we?"

As the lawyer fell into the drone of legalese, reading the last will and testament of Luther Alexander Beaumont, Raleigh's gaze strayed past him to the window. Just a little while longer, then he'd finally be free to speak to the hands and their families, giving them the reassurance that nothing would change. They wouldn't lose their homes or jobs. His mind shifted to what needed to be his first orders of action. He'd had plenty of time to consider that, but he had to think about the season and what expenses the ranch would have coming up.

Abruptly, Raleigh realized Hamp and Twila were staring at him.

"I'm sorry. I zoned out there for a minute. Can you break it down into layman's terms?"

Hamp glanced at Twila, then back at him, his expression apologetic.

What the hell had he missed? Fighting not to curl his hands around the arms of the chair as a bad feeling set up like Quikrete in his gut, he waved at Hamp. "Go ahead; spit it out. I don't care about the money. I just want the ranch."

The old man winced. "Your father left everything to Twila."

That couldn't be right.

Shock was the only thing that kept his voice level. "I'm sorry. What?"

"All of it. He changed his will a few years ago. The stock, the land, the house. It all belongs to her now."

Raleigh exploded up, sending his chair skidding several feet back as he rounded on his father's wife. "This is fucking bullshit. This is my birthright. My mother's family's land. You have no right to it whatsoever. You don't want this place. You have no interest in running a ranch."

Unperturbed, she lifted her chin, somehow managing to look down her nose at him from where she stayed seated, her long legs crossed neatly in the slim pencil skirt. "You're right. I don't. Which is why I've already made arrangements to sell it."

The blood drained out of Raleigh's head. "Sell it? To who?"

She named a developer who'd been sniffing around for years with designs on turning their several thousand acres into cookie-cutter suburban houses.

As he let loose a string of profanity and began to pace, Twila examined her manicured nails. "You're welcome to try to beat the price." The figure she quoted was stratospheres above what Raleigh could afford.

When he said nothing, she flashed a smug little smile. "That's what I thought." She turned back to Hamp. "If that's all?"

At his short nod, she picked up her designer purse. "You have a week to clear out." Then she strode out of the room without a backward glance.

Raleigh scrubbed a hand over his head. "This can't be happening."

Hamp shoved up from the chair, looking about ten years older than he had when he'd sat down. "I'm sorry, son. There's nothing we can do."

"Can I take her to court? Contest the will?"

"You can try. But in my professional opinion, it's going to cost you more than you've got, and you're not going to come away with a ranch in the end. Luther was in his right mind when he changed his will. The bastard screwed you right and proper. There's no two ways about it."

The sucker punch of it had Raleigh swaying on his feet in a way the loss of his father had not. It threw him back to the devastation of his mother's death. He'd promised her he'd take care of the ranch. Take care of the people who worked there. Carry on their family legacy. And all of it had just been ripped away.

He didn't even remember leaving the room, not until he almost ran over Charlotte.

"Honey, what happened?"

Raleigh just shook his head and kept going. He needed out of the house, into the hot, humid air.

As soon as he hit the front porch, Zeke pushed up from the rocking chair he'd commandeered. "What the hell happened?"

"I got fucked, that's what happened. The old man left her everything. All of it. The entire ranch. My *mother's ranch.* She's selling it to fucking developers. It's gonna be a goddamn neighborhood here next year. My home is liable to be bulldozed or turned into some kind of clubhouse. Not to mention what the hell happens to all the hands and their families." Heart sinking, he scrubbed both hands over his face. "I promised them I'd look out for them, and there's not a damned thing I can do about it. She gave me a fucking week to get out."

His gaze caught on Charlotte's face. Her expression had turned carefully neutral, but she'd lost all color. He realized he wasn't the only one out of a home.

"Fuuuuuck." Zeke drew the word out. "Man, I'm sorry. I don't even know what to tell you. I mean, I could—"

Raleigh held up a hand, knowing what he was about to suggest. "Not an option. Thank you, but no."

"Alright. Well, in that case, I'm thinking the best option is gonna be for you to get the hell out of town before you do something you're gonna regret."

Raleigh had no idea what he might do if he stayed and wasn't much inclined to risk ending up behind bars. And yet. "I can't just leave. I need to break the news to the hands. Do what I can to help them find other placements. And I should pull together the family momentos before that bitch tosses them all." The idea of losing anything else of his family history made Raleigh sick.

"I've already done a lot of that, setting things aside for you over the years," Charlotte assured him. "It won't take long to pull together the rest. We should probably hurry before that harpy gets it in her head you don't have a right to them."

Zeke pulled out his phone. "I'll make the arrangements for boxes and storage."

As his friend stepped away, Raleigh took Charlotte by the shoulders. "I don't know where I'm gonna land with all this, but wherever it is, you'll have a place there. Always. You're family."

She cupped his cheek. "You're a good boy, Raleigh, and you grew into a fine man. Your mama would be proud. Now, let's go get to work."

———

"Maybe no one will notice."

Kyla MacKean briefly shot her brother some side eye. "Aye. Right. No one will notice the six-foot-wide chunk of plaster that's crumbled off the wall." The remains of that plaster lay in a heap on the scarred hardwood floors she'd only just waxed and polished for the wedding reception set to be held here in a matter of days.

Connor shrugged with his usual insouciance. "It's a six-hundred-year-old castle. We'll say it's part of the ambiance."

"Be serious, Con. This is important. We can't afford for anything else to go wrong. Too much is riding on this weekend."

The reality of living in a centuries-old castle in the Highlands of Scotland was nowhere near as romantic as books and movies made it out to be. It was cold, drafty, and often wet. Parts of the castle were fully uninhabitable. The estimates they'd received from various contractors for truly weatherproofing the place were astronomical. Every single problem they discovered was usually a sign of a bigger, deeper issue that called for bigger, deeper pockets than they had. The truth was, they were land rich and house poor, and without a massive influx of cash, the home they both loved would fall to ruin. And while Scots did love their ruins, Kyla wasn't keen on living in one.

She had a plan. One that involved using her brother's wedding as an opportunity to show the world that Ardinmuir could be a premier wedding destination. People paid big money for that sort of thing. But not if the bloody walls of the great hall were falling down around their ears.

"Dinna fash yourself. It's stood for this long. It's no' gonna crash onto our heads this weekend."

"So say you."

He swung an arm around her shoulders and squeezed. "Aye, I do."

"Oh good. You've got your line down." She teased him out of long habit, but in truth, she was worried.

"That's right. Until I do my bit as the sacrificial groom, your bit hardly matters."

Kyla spun into him, clutching his shirt. "You're not thinking of backing out, are you?"

His beleaguered sigh didn't make her feel any better.

"No. I know my duty. I've had a lifetime to accept it. This

wedding will happen, and the terms of the marriage pact will finally be satisfied."

Then the axe hovering over all their heads because of an agreement made by ancestors who'd long since turned to dust would be gone, and they could get down to the serious business of actually saving the estate.

"I hope you know how much it means to me that you're doing this. I know Afton isn't who you'd have chosen."

"I'm certain I'm not her first choice, either. But it is what it is. We're friends. That's a far better basis than many have in arranged marriages."

Afton Lennox was the remaining heir to the barony of Lochmara, the neighboring estate. Her legacy fell under the same threat as their own, and Kyla could only thank God that she was willing to adhere to the terms of the pact. Then again, if she didn't, both their estates were forfeit to the Crown. Kyla would never stop cursing their ancestors for the addition of that little failsafe to the agreement meant to ensure the alliance between their families actually happened.

Knowing there was no changing their situation, she shook off the frustration. "We need to get someone out to look at it to make sure it's not going to get worse before the wedding. I don't want to have this place full of guests only to have plaster crashing down onto plates at the reception." Already feeling the beginnings of a headache, Kyla headed for the door. There was no getting a mobile reception inside three- to four-foot-thick stone walls. "Maybe we can have a quick patch job done to get us through, then deal with the more permanent repair after."

It wasn't ideal, but she simply didn't have the bandwidth to deal with more disasters right now.

Connor followed her out. "I'm gonna go check in on Uncle Angus. The latest iteration of the wedding cake should be about ready."

"But the cake was decided on weeks ago! Why is he mucking around with it?"

"He reckons it'll be good practice for his audition for the *Great British Baking Show*, and who am I to turn down more cake?"

Kyla closed her eyes and prayed for patience. She loved her great uncle and her brother, both, but sometimes dealing with them felt like wrangling a couple of cheerful puppies rather than grown adults. At least if Angus was baking, he wasn't out getting into some other sort of trouble. And, really, she wasn't going to turn down more cake, either, given how the day was shaping up.

It took longer than she wanted to get ahold of Theo Gordon, the contractor who'd done the most work on Ardinmuir. And longer still to convince him to come out today, after he finished up the job he was working the next village over. If a batch of Angus's jaffa cakes had been promised as a bribe, well, she'd run into Glenlaig to pick up ingredients herself, if she had to. It wasn't like they could finish setup until this was sorted, anyway.

Satisfied that she'd done all that could be done for the moment, Kyla made her way down to the kitchen, which was housed in the newer portion of the castle. New being relative, having been added on in the nineteenth century, when James MacKean, head of the family at the time, had been flush with cash from a shipping empire that later collapsed. But at least that part of the house had been comparatively modernized.

As she stepped into the kitchen, Angus straightened at the heavy wooden island, lifting his piping bag in triumph from a truly lovely confection of swirls and flowers.

Kyla sniffed the air and caught the tang of citrus. "If that's a lemon chiffon cake, I just might fall to my knees and weep with gratitude."

Angus's blue eyes twinkled. "Then ready your tissues, lass. But you'll have to wait until I take a picture for my blog."

"We have a deal. Although you may take that back when I tell you that the only way I could get Theo out today to look at the wall in the great hall was to promise him a batch of your jaffa cakes."

One white brow winged up. "And what'll you trade *me* in this bargain?"

"My undying gratitude." Kyla slid her arm around him, and pressed a smacking kiss to his leathery cheek, feeling a bit of a pang as she realized he'd gotten a little more frail over the winter. Other than Connor, Uncle Angus was the last of her immediate family. When had he last gotten a checkup? She added that to the never-ending list in the back of her brain. Something to address after the wedding.

Connor snagged an Irn Bru from the avocado green refrigerator and kicked back against one of the long stone counters, smirking. "That disnae sound like much of a deal to me."

She pointed a finger at him in warning. "You stay out of this."

Angus considered. "You do the second round of dishes, and we have an agreement."

"Done."

As they shook on it, someone knocked on the door.

Connor pulled it open. "Malcolm! Welcome. Did you come to help with the setup for the reception, or did you hear a rumor that there's more cake?"

The brawny, fifty-something man stepped into the kitchen, kilt swinging, his thick-soled boots thumping on the hardwood floors. His hazel gaze slid over the cake on the island, but his expression didn't change. There were some in Glenlaig who believed Lochmara's estate manager to be surly, but Kyla knew the truth. He just preferred animals to people. In social settings, he tended to be a man of few words. Still, the prospect of cake usually would have garnered at least some interest.

A frisson of unease traveled down her spine as she registered the tension in his burly shoulders and jaw. "Is everything all right, Malcolm?"

"No." His throat worked. "Afton is gone."

The words hit Kyla like a well-aimed stone to the gut. "Gone? What do you mean she's gone? The wedding is in less than a week. She can't be gone."

"I found a note."

"Saying what?" Connor asked.

"That she's sorry."

"That's it?" Kyla knew her voice was edging into the realm of shrill, but couldn't seem to control it.

"That's it."

Like a puppet with cut strings, she dropped into a nearby chair. "You can't be telling me what I think you're telling me. If she's gone... If she doesn't go through with this wedding, we're all screwed. The Crown has been watching since we filed the paperwork for the marriage. We have to find her."

"Her car is still in the village. I tracked her that far before I came here. But she's gone. She could be anywhere."

"What about the police?" Angus asked.

"Since she left a note, we have no reason to get them involved. She's not a missing person since she left voluntarily." Malcolm spread his hands. "Unless you want to pour money into a private investigator to track her down..."

That was money they didn't have.

This was terrible. Disastrous.

Connor tunneled a hand through his mop of blond hair. "Maybe she'll come back."

Kyla shot a hard stare in his direction. "Are you willing to wait until the eleventh hour to see? I'm not. We all need to turn our efforts to tracking her down. She has to go down that aisle if I have to march her there in handcuffs myself."

Two

Raleigh stood in the middle of the casino floor, amid countless people and unfathomable noise, missing home so much it hurt. He should never have let Zeke talk him into this insanity. Sin City certainly wasn't the cure for what ailed him. There was no cure. The old bastard had seen to that from beyond the grave.

Needing to escape the chaos of flashing lights and the haze of smoke, he wandered into one of the hotel bars as far from the casino floor as he could get. It wasn't the wide-open spaces and silence he craved, and the high-backed stools sure as hell weren't a saddle. But they'd have whiskey. That would have to do. Never mind that Zeke had dragged him out of a bottle to get him here. Better the bottle than needing bail money. It had been a close call after he'd found out that his horse had been among the assets left to his stepmother. He'd raised Zodiac from a colt, done all the training himself. He was one of the best damned cutting horses in Texas. The rodeo cowboy who'd bought him had been sympathetic, but unwilling to sell back to Raleigh. So he truly had almost nothing left. Having lived on the ranch almost his whole life, he'd never had reason to kit out a house with furniture, so the only things that had gone into storage were his saddle and the dozen or so boxes of family memorabilia Twila wouldn't have been able to sell. He'd call for them once he figured out where he was gonna land. Zeke or Charlotte would get them to him.

The sounds of the slot machines and crowds were more muted here, so he could breathe a little easier.

The bartender wandered over. "What's your pleasure?"

"Whiskey. Neat."

With a nod, the guy flipped over a glass and poured two fingers of something from the top shelf. That'd probably cost a pretty penny. Raleigh ought to be mindful of that, what with being jobless. But Zeke was bankrolling this trip, and for once, he wasn't gonna argue. Taking the drink, he held up a finger for the man to wait and tossed it back in one swallow. Wincing at the burn, he set the glass down. "Another."

The bartender didn't even raise a brow, just refilled the glass and moved a little way down the bar to serve someone else. Raleigh took his time with this one, slowly spinning the glass between his fingers and having what his mama would've dubbed a good brood. He figured he'd earned it.

A frisson of irritation skittered over him as someone slid onto the next stool over. There were more than a dozen empty seats. Why had she chosen that one? He sure as hell wasn't looking for company. The weight of her gaze settled on him briefly before she ordered a whiskey for herself.

The bartender filled another glass and pushed it to her. With a silent toast to no one in particular, the blonde drank. Raleigh didn't miss her grimace of disgust in the reflection of the mirror behind the bar.

"What's wrong with you Yanks, having the temerity to call this piss whisky?" The accent made him glance up because she was definitely not from around here.

"My advice is drink more. After number two, you won't care anymore." With that in mind, he finished his second, which was starting to dull the edge of annoyance at all the people.

With some amusement, he watched as the woman eyed her

drink before tossing it back and pulling another face. "You're sure two will do it?"

Recognizing someone drinking to forget something, and sensing a kindred spirit, Raleigh signaled the bartender for two more, one for each of them.

"Thank you." She shifted far enough in her seat to study him as she sipped at the drink. "You should know, I'm not emotionally available."

Raleigh snorted into his own glass. "Sugar, no offense, but getting tangled up with a woman is the last thing I'm looking for. One just ruined my life."

"Did she break your heart?" Ah ha. Those rolling r's finally identified her accent as some kind of Scottish.

"Not like you mean. But yeah."

"Want to talk about it?"

He gave her some side eye. "You actually want to hear about it?"

"It might distract me from my own problems."

Well, all right then. Shifting on his stool, he clasped his glass loosely between both hands. "I'm from Texas. Old ranching family. My great-great-great-great granddaddy, James Hepburn—"

"Hepburn. Your family is Scottish?"

"Way on back there somewhere, yeah. Anyway, he started the spread—fourteen-thousand acres—and passed it on down through the family. That'd be on my mama's side. She died about fifteen years ago. Cancer."

"I'm sorry." The soft voice was full of a legitimate empathy that told him she'd lost someone, too.

"Well, at that point, I wasn't considered old enough to run it yet, so it passed to my daddy. Then he remarried—a pretty little viper who was barely older than me. I never dreamed a city-girl like her would stick, but she did. Made me feel like a stranger in my own home. If not for Charlotte, I don't know what would've happened to me."

"Who was Charlotte?"

"My mama's best friend. She stayed on at the ranch as housekeeper and more or less finished raising me. Anyway, the old man died recently and left everything to Number Two. She sold the place out from under me. Every stick, stone, and cow. Even my horse."

A faint trace of sympathetic amusement lit his companion's brown eyes. "I'd say that makes you a walking country western song."

He huffed a humorless laugh. "You're not wrong. There probably is one out there somewhere. Anyway, the stepmonster's turning it over to a developer. I lost everything. All the people we were responsible for are out of work, out of a home. And I can't do a damned thing to help."

With a wry twist of her painted lips, the stranger lifted her glass. "That kind of responsibility isn't everything it's cracked up to be."

"Maybe not for everybody, but I spent my whole life, my whole education, getting ready to take over my family's ranch."

"Isn't there a part of you that's relieved to not have the burden of that responsibility?"

Raleigh didn't even have to think about it. "No. It's what I was born for. What I always wanted. It wasn't a burden, it was a privilege. It wasn't just about my family's legacy. It was about making sure we were good stewards of the land. I had all these ideas for how to innovate, reduce our carbon footprint, and bring the place into the twenty-first century. Hell, I got a damned graduate degree in all that. And now? I've got nothing. No job. No horse. No home. No prospects."

"So why did you come to Vegas?"

"A friend dragged me. He thought it was sensible to get me the hell out of Dodge before my temper got the better of me and I did something I might regret."

"You didn't come to gamble?"

"I'm not normally much of a risk taker."

"Neither am I. But recent circumstances are changing my mind." She finished off the drink. "Are you single?"

After her announcement that she wasn't emotionally available, Raleigh hadn't expected the question. "Uh... yeah?"

"Do you play poker?"

"Used to have a weekly game on the ranch with chores as the stakes. That's about as far as it goes."

Leaning across the bar, she snagged a napkin. From her tidy little purse, she pulled out a pen and scribbled something before shoving it across to him. "Meet me in this room in half an hour."

"For what?"

Her gaze seemed far too assessing as she looked him over. "An opportunity."

———

"You look like you could use this."

Kyla watched as Ewan McBride, her distant cousin who owned The Stag's Head pub in Glenlaig, poured amber liquid into a glass. When he started to step back, she simply lifted a hand. "You may as well leave the bottle."

He arched a dark brow. "It's like that, is it?"

"Sit, if you can. You can hear the update along with everyone else."

Crossing to the doorway, Ewan scanned the few patrons out in the pub's main room before coming back to take a seat at the table with the rest of their rag-tag search party. Connor had taken over pouring and passed out glasses to Angus, Malcolm, Kyla's friend, Sophie Cameron, and his oldest friend, Hamish Colquhoun, who'd come up from Edinburgh for the meeting.

Two days had passed since Malcolm had broken the news, and none of what they'd uncovered since was good.

Kyla tipped back the whisky, wishing it would burn away the worry eating her from the inside out. "As you know, I had David call in some favors in an effort to track Afton down."

Her long-term, long-distance boyfriend was nearly as motivated as she was to see this wedding through. He wanted her focus to be freed of the danger to Ardinmuir so she could finally, truly consider their future—something she hadn't been willing to commit to until her family legacy was safe.

"His contact was able to track her to Glasgow, where she took a flight to the U.S., to Los Angeles. From there, she hired a car."

"To go where?" Sophie asked.

"We don't know. The trail went cold there."

"Should one of us head to the States after her?" Connor asked. "I could go. She might listen to me."

If only. Kyla sipped more whisky. "She hasn't been willing to answer any of our phone calls or emails. That seems like throwing good money after bad. Without knowing where to look, you'd be looking for a needle in a very large haystack. And much as I would like to, we can't very well extradite her for the sake of a wedding." She glanced to Hamish, their resident legal expert, for confirmation.

He inclined his head in concession of the point, but otherwise stayed quiet, his expression grave.

Sophie rolled her glass between her palms. "I understand that the idea of an arranged marriage must be incredibly hard, but to leave everybody in the lurch like this, with so much at stake..."

"It's selfish." Kyla couldn't keep the judgment out of her voice. "If Afton harbored doubts, the time to bring them up was years ago, not days before the wedding."

"To what end?" Connor demanded. "There's no other solution. Hamish has been trying to find one his entire legal career."

"If she'd brought up her fears sooner, at least we could've tried to address them. Gotten her into therapy. Something."

Her brother snorted. "You can only say that because you aren't the one whose life is on the line."

Kyla bristled. "If circumstances had been different, if she'd had a brother and it was me, you can be damned certain I'd have done my duty." The good of the many who'd be impacted by the Crown taking control of all that property was worth the sacrifice.

But there was no one else. Darcie Lennox had struggled with fertility, and ultimately, Afton was the only child she'd been able to carry to term. So all that weight of responsibility had fallen to her. For better or worse.

Was it right or fair? No. Nothing about this lunatic marriage pact was. Then again, its authors certainly couldn't have predicted that illness and disaster and quirks of birth would make it so three entire centuries would go by before two eligible heirs even could marry. Either way, this was the reality they'd all grown up with, so a last-minute abdication of responsibility was unconscionable to Kyla's mind.

She didn't even want to think of all the money they'd put into this wedding that would go to waste if she didn't return. And that hardly mattered when their very homes were at stake. Kyla's heart ached at the thought of it. More than six-hundred years of her family history lost because of one woman's selfishness.

"Laying blame is hardly productive, at this point," Ewan pointed out. "It seems like we need some sort of plan."

Sophie knit her hands. "Should we send out notice that the wedding is cancelled?"

"What if we do that, and she comes back?" Connor asked.

"What if we don't, and an agent of the Crown shows up and sees the wedding not happening as planned?" Kyla challenged. "At least if we put the word out locally, we can control the narrative. Suggest that it's been postponed. We have six months from the submission of the marriage paperwork to see it executed. That's time enough to find her and get some answers, isn't it?" Again, she looked to Hamish.

"In theory. The truth is, we don't know exactly what they'll do. It's not as if there's a lot of newer legal precedent around situations like this. But make no mistake, they *are* watching, because they want this land. If they have reason to believe she's going to renege on the terms, chances are, they'll move to start reclamation."

Anxiety twisted Kyla's gut. "There has to be some way to slow things down."

"I'm trying to find one. I can attempt to file for an injunction. I don't know that it'll be accepted or how long it'll hold. But by dint of it taking time to actually go before a judge, it'll buy a little time."

"Do what you can. At this point, we simply have to pull out all the stops. We cannot give up our home."

THREE

"What is there to think about?" Zeke asked. "An attractive woman asked you back to her room."

Raleigh stared at his friend. "I'm not here for some random roll in the hay with a woman I just met."

"A good romp would probably do wonders for your stress level. When was the last time you let yourself loose enough for that?"

He ignored the question. "Doesn't matter. I don't really get the sense that's what this was about for her. She specifically asked if I played poker."

"And if you were single," Zeke reminded him. "Maybe she's angling for a game of strip poker. Why else would she invite you back to her room?"

"I don't know. But she made a point to say she wasn't emotionally available."

"Which makes nameless hookup seem more probable to my mind. A chance for both of you to scratch an itch with no complications."

Raleigh shook his head. "You weren't there. You didn't see her. I just don't think that's what this is about."

Zeke opened a can of nuts from the room's minibar and

popped a handful in his mouth. "Well, you can either go or not. Personally, one way or the other, I'd have to go, just to satisfy my curiosity. If you're not into whatever she's offering, there's nothing stopping you from turning around to leave."

"Fair point. Guess I'm going."

Fifteen minutes later, he found himself outside room 713. After only a few moments' hesitation, Raleigh knocked. The door opened almost immediately, and he was relieved to see she hadn't changed into some kind of slinky lingerie or sexy dress. In fact, she'd changed out of the pantsuit she'd been wearing at the bar and into some yoga pants and a light sweater. The casual attire instantly put him more at ease and made her feel approachable, as did the smile she offered.

"I wondered if you'd change your mind. Please, come in." She stepped back.

As soon as he entered the room, he spotted the poker table that had been set up in the open space beyond the king-size bed. One of the hotel's dealers, a stone-faced woman with dark hair pulled back into a neat bun, was arranging chips in stacks on the green felt surface.

"Guess you really were serious about playing poker."

She lifted a brow. "Yes. Is that a problem?"

"Not at all."

"Then have a seat."

He removed his black Stetson and faced her. "I don't play poker with total strangers. What's your name?"

Her mouth curved a little at that. "Afton Lennox. And you?"

"Raleigh Beaumont."

"Nice to meet you, Raleigh Beaumont." With an elegant hand, she gestured toward the table again, inviting him to sit.

Taking the chair closest to the door, he set his hat to one side. "What's the buy-in?"

Afton waved that off. "I've already taken care of that."

Raleigh frowned. "That hardly seems fair."

"I'm just here to play, Mr. Beaumont. Indulge me."

"Fair enough, I guess. It's your money."

"Indeed."

At her nod, the dealer began to shuffle.

"What form of poker are we playing?"

Again, the edges of her smile flickered. "Texas Hold-'em seemed most appropriate, as you're my guest."

The dealer passed out the initial hole cards, and Raleigh peeked at his options. Because it was his habit from those weekly games on the ranch, he felt compelled to start a conversation as he tossed a chip in for the small blind. "You've already heard why I'm in Vegas, what I'm running from. What about you? Why are you here? You're even further from home than I am."

Afton carefully studied her cards. "I'm running from family expectation and a responsibility that should never have been mine to begin with. I'm here to reclaim my life." She placed the big blind.

Raleigh tried to imagine what kind of reclamation a place like Vegas would offer. Seed money for a new beginning? "Do they expect you to take over the family business?"

She hummed. "Something like that."

The dealer laid down the flop.

"You playing mysterious on purpose?"

"Just keeping my hand close to my vest." With a Mona Lisa smile, she made her bet.

He huffed a laugh and matched. "All right, then."

At the turn, she raised again, and he checked. Then the dealer laid down the river. Again, she raised, and he stayed. Raleigh's three of a kind beat her hand of nothing. It didn't mean anything. Opening hands were about learning your opponent. But after they'd gone through two more hands with similar results, Raleigh had to question the fairness of continuing. "You sure you wanna keep going with this? Poker doesn't seem like your game."

"Definitely."

She cheerfully continued her betting streak. "You mentioned you've lost both your parents. Do you have any other family?"

Resigned to letting her lose her money if that was her true desire, he settled in and played the game. "No. Not by blood, anyway. I was an only child."

"Me, too. It's hard being the only one left."

"You've lost both your parents, too?"

A curtain of sadness draped over her. "Aye. In a plane crash some years back."

"Oh damn. I'm sorry." He regretted that his curiosity had put that haunted look in her eyes.

"Tell me about the ranch where you grew up. What sort was it? Beef cattle? Dairy? Something else?"

"Predominantly beef, some dairy. My true love is horses, though. There were a lot of changes I wanted to make that my dad wasn't on board with."

"What kinds of changes?"

"Well, the beef industry has a pretty steep toll on the environment, and it can be a volatile business. I wanted to diversify and modernize the way we did things. Expand into other sectors that helped balance out environmental impact, so the business could continue for generations to come."

"So you're an environmentalist and an idealist."

"At the heart, I'm a practical man who believes in responsibility to the world that he was born into."

She inclined her head in acknowledgment of the point. "Seems there are very few people who fall into that category who are willing to make the changes that are necessary to the way things were done in the past, in order to ensure a future."

There was something more in her tone, but Raleigh had learned by now she wasn't going to elaborate, so he didn't ask the question. Why bother, when he didn't expect to see this woman again after tonight?

As the river was dealt, Afton smiled. "I'm all in."

Raleigh thought about folding, but he had a full house. That was pretty damned solid, and so far, it seemed she didn't have even the vaguest handle on what hands beat what. Deciding to call her bluff, he stayed in.

When she triumphantly laid down a jack and a two, he tried to find some combination of anything with the community cards. But there really was none. So why the hell was she beaming?

"Congratulations, Mr. Beaumont. You've just gotten what you wanted."

"What are you talking about?"

"You wanted the responsibility of managing an estate—the land, the people. Now you've got it. You're the new Baron of Lochmara."

She was talking outright nonsense. "Excuse me?"

Afton shoved back from the table and waved from the dealer to him. "Please cash him out."

"I don't understand what you mean."

"I was, until now, the most recent Baroness of Lochmara in Scotland. But I've just gambled it away. To you. The title, the lands... all of it is now your responsibility. I wash my hands of it. I'm free."

And indeed, a weight seemed to have visibly slid off her shoulders.

As Raleigh stared at her, the dealer handed over an envelope. He opened it, carefully unfolding the paper inside. It was old. Clearly, very old. He could barely read the scrawl, but it seemed to be a deed of some kind.

"The contact information for the lawyer who will handle the transfer of all the legal paperwork is also inside. Hamish Colquhoun."

His head was spinning with disbelief. "You bet me your... land?"

"Your land now."

"This can't be real or legal."

"Oh, I can assure you that it is. That's why I had Sharon here as dealer. The casino has verified the collateral I put up. Everything is on the up-and-up."

The stone-faced Sharon nodded in confirmation.

Raleigh wilted back in his chair in stunned disbelief.

Afton beamed. "Have you ever been to Scotland, Mr. Beaumont?"

———

By Thursday, they'd heard nothing.

Because Kyla was no good at simply waiting, she threw herself into setting up for the reception—placing tables, unfolding chairs, ironing and laying out tablecloths. She told herself it was optimism rather than desperation. The plaster in the great hall had been patched and painted, which really just highlighted how the entire room needed to be repainted. But they didn't have the time for that.

"I think the mood lighting from the cafe lights will help hide the imperfection." She eyed the crisscross of strands they'd hung from the balcony overlooking the hall to the far wall. Those had been her budget-friendly idea for solving the poor lighting issue in the space that had been originally lit by torches. "And really, with your stunning flowers and the other decorations, nobody should be looking up."

Kyla dropped her gaze to find Sophie staring at her with an expression of pity in the striking gray eyes she'd inherited from her white father.

"We have to make a real decision here." Sophie's voice was gentle but firm. "I've already put off the work past when I really needed to start. It's do or die. If you want me to push forward and do the work as if this wedding is really happening, I'll do it. If it's not, then I need to be able to turn those flowers I ordered into something else that I can sell to offset the cost."

Kyla choked down the fresh spate of anger that flared at Afton. Her selfish abdication didn't just threaten everyone associated with Lochmara and Ardinmuir. It also risked Sophie's livelihood. She needed this wedding business to work, needed the extra income to make a true go of her fledgling flower shop and finally move out of her stepmother's house. The two of them had invested so much time and money in launching things, and without this wedding, there was nothing to launch. No way to recoup the costs of all those tables, chairs, and tablecloths they'd purchased, believing them to be a solid investment. Because if this wedding didn't happen, they'd lose the very venue they were trying to promote.

There was no sense in voicing her frustrations again. Everyone well knew where she stood on the matter. Instead, she turned to her uncle. "What do you think?"

Angus nudged his wire-framed glasses up his nose. "It's hard to say," he hedged. "She might show up at the eleventh hour."

She shifted her focus to her brother. "And you?"

Connor hesitated. "I think if we were going to hear from her, we would have by now. It's no' too late to cancel the caterer. We'll lose the deposit, but that's better than losing all of it."

Kyla's breath whooshed out on a heavy sigh. "I don't want to give up."

Sophie squeezed her shoulder. "There is one other option."

"Then, by all means, share it."

"We find another couple who wants to get married."

Kyla blinked at her. "I'm sorry?"

"It's possible we might be able to find another bride and groom in need of a venue."

"You think, in two days, we can find someone else to basically take over the wedding we've planned?"

"Maybe not fast enough to keep the flowers and food from going to waste, but we can still find another couple. We can still launch our business."

Aching at the hope in her best friend's face, Kyla spread her hands. "What good is that if we're going to lose this place? If this wedding doesn't happen, the Crown is going to start reclamation."

Connor folded his arms. "Even if they do, it's no' as if they'd be evicting us at the end of the week. It'll take time. All governmental shite does. And I'm sure Hamish will find some way to slow things down. I think it's a good idea to try to find another bride and groom who'd be willing to pay for the privilege of having a reception, possibly a ceremony, here. Highland weddings are big business. That's why you both chose this option. At the very least, it would be a solid effort to recoup some of the costs you put into this, which is a damned sight better than losing it all."

Sophie blinked at him. "That's a surprisingly mature perspective coming from you."

"I'm no' just a pretty face, darlin'." The exaggerated batting of his unfairly long lashes and the mile-wide grin took all seriousness out of his reply.

Numbers began scrolling through the spreadsheet Kyla kept in her head. How much could they charge for a last-minute wedding where the couple wouldn't have a lot of choice in terms of options? She didn't know. But even if they offered the package at a steep discount, there was significant appeal in making any money back on what they'd already spent.

"How would we even go about finding someone?"

"There are places we can post online," Sophie said. "Maybe we'll get lucky and find some tourists who already planned to elope and haven't settled on where yet. I'll see what I can find out."

"Do it." At least one of them could take positive action.

Sophie leaned in to hug her. "It'll work out. You'll see."

Her optimism had always been a wonder to Kyla, given the circumstances she lived in. Squeezing her back, she prayed Sophie was right.

"I'll let you know what I find out."

The rest of them said nothing as her footsteps faded. What was there to say?

Angus wrapped an arm around Kyla's shoulders. "I think we could all do with a cuppa."

She tipped her head to his, appreciating that he was here. "I wouldn't turn one down."

"I'll go put on the kettle, then."

"We'll be along shortly." It was time for some real talk with her brother. When they were alone, she voiced the question she hadn't been able to banish. "How are you so calm about all of this? Don't you care?"

"Of course, I bloody care. I can be calm because I've never had the illusion of control over my life."

She frowned at him. "What are you talking about?"

"I've been promised in marriage to someone not of my own choosing from the day she was born. I've pursued women all these years, but never a meaningful connection because the expectation was always that I'd be the one to save Ardinmuir. I know you think I've wasted years gallivanting rather than slaving to save our legacy as you have, but I've always felt like what was being asked of me was more than enough."

Speechless, she could only stare at him. "You've... never said."

"What was the point? No one ever considered walking away from this place an alternative. Not even me. But I'd be lying if I didnae admit that a part of me is impressed as hell that Afton had the stones to do this, even as the rest of me is livid about the consequences."

"Did you know she'd leave?"

"No. I never would've imagined it. But now that she has..." He offered another of those trademark insouciant shrugs. "Worrying over it will change nothing. So I'm living in the moment and taking things as they come. I suggest you do the same before you burn a hole in your stomach lining from all the stress."

"Easier said than done."

"C'mon. Uncle Angus will have the tea."

Kyla stayed quiet as Connor escorted her to the kitchen. She'd never truly considered what it must've been like for him to bear this burden. Would she have held up as well? She wanted to think so. Wanted to believe that if the responsibility had been hers, she'd have stepped up to it without qualm. But that was easy to say when things were just hypothetical.

An electric kettle whistled from the counter beside the gas hob their mother had insisted on when she took up residence in the castle. It was the newest appliance in the room and had, at this point, been well-used. Angus lifted the kettle, pouring water into a waiting teapot and setting a small egg timer in the shape of a chicken. As it began to tick down, he pulled plates from the dark wood cupboards and sliced more of the lemon chiffon cake he'd made earlier in the week.

A quick knock sounded on the back door before it opened and Hamish strode in. He was dressed for work—or had been. His tie was loosened, his shirtsleeves rolled up, and his suit jacket was nowhere to be seen. His hair stood on end, as if he'd spent much of the drive from Edinburgh tunneling his fingers through it.

Kyla gripped the edge of the island. "Did you find her?"

Hamish glanced at the steeping tea. "Is there enough for me?"

"I'll make it so." Angus retrieved another mug and plate.

"Hamish, did you hear from Afton?" Connor demanded.

"Not directly."

"But you know where she is?" Kyla prompted. She didn't know how to read the look on his face. He'd lost some of the color there, as if he were ill.

"I know where she's been."

A frown bowed Connor's lips. "What's that supposed to mean?"

Hamish exhaled a slow breath. "There's a new owner of Lochmara."

Whatever she'd expected him to say, it wasn't that. "How? Part of the terms of the marriage pact are that the estate can't be sold to anyone but us."

"It can't be sold. But it could be gambled. She went to Las Vegas and has gambled the entire estate away to an American."

Gambling. The worst of vices. A huge part of the reason they were in the state they were in. Kyla's fingers flexed so hard against the island, the knuckles turned white. "Are you serious?"

"Aye. I've just gotten off the phone with his lawyer. It's real, and it's done."

The timer dinged, as if punctuating the statement. Angus moved to pour tea into the waiting mugs.

Connor broke the shocked silence. "So the wedding is definitely off?"

"That would seem to be the case."

He couldn't or didn't hide the relief that swept over him at the news. Kyla couldn't blame him for that after what he'd said. But this presented a whole new set of problems.

"What do we know about this Yank?" she asked.

"Very little. But he'll be arriving at the beginning of next week to take possession."

Angus slid a cup of tea and a plate of cake in front of Hamish. "He?"

"Thanks. Aye, it seems she gambled it away to a man."

Absently, she accepted her own tea as her brain began to process implications. "Does... does he have a family?"

With a look of apology, Hamish shook his head. "He's single."

All eyes turned to her.

"Fuck."

Four

Kyla left for Edinburgh barely an hour after Hamish broke the news. There were a thousand questions with very few answers, but she knew she had to tell David, and she had to do it in person. This wasn't the kind of thing to be shared over a phone line. Over the hours of the drive, she had time for a good cry as the reality of what this could mean began to truly sink in. She'd thought she'd understood what it had been like for her brother. But she hadn't. Not really.

Unlike Connor, she'd been free to pursue relationships like any normal person. She'd had a few boyfriends through university, a handful of casual affairs in the years after that had left her feeling unsettled, in search of something more. When she'd met David Murray at an antiques auction, the restlessness she'd been wrestling with finally quieted. He was comfort and stability. While he respected her legacy, he didn't expect it to rule her life. She'd needed that perspective. Needed that subtle and constant reminder that there was life beyond this lunacy she'd been raised with. They'd necessarily been long distance. His job as a banker kept him in Edinburgh, as her efforts to protect Ardinmuir kept her in the Highlands. For two years, they'd made do with frequent weekends and holidays. The understanding had always been that once the pact was satisfied, she'd be free and willing to discuss the possibility of relocating so they could finally start their life together. But all that had been predicated on Connor fulfilling his end of the marriage pact. She'd never considered that Afton would make such a rash decision that would impact them all.

The noxious curl of anxiety in her belly tightened as she pulled up in front of a row of terraced houses. David had been slowly rehabbing the narrow, three-story mid terrace for the past two-and-a-half years. He'd said he'd bought it because he was ready to settle down and make a life with someone, and he'd considered it a sign that he'd met her on a quest for period-appropriate hardware at that antiques auction in Perth. They'd spent so many joyful hours bonding over restoration projects. Given her connection to Ardinmuir, restoration had been a necessity as much as passion for her, and she'd taught him a great deal. As she let herself into the house with her key, her gaze automatically scanned the space, looking for changes, spotting all the little signs of her. The carved wooden bowl on the entryway table where he kept his keys was currently empty. The series of framed architectural sketches of some now defunct estate on the West Coast that they'd picked up for a song at a hole-in-the-wall junk shop on one of their holidays marched along the wall in a neat line above the crisp, white chair rail. The bright, Indian-print cushions were tossed onto the Harris tweed sofa, along with a plush red throw she'd given him as a birthday present that first year. There were little signs of her—of them—everywhere. And she couldn't help but wonder if this would be the last time she saw it all. Would this finally be David's breaking point?

She was waiting on the sofa, knees up-drawn, arms tightly hugging one of those cushions when he got home. The moment she heard his key in the lock, she scrambled up. He'd barely made it in the door and spotted her before she was moving into him. He dropped his briefcase with a thunk and wrapped his arms around her.

"Here now. What is it?"

Kyla couldn't answer him. Not yet. She tipped her face up to kiss him, framing his face in her hands and pouring out all the uncertainty, all the need. He gave back comfort and ease, slowing her frantic pace, rubbing her back. This was why she endured the long distance. Because he was a safe place for her amid the chaos of her normal world.

At length, he eased back, skimming his hands through her hair. "What's happened, love? Did you find Afton?"

There was no putting this off. "Not exactly." With a sigh, she pulled him over to the sofa and down, keeping hold of his hands as she repeated what Hamish had told them.

David listened, quiet and calm, as was his way. "A new owner? What does that mean, exactly?"

"Well, we're still sort of figuring that out. But it does mean that the wedding is off. Connor is free of his role."

"That's a good thing, isn't it?"

She hesitated. "Aye. For him."

He angled his head, brown eyes intent on hers. "What is it you're not saying?"

"Well, Connor is free of his role because the new owner is a single man."

David's hands tightened on hers as he realized the implication. "No. You can't mean that you're expected to just jump into this and marry some total stranger. What about us?"

"I don't know. I do know that our relationship, for the purposes of the pact, doesn't matter. If we were already married, that would be one thing, but—"

"Then we'll get married."

She appreciated the swift, matter-of-fact conclusion. As if it were the most logical thing in the world. She wished he'd thought of it last week. "It's too late for that. We haven't filed the paperwork. It takes at least a month here. Even if we eloped somewhere else, it would have had to predate the transfer of ownership. That's not the solution."

With uncharacteristic agitation, he shoved up from the sofa and began to pace. "What is the solution?"

"I don't know."

He stopped, one hand combing through his hair, the color draining out of his cheeks. "Are you here to break up with me?"

Kyla rushed to him, taking his hands again. "No! No, I don't want to break up. I just... I needed to see you. I needed to tell you this in person. Afton's actions have thrown a spanner into the works."

"But you're expected to marry this guy."

"In theory. But I guarantee he doesn't yet know about this part of the estate he's inherited. What happens next is largely going to depend on him. The easiest solution would be for him to transfer ownership to us. To sell the estate to us. It's the only variation that completely circumvents the pact." That had been her conclusion after spinning the problem round and round on the drive down.

"But what about the money? You don't have that kind of cash."

"You're right. I don't. But maybe we could borrow it." Hating what she was asking of him, she stared into his eyes, pleading, waiting for him to understand.

Realization dawning, he drew back a little, but didn't let her go. "I don't know."

She squeezed his hands. "Can you find out? At least try, just so that we have a potential option on the table. I mean, it may be that he decides that he doesn't want any part of this, in which case—hell, I don't know what will happen. The terms of sale are still the same. He can't sell it to anyone but us. So if he refuses it, everything reverts to the Crown, and it's all over. Or he can opt to do exactly what Afton did and gamble it away to someone else. And then we start all over again. I don't know where we are with any of that, and I don't think we'll find out until he arrives next week. But it seems like the clearest, easiest, most logical response is purchase, and I need your help for that."

For a long, interminable moment, David said nothing, and Kyla was convinced she'd pushed too far, asked for too much.

Then his face softened, and he pulled her in. "Alright. I'll see what I can find out."

She burrowed in, soaking in his comfort, grateful that for today, at least, her relationship wasn't over.

———

The attorney, Hamish Colquhoun, had offered to pick Raleigh up at the airport and take him to the estate personally. But he didn't fully know what he was getting into at Lochmara, and he wanted some quiet to reset after the long flight and all the airport time, so he opted to rent a car and drive himself. Hamish would be meeting him there to make introductions and answer some questions.

He still couldn't get over the fact that this lunacy was actually real. He legit owned a Scottish estate with several thousand acres of land, some number of tenant farmers, and apparently an estate manager who came with the property. The retention of Malcolm Niall had been the one point Afton refused to budge on. She'd said that Lochmara had been Malcolm's home for more than twenty years and that no one knew the place better than him. There was no keeping one without the other. She'd insisted he be able to keep his home and his job, regardless of any other changes Raleigh might decide to make. As the man sounded like a real resource, it hadn't been a difficult promise to make. Only a fool would fire the existing employees for no reason, just to bring in their own people.

The drive out of Edinburgh was a little hair-raising. That whole switching to the other side of the road was a challenge, and the little Fiat they'd given him at the rental counter felt like one step up from a bumper car as he hit his first roundabout. But by the time he made it out of the city and onto the A9 headed north, he'd more or less gotten the hang of things. It was a gorgeous drive through green, green hills and on into mountains that were so far from the gentle, rolling expanse of East Texas as to be a whole other world. Raleigh took his time, appreciating the view and feeling the tension unwind from his neck and shoulders with every mile that passed. He saw lochs and rivers and countless sheep. The rancher in him wondered about their use and profit margin.

His phone's GPS took him right down the main street of Glenlaig, the nearest village to Lochmara. It was a picturesque little place, full of stone houses with slate roofs. He spotted an ancient stone church, a post office, some kind of convenience store, a petrol station, and, of course, a pub before his route took him out of town and onto another winding road framed by centuries-old trees. The green darkness of their canopies felt like an embrace for the last leg of his journey.

By the time he pulled through the stone pillars marking the front gate of Lochmara, he'd found some equilibrium and a healthy dose of curiosity. The heavily forested slopes opened up to a small valley. Two stories of red brick and dark gray stone, the house itself sat atop a hill, overlooking everything. It was a huge house, but not particularly ostentatious, which suited him just fine. He was having a hard enough time with the idea that he now technically had a title. There was a scattering of outbuildings, some kind of wall he thought marked the edge of a formal garden, and he spotted more sheep and a small herd of shaggy Highland cows beyond the stone fence. Somewhere past that, in the distance, was the glitter of water. The loch this place was named for? The whole thing looked like a painting, and he couldn't quite believe that all this was his.

Another car sat in the circular drive. As he parked behind the sleek sedan, two men came out of the house. One wore a suit and an air of professionalism. Raleigh pegged him to be in his early thirties. The other man was older. Maybe fifty-something. Clad in a t-shirt, kilt, and combat boots, his face was set in lines of unmistakable distrust that Raleigh could hardly blame him for.

Grabbing his hat, Raleigh climbed out of the car.

The suit stepped forward, offering a hand. "You must be Mr. Beaumont. I'm Hamish Colquhoun."

"Raleigh Beaumont. Nice to meet you."

"And this is Malcolm Niall. He's the gillie and estate manager."

Malcolm didn't unfold his massive arms.

Raleigh nodded in his direction. "Nice to meet you, too. What's a gillie?"

After a moment's pause—probably to see if Malcolm would answer himself—Hamish responded. "It's a fishing and hunting guide. Absolutely no one knows this land better than Malcolm. But as estate manager, he's responsible for the broader land management of the property."

Hoping to establish some common ground, Raleigh fixed the man with a steady gaze. "I served more or less the same function on my family's ranch. I look forward to learning from you, sir."

The man grunted. Raleigh didn't let it bother him. A lot of the horses he'd worked with were slow to warm up, too.

He crossed his arms and focused back on the lawyer. "Look, I know we cleared all this over the phone, and you squared things with my attorney, but I'm having a hard time wrapping my brain around the fact that this is really a thing. That it's really... well, real. That all this is actually mine. That I'm a friggin' baron."

"You really are the Baron of Lochmara. Should the estate pass out of your hands, the title goes with it. It does not go with you."

"Fine with me. I don't have airs of being something I'm not."

Hamish seemed to weigh his words. "If I may ask, Mr. Beaumont, what are your plans?"

"I hardly know. I've been on a plane or in a car for the better part of twenty-four hours. I was hoping to stretch my legs, maybe get a tour of the place, a bite to eat, and hit the hay. My body doesn't have a clue what time it is."

Again, it was Hamish who answered. "Well, I'm not sure what

there is in the house to eat. There's not been a housekeeper in some time, and that's not part of Malcolm's duties."

"Of course not. I can fend for myself on that front." Charlotte had made sure of it.

"You can certainly go into the village and get a bite at the pub. The Stag's Head. It's owned by a friend of mine, Ewan McBride. There's also a wee cafe, but it closes after lunch. There may be something in the cupboards. We weren't exactly prepared for your arrival. The... uh... previous owner left in rather a hurry and hasn't packed up all of her belongings. I'm not sure what you intend to do about that."

"I've got no interest in keeping Afton's stuff from her. I'll pack it up and see that she gets it wherever she lands." Raleigh sure as hell understood that kind of starting over. It was the least he could do for the woman who'd given him this second chance. "I haven't made arrangements for my own things to be shipped yet. I was waiting to see what was what."

A curious intensity seemed to light Hamish's sharp blue eyes. "You know where Afton is?"

"Not right now. I'm not sure where she was headed after she left Vegas. I'm not sure she knew. But she has my contact information and promises she'll be in touch when she's settled somewhere."

The two men exchanged a look.

Hamish seemed to decide something. A little of the stiff professionalism melted away. "Look, Afton's a friend. We've all been pretty worried about her. She disappeared practically without a word. We're just trying to make sure she's all right."

"I can see how that would upset folks. But she was okay when I saw her, if that puts your mind at ease at all."

"Thanks for that."

The piercing whinny of a horse split the air. Raleigh turned to see a small cluster of them coming over the hill. His breath caught as a white horse broke into a gallop, heading in their direction. If his eye wasn't mistaken, she was a Thoroughbred, and a damned good one, judging by her lines.

"She didn't tell me there were horses."

"Are you a horseman, Mr. Beaumont?" Hamish asked.

"I'm a cattle rancher by upbringing. Land manager by training. But I'm a horse trainer at heart."

As the mare ran the length of the stone fence, Raleigh moved closer. She wheeled and ran back toward him, skidding to a stop about ten feet away, her nostrils flared. Inching closer to the wall, he crooned to her. "Aren't you just gorgeous? All that fire and spirit."

"That's Titania. She does what she pleases." Malcolm's voice sounded from somewhere behind Raleigh's shoulder.

"As any woman should."

Ears twitching, Titania eased forward. Moving slowly, Raleigh extended his closed hand, knuckles up. The mare kept coming, and he saw curiosity warring with distrust in her eyes. Knowing this routine, he held himself perfectly still. No one spoke as she edged closer, closer, until the velvety tip of her nose brushed up against his fist, testing his scent.

"Brave, beautiful girl," he murmured.

Moving slowly, and only because she allowed it, Raleigh gave her a gentle scratch along the cheek. The moment he dropped his hand, she stepped closer, bumping her head against his arm as if it say, "I didn't give you permission to stop, manservant."

Raleigh laughed and obliged her with a longer scratch. "I'm looking forward to getting to know you, pretty girl. After I've had time to do some grocery shopping, I'll bring you some carrots. How 'bout that?"

"It's apples for this one."

Raleigh glanced back at Malcolm, wondering if it would be the horses that they'd bond over. "Apples it is, then. Mr. Niall, I'd appreciate it if you'd be willing to give me a tour. Show me the place—the house, the grounds, the rest of the property."

Malcolm grunted. "You're on your own for the house. No' my area. But I'll show you the rest. Come on."

Hamish spoke up. "We should set up a time to talk. Perhaps tomorrow? There are things you should be apprised of after you've had a little rest. My parents live in town, so I'll be staying with them for a couple of days while we get things sorted."

"I appreciate it." Realizing that Malcolm had left him on his own, he offered a quick wave to the lawyer. "I'll be in touch."

Racing to catch up to his estate manager, he wondered exactly what it was he'd gotten himself into.

FIVE

"I dinna think this is a good idea."

Kyla didn't spare a glance for her brother in the backseat. "Your opinion is noted." But she didn't slow the car or turn around.

Angus twisted toward her from the front passenger seat. "Perhaps the lad is right, dear girl. We should wait and go with Hamish."

That certainly would have been preferable, but she was past the point of patience. "Hamish got called back to Edinburgh for work. We don't know when he'll be making it back up this way, and I'm not waiting to meet this man. I need to know what sort of person we're dealing with."

What sort of man she might be trapped with.

All Hamish had told her was that Raleigh Beaumont was from Texas, he was about her age, and he was reckless enough to play high-stakes poker in Vegas. That was it. The sum total of her knowledge of the man she was now expected to blow up her life to marry.

The lack of information had done nothing to ease her anxieties. As she firmly believed that knowledge was power, she'd loaded all of them in the car for a friendly trip over to Lochmara to meet the new baron. Because she wanted to make a good impression, she'd dressed to the nines. She might not be a wealthy heiress, but he didn't know that. Right now, that was to her benefit. As Mr. Beaumont had not shown up on her doorstep with the predicted, "What the hell?" reaction that everyone had to hearing of the marriage pact, she remained certain he was ignorant of the stipulation.

Nobody wanted to marry a stranger, so she felt sure they could come to an agreement of some kind. Connor and Angus weren't wrong that Hamish should be the one to explain the details of the pact itself. She'd hold off on that. Today was a fact-finding mission. They'd introduce themselves, get to know him a little, and hopefully, she'd leave with a better handle on the best way to approach him. Perhaps they'd luck out and find out that he'd impulsively acquired a wife while he was in Vegas as well, and she'd be saved from all of this.

Hope springs eternal.

She imagined a formal visit in the house, a notion that almost had her snickering with laughter because it was so redolent of the Regency romances she occasionally enjoyed reading. And they were, in reality, so far from the nobility. But as she pulled into the circular drive, all thoughts of formality or propriety bled entirely out of her head as she spotted the man himself.

She couldn't see his face. His back was to them, all his focus on the mare in front of him in the paddock. Dimly, she was aware of Malcolm watching from the side, but she couldn't take her eyes away from Raleigh. It had to be him. Tall and lean, with broad shoulders, he wore a blue plaid flannel shirt with the sleeves already rolled, and jeans that fit him like a second skin. She could just make out sandy curls at his nape, beneath the black hat he wore with all the confidence of a prince with his crown. As she watched, he extended his arm toward the mare. Something was coiled in his hand. Rope, maybe? The horse trembled, then spun, breaking into a canter around the perimeter of the small space. He pivoted with her, and Kyla caught her first glimpse of a rugged face, highlighted with golden stubble.

He was a Wild West cowboy fantasy come to life.

Pulled by the vision the pair of them made, Kyla eased quietly out of the car.

As she watched, the mare slowed and finally stopped, quivering, just a few feet from the man. He waited, patient, until she edged forward close enough to sniff him. He stroked a hand down that long, muscular neck. The mare bumped him in the chest with her nose. Raleigh murmured something Kyla couldn't make out, but apparently the horse didn't appreciate his answer. She bounced her head, quite deliberately knocking his hat to the ground.

Raleigh laughed. The sound of it rolled across the grounds, rich and full. That laugh wrapped around Kyla, drawing her closer still for her first good look at his face. It was a hell of a face. Wreathed in smiles, with crinkles around his eyes that suggested he did it often, he wasn't classically handsome. He looked too—real—for that. Like a sculpture the artist hadn't bothered to smooth. And there was a beauty in that rough imperfection that she couldn't stop herself from responding to with a primitive yearning to know how those working man's hands would feel on her bare skin.

Oh, hell.

She shook off the blast of lust. Him being attractive hardly mattered. She wasn't free.

Reminding herself why they were here, she walked quietly in his direction. Only when she'd reached the fence did he turn his focus away from the horse to her. His eyes were a rich, golden brown. Like a lion or a wolf.

"Can I help y'all?" His drawled greeting flowed over her like warm, golden syrup.

Kyla's insides went melty at the sound of it. Damn, if she hadn't always had a thing for Southern accents. Mortified by the schoolgirl reaction rioting inside her, she struggled to remember the speech she'd planned.

"I'm Kyla MacKean. This is my brother, Connor, and our uncle, Angus. We're from Ardinmuir, the estate on the other side of Glenlaig. That'd be the nearest village, if you haven't made it there yet."

"Raleigh Beaumont. And I drove through there yesterday. So we're in the way of bein' neighbors?" He stroked a lazy hand down the mare's neck. Sensing his attention shifting away from her, she head-butted him again. "Patience, pretty girl. I'll get back to you."

Was he that sort of man? Easy with his affections and ready to share them with women far and wide?

"You could say that," Connor replied. "You've quite a way with her. I know Titania's a fussy sort. She wouldn't do more than tolerate many, other than Afton."

"You were a friend of Afton's?"

Connor grimaced. "Ah, well, yes. I'm also the groom she jilted."

Raleigh's eyes widened at that. "She mentioned she was running from something. Didn't say it was a wedding. Sorry, man."

"What, exactly, *did* she say?" Kyla asked.

Those leonine eyes swung back, pinning her in place. "That she was reclaiming her life from some family expectation and a responsibility she didn't think should've been hers to start."

"Did she mention *what* that responsibility was?"

"No. Didn't seem like she wanted to talk about it, so I respected her privacy." With a final stroke to Titania's nose, he strode toward them. "What's all this about? Are you expecting some kind of recompense for the wedding or something?"

"No. I'm here to ask you what you want, Mr. Beaumont."

"Want?" The low rumble of his voice made her insides shimmer and her mind slide down a rabbit hole of a multitude of things she might want from him.

Steeling her spine, she made a sweeping gesture to encompass the house and the rest of the estate. "This place is obviously a very long way from home for you. What will it take for you to sell the property?" The moment the words were out of her mouth, she cursed herself. That wasn't how she'd meant to put it. He just flustered her.

She could feel Connor's eyes on her. He knew they didn't have the money to buy this place. David hadn't gotten back to her about the potential for a loan yet, but she was desperate.

The friendly smile slid off Raleigh's face. Those warm eyes chilled, and everything about him seemed to harden as he straightened. No more tame house cat, but a lion roused to anger. "I'm not interested in selling, Miss MacKean."

It wasn't too late. She could salvage this. "Come now. You can't possibly want to move your entire life across an ocean, to a whole other country, away from everything you've known. You don't know what you're taking on here."

A muscle ticked in that granite jaw. "With all due respect, *ma'am*, you know nothing about me, or my life, or what I'm capable of. I won't be selling. Period. Not to you or to anyone else. If that's the only reason you came out here, I'm afraid y'all have had a wasted trip. Now if you'll excuse me, I've got to go meet my tenants."

He strode to the gate between the paddock and the pasture, opening it wide to let Titania loose. Then he crossed to join Malcolm in the ancient Land Rover.

As they drove away, Connor folded his arms. "Well, I don't think that could have gone a whole lot worse. You're not winning any favors with your groom-to-be."

"That wasn't my intention," she bit out, furious with herself for losing her cool and straying from the plan.

Angus slid an arm around her shoulders. "It'll be all right, lass. I've taken care of everything."

They both turned to their uncle.

"What did you do?"

Raleigh's temper continued to simmer as the Land Rover bumped down the rutted road. How dare that woman show up the day after his arrival, trying to buy the place? In her little suit and fancy shoes, with all her implications that he'd fall flat on his face trying to take on something like this? No doubt she saw some country boy. Some parody of an American bumpkin, or shiftless rodeo rider, or whatever spaghetti western bullshit they had for reference over here. She didn't know him. And maybe he wasn't familiar with how they did things, but by damned, he was going to learn. He had a good mind and a strong work ethic. He'd make a success of it for himself. For his tenants. Not just to spite Kyla MacKean.

Though spiting her felt like a pretty solid plan just now.

No wonder Afton had been so desperate to get away. Connor hadn't seemed that bad, but what did five minutes of interaction actually prove?

"I can't say I blame Afton for not wanting to hitch her wagon to that family."

Malcolm didn't take his eyes off the road. "It wasnae about the family. It was more complicated than that."

Afton had insisted he keep Malcolm on. He'd obviously known her for years, so presumably he'd have been privy to a lot of her day-to-day life. Curiosity piqued, Raleigh turned toward the estate manager. "Complicated how?"

But Malcolm's allegiance definitely hadn't transferred with the deed. "It's no' my story to tell. You're here for a tour of the crofts."

Understanding that he wasn't going to get anything more about Afton's story out of the older man, Raleigh pushed the MacKeans from his mind and focused on learning about the estate he'd inherited. "A croft is a small farm, right?"

"Aye. Around five to twelve acres, focused on food production. And all the crofters have access to common grazing lands.

Nearly forty percent of Lochmara's holdings are tied up with crofting."

"And the other sixty percent?"

"Split between woodlands, heathlands, and cultivable lands for the baron's use."

"I assume there are harder numbers and maps indicating each of those?"

"Aye."

"I'll want a look at those later."

Malcolm grunted an affirmative.

"Those cattle and sheep I saw yesterday, are they ours, or is that part of the communal grazing lands?"

The "our" seemed to surprise him. One thick brow twitched up, and Malcolm glanced over briefly. "They belong to the estate, hence to you."

Raleigh made a mental note to dig into the books associated with the estate. Figure out how much he had in land, in equipment, in stock, and whether he could afford to offer Malcolm a stake in ownership of the lot. That probably wasn't how things were done here, but as Kyla MacKean had pointed out, he wasn't from around here, and some things deserved to change. He firmly believed people worked harder for things they had ownership of.

As they drove along the rutted lanes, his estate manager pointed out this croft or that, giving a brief sketch of who lived where. He explained that few Highland crofts were sufficient to support their residents entirely financially, so most of the tenants held other jobs or did other things in order to make ends meet. Hence, most of those tenants weren't home in the early afternoon on a weekday.

But one tenant definitely was. As they pulled up to a little stone house, Raleigh spotted someone bent over into the engine casing of a tractor. The person didn't emerge as Malcolm parked nearby, a mystery explained as soon as they opened the doors. Music blasted from a radio somewhere. Above the cheerful drums and pipes, a male voice rang out, swearing a blue streak. Raleigh didn't actually understand anything the guy said, but the tone was clear enough.

He straightened on a curse and hurled some tool. It landed in a large toolbox with a clang. Then he spotted them.

"Malcolm."

"Hugh. You'll have heard about the new owner of Lochmara."

"Aye, I have."

Malcolm jerked a thumb toward Raleigh. "This is him. Raleigh Beaumont." He nodded toward the man climbing down from a stool on the other side of the tractor. "Hugh McGowan."

The guy could've been anywhere from sixty to eighty. His skin had that weathered look that said he'd lived most of his life outdoors. Raleigh could relate to that.

He offered a hand. "Nice to meet you, sir."

"And you, Mr. Beaumont."

Raleigh took a few steps toward the tractor. "What seems to be the trouble?"

Hugh exchanged a questioning look with Malcolm.

"I grew up on a ranch. I've been working on tractors and farm equipment most of my life," Raleigh explained. "Maybe I can help."

The old man shrugged. "You're welcome to try. The bloody thing willnae start."

Feeling far more comfortable with an actual task, Raleigh rolled up his sleeves. It took more than an hour, but between the three of them, they managed to locate the problem and make the necessary repair.

Hands covered in grime, Raleigh stepped back from the engine compartment. "Try it now."

Climbing into the seat, Hugh turned the key. With a groan and a wheeze, the engine caught, quickly settling into a comfortable chug.

Hugh whooped. "Fuck me sideways! It works!"

Grinning, Raleigh began placing tools back into the box. "Happy to help."

The old man turned off the tractor and leaped down with an ease that had Raleigh edging that age estimation closer to the sixty end of the spectrum. "Of course, you'll come in for a cuppa. My wife just made some fresh biscuits."

Raleigh wasn't particularly keen on tea, unless it was iced, but he knew it would be rude to refuse, and his mama and Charlotte had raised him better than that. Besides, he could go for a snack. The three of them scrubbed up at a sink in the mudroom, washing off dirt and grease and carefully wiping their feet before stepping inside the little house. Raleigh automatically removed his hat.

"Flora! Put the kettle on. We've visitors."

"Already done, love." A comfortably round woman with pink cheeks and lively green eyes set off by her silver hair turned from one of the kitchen counters. "And you'll be the new baron. There's been lots of talk about you."

Raleigh wasn't quite sure how to take that. He offered a hesitant smile. "All good, I hope."

"All questions, mostly. And they're overshadowed by the gossip about young Afton running off."

"I expect that was pretty big news."

"It's certainly got the village in a dither. Please, sit."

They all took chairs around the kitchen table as Flora bustled around, bringing mugs to the table, along with a plate of cookies. Thanks to Charlotte's addiction to *The Great British Baking Show,* Raleigh knew these were what the UK referred to as biscuits. As he'd never met a cookie he didn't like, he followed Flora's urging to help himself.

"Tell us a little about yourself, Mr. Beaumont."

"Oh, please, call me Raleigh." To give himself a moment, he bit into the cookie, his eyes widening at the sharp, sweet bite of ginger in his mouth. "Oh, this is delicious."

Flora's cheeks flushed with pleasure. "Thank you."

Taking a sip of the tea to wash it down—yeah, he was definitely gonna need some sugar and cream there—Raleigh tried to think what they might want to know. "Well, I'm from Texas, from a multi-generational ranching family. Cattle, mostly. Some crops. Some horses. I've got a passion for working the land, and I'm hoping to do the same here."

The older couple didn't quite manage to hide their worried looks.

Raleigh leaned forward. "Look, I don't have any intentions of making sweeping changes. I'm here to learn how y'all do things around here. It's not my place to go overturning things just for the sake of overturning."

Their shoulders relaxed.

Flora picked up her mug with a smile. "Aye, and it's nice to see someone stepping in who really understands what it means to work with their hands and wants to work with the land. We havenae had that since Peter Lennox was killed."

Raleigh reached for another ginger biscuit. "Peter Lennox. That was Afton's father?"

"Aye. A good man was Peter. And his wife Darcie. Such a tragedy what happened."

"What happened?" He remembered her saying they'd died in a plane crash, but he was hoping they'd tell him a little more of the tale.

"Oh, terrible thing. Both of her parents and both of the MacKean parents were good friends. They'd gone on holiday, and the small plane they were on crashed on the return trip. Killed the lot of them nearly ten years ago now."

"Aye," Hugh agreed. "All those kids had to step into a hell of a lot of responsibility at a verra young age."

Was that the responsibility that Afton said should never have been hers? The full running of an estate that should have been under the purview of her father for years to come?

And Flora had said the MacKeans had also lost their parents. Maybe that loss was what had shoved that stick so far up Kyla's ass. It didn't make him like her any more, but he did feel some sympathy. He knew what it was to lose a parent young.

They chatted for a few more minutes as Raleigh and Malcolm finished their tea.

Shoving back from the table, Raleigh offered a genuine smile. "I thank you for your hospitality, Mrs. McGowan."

"Oh, of course. And thank you for the help with the tractor. This one would have been in a bear of a mood the rest of the day over it."

"Not a problem." He settled his hat on his head.

"Oh, and congratulations to you, Raleigh."

"Ma'am?"

"On the wedding."

He blinked at her. "Wedding? I'm not getting married."

Flora looked as confused as he did. "Oh, but the banns were posted this morning."

"The what now?"

She pulled out her phone, punching and swiping, before turning the screen toward him.

It appeared to be a post on the village's Facebook page announcing the intended marriage between himself and one Kyla MacKean.

What the actual fuck?

Putting a lid on his straining temper, Raleigh forced a smile. "If you'll excuse me, Mrs. McGowan, I need to go have a word with Miss MacKean."

Six

Raleigh's temper had hit full boil by the time he drove through the gates at Ardinmuir. He'd taken the time to drop off Malcolm, who'd had nothing to say on the matter, except that Raleigh needed to speak to the MacKeans. He'd be speaking to them all right. Likely at high volume, with probable profanity. He came around a curve in the drive a little too fast and tapped hard on the brakes as the castle came into view.

"Holy shit."

Because this *was* a castle. Or part of it was. He saw ramparts and battlements and a tower that half made him imagine a trebuchet in the yard. Clearly, the original structure had been added to over time. He recognized some architectural features that were of the same style as Lochmara. But this was much larger, much grander than the house he'd acquired. He actually preferred his. At least it felt like a home you could actually live in. He couldn't imagine calling a place like this home.

But that hardly mattered. He wasn't here for a tour. He'd come for answers.

Driving the rest of the way to the castle, he parked in the drive and stalked up the short flight of stone steps to the massive, carved-wood door he presumed was the main entrance. He pounded on it with his fist, wondering how long it took people to get from one part of the building to the other and how long he'd have to stand here waiting.

Not long, as it turned out.

The door opened to reveal a very different Kyla MacKean from the neatly turned out woman he'd met this morning. Her hair was down from the careful knot, now curling around her shoulders in thick red waves. She'd changed to jeans and a button-down shirt, and her feet were clad in bedroom slippers. Something about those damned slippers made her feel far more human, a fact that made his temper falter slightly.

"Mr. Beaumont. I've been expecting you."

He had only a moment to register that her tone held none of the supercilious condescension from this morning, before he was spewing the words that had been simmering in his mind the whole drive.

"What the actual hell is wrong with you, lady? I say no to your incredibly insulting business proposal, and you immediately turn around and publicly announce we're getting *married*?"

Kyla sighed, her shoulders drooping, her face set in lines of exhaustion and defeat. "That wasn't me."

Something about her posture got to him, but Raleigh shoved the reaction aside. It was probably more manipulation tactics. "Then who the hell was it?"

In contrast to his near shout, her voice was quiet and level. "Please, come in, and I'll explain."

He stalked in after her, following her through a grand entryway, up a short flight of stairs, and toward what was apparently the newer part of the house. The room she led him to was some sort of parlor, full of once grand furnishings that were threadbare with use and coated with a patina of age. It reminded him of a museum. How old was this stuff?

"Take a seat."

"I don't want a seat. I want some goddamned answers." He

didn't take off his hat either. He wouldn't be staying long enough for it to matter.

She jerked a shoulder as if to say, *Suit yourself,* before walking over to a cabinet and pulling out two crystal lowball glasses. Lifting a decanter of rich golden liquid, she glanced back at him. "Whisky?"

"No." This wasn't a damned social call. He didn't want to be here any longer than necessary.

"You'll probably want one by the time this is through." Kyla poured herself a generous glass and tossed it back.

Raleigh couldn't fight back the reluctant admiration at the fact that she did it without a single flinch.

She blew out a long, slow breath, bracing her hands on the top of the cabinet. "Hamish should have told you this already. Really, you should have been told by Afton herself, because she never should have done away with the property the way she did without disclosing all the strings that come attached to it."

The first flickers of unease began to push through his temper. "What are you talking about? I was told I owned the place free and clear."

Her flash of a smile held no humor. "Freedom is an illusion. That's something my brother said to me recently, and I'm only just coming to understand what he meant."

Crossing to one of the chairs, she lowered herself slowly, as if struggling under a great weight. The Texas bluebonnet eyes she lifted to his were direct, with no trace of guile. "Before I get into the necessary history lesson, I'd like to apologize for earlier today. I've been pretty rattled by all of this, and I handled the situation poorly. You deserved far more consideration than that. Especially, as you have no idea what you've walked into."

He hadn't expected an apology and wasn't entirely sure what to make of it. He got the impression she seldom made such overtures.

"Rattled by what?"

"I'm getting there. Has anyone told you the history of your estate?"

"Not really. Malcolm told me a little about how different parts of the land have been used over the centuries, the history of some of the buildings. But that's about it."

"The story actually begins here, at Ardinmuir. The history of this place extends back through my family for nearly nine hundred years. It's seen uprisings and changes, survived siege and famine. Survived the bloody English. It wasn't the main seat of the MacKean clan—that was in the West of Scotland—but it was one of their strongholds. The original structure that was constructed in the twelfth century was destroyed. The oldest part of the castle you see today was built in the fifteenth century. It was passed down, as such things were, from father to son, laird to laird, generation after generation, with each defending and expanding the MacKean holdings."

Her words held the tenor of a story told often, and Raleigh found himself listening intently despite himself.

"Around four hundred years ago, the king was on a hunting trip in the area. He was nearly skewered by a wild boar and would certainly have died if not for the bravery of William Lennox. Being grateful for the farmer's intervention, the king gifted him land and the title of Baron to go with it. That would be the start of Lochmara." She linked her fingers, clearly pausing for effect.

"Now, my ancestor at the time, Robert MacKean, had no respect for William Lennox. Our family had fought and bled and protected this land and its people for centuries. What did an upstart farmer know of such things? Robert didn't go quite so far as to declare outright war, for he didn't wish to anger the king, but that was the beginning of a feud that lasted for several generations. It was bloody and ugly and violent, as history often is. So, about three hundred years ago, the wives of the heads of each respective household decided they'd had enough. Knowing their husbands were more stubborn than mules and would never agree to terms purely on their own, the women sought an audience with the king. They wanted him to apply political pressure for the two families to forge an alliance and put an end to the feud. The heir from one family was set to wed the heir from the other. As an incentive to make certain that the marriage actually took place, both estates were pledged to return to the Crown if the wedding didn't happen. Because they didn't want to lose favor with the king, both families agreed, and the marriage pact was signed.

"Well, it turned out that there was a carriage accident and the intended groom was killed. As there were no other Lennox sons in that generation, there was no one to fulfill the pact. So the king made an amendment to the bargain that the pact should hold until such a time as it could be fulfilled. So, basically, it got passed on to the next generation. And so it was, through a series of unfortunate events involving childhood mortality, accidents, and flukes of birth with generations where both sides were born the same gender, that this pact has been passed down for three hundred years."

At her expectant expression, Raleigh narrowed his eyes. "You're telling me that this marriage pact thing that was signed some three centuries ago is still active?"

"Yes."

"And you don't find this absolutely insane?"

"Oh, I do. But this is something we were raised with all our lives. Afton was supposed to marry my brother, you see. That was finally supposed to be the end of it. Both estates would be saved from reverting to the Crown, and this lunacy would finally be over."

"Except she didn't go through with it."

"Correct. She apparently found the prospect of marrying Connor so abhorrent that she ran away and gambled her entire family history away to you."

"But I'm not part of the Lennox line."

"No. The pact is tied to the land, not to the Lennox family, in particular. So you, as a single male of appropriate age, have walked in as the new owner, and according to the terms of this pact, you and I are supposed to marry or both of our estates are forfeit. Hence, my uncle posted the banns this morning. Without my knowledge or approval."

"Forfeit. You mean, I won all of this, and I can turn around and lose it all if I don't marry you?"

"Yes."

"I don't even know you."

Her laughter held a slight edge of hysteria. "I am aware. I'm already involved with someone else. I have no interest in marrying you. *That* is why I made the offer that I did. Part of the complicated details of the thing mean that Lochmara cannot be sold to anyone but us. It's the only option that avoids either of us having to be tied to the other and the land reverting to the Crown."

Raleigh took off his hat and began turning the brim through his fingers.

"Look, Mr. Beaumont—"

"Under the circumstances, it seems like you should probably call me Raleigh."

"Look, Raleigh, I apologize for my blunt and inelegant delivery earlier today, but you have to understand, I am not willing to let nine hundred years of my family history go up like a puff of smoke. Is that kind of legacy and family history something that you can understand?"

Oh, the irony that they held far more in common than he'd first believed. "Yeah. Yeah, that's something I understand."

Deciding to take her up on that drink after all, he crossed to the bar himself to pour a two fingers of whisky, then filled the glass she'd left behind.

A faint glimmer of humor lit her eyes as she accepted the drink. "Thank you."

"So, let me get this straight. My choices are to marry you and keep Lochmara." He began ticking the options off on his fingers. "Let you buy the place and go home. Or do neither, and we both end up ass out with nothing."

"That's about the size of it, yes."

"And I presume this is all legally verifiable?"

"Of course. Hamish had intentions of telling you before he got called back to the city."

"And I assume, at some point in the last three hundred years, y'all's families went to the king or queen or whoever to ask that this whole thing just go away?"

"I don't think anyone managed to get an actual audience with Her Majesty before she passed, but the request has been run up the line. It boils down to the fact that our land is valuable and the government would love to get its hands on it. And they're certainly paying attention, since we submitted the paperwork for the marriage between Connor and Afton. There's a housing crisis in Scotland, and I know for a fact that the man currently in charge of enforcing this would love nothing more than to develop the area with that in mind."

Raleigh shuddered. "People need places to live, but why the hell do we have to give up pristine wilderness to build them?"

Kyla's eyes widened slightly, and she lifted her glass. "Here here."

He dropped into a chair and sipped at a truly excellent whisky to consider what she'd said. He'd been here for all of two days. He hadn't had a chance to get attached. Not really. Lochmara was a beautiful property, and he already had a soft spot for Titania. But he could walk away. At this point, he could take the money and go home, buy his own small spread, and start over. It wouldn't be the ranch that he loved, but it would be something. And it did make more sense than staying here.

"If this is a legit thing—"

"I assure you, it is. You can verify with Hamish. Believe me, if there were another way out, we'd have found it in the past three hundred years."

"If he verifies that these are my only legal options, then I'll accept fair market value on the property."

Her shoulders relaxed somewhat at that. "Thank you." She set her glass aside and leaned toward him, those eyes beseeching. "It's not personal. I'm just trying to protect my family legacy."

Perhaps nothing else could have convinced him to listen. But he understood what it was to lose a legacy. Needing some distance and a chance to mourn what he'd barely even seen, he rose and donned his hat. "I understand. I'll touch base with Hamish, see what's what."

She rose, too. "And I'll be in touch when I have the money."

This time, when she offered her hand, he took it. Her palm was warm, her fingers surprisingly callused. There was more to this woman than first met the eye.

"I guess this is grounds for a truce."

Kyla smiled, a real one this time, and Raleigh felt the kick of it somewhere in his chest. "I'll gladly take that truce."

As he followed her back to the door, he reflected it was probably a good thing the crossing of their paths would be fleeting.

———

For the first time in days, Kyla felt hopeful. When she'd found out what Angus had done, she'd known Raleigh would be on their doorstep as soon as he found out. But she hadn't expected him to truly listen. Nor had she thought he'd agree to sell so easily. She supposed any reasonable person would recognize that a bird in the hand was worth more than... well, no birds at all.

All in all, the entire thing had gone smoother than she'd expected. There was still the matter of actually getting the money, but she had faith that David would come through for her.

As she walked Raleigh out, they ran into Sophie coming up the front steps. She came to a stop and did a legitimate double take at the sight of Raleigh. Kyla couldn't blame her. He truly was a pleasure to look at.

"Raleigh Beaumont, I'd like you to meet my friend Sophie Cameron. Sophie, the current owner of Lochmara."

"Nice to meet you, ma'am." He extended a hand and flashed a smile. And holy hell, the man had dimples.

Sophie took his hand and shook briefly, the faint blush blooming in her brown cheeks proving she wasn't immune to all that Southern charm, either. "Welcome to Scotland. I hope you're finding it to your liking."

"It's been... an education." Those leonine eyes flicked to Kyla for a moment before moving back to Sophie. "If you'll excuse me." With a tip of his hat, he turned to go.

They both watched as he trotted down the steps and climbed into the Land Rover. Not until he'd cranked the engine did Sophie turn to her with wide eyes. "I never knew I needed to see Charlie Hunnam in a cowboy hat. Bloody hell, Kyla. *That* is the guy you're technically supposed to marry?"

"I'll concede he's attractive in a rugged sort of way. But it's a moot point. We've just come to terms."

"What kind of terms?"

"He's going to sell me Lochmara."

"How are you going to afford it?"

"David's working on it." That was all she wanted to say about that until the details were ironed out. "What brings you out here this evening?"

"Well, that's all good news, and I come bearing more. I have a couple who wants to get married here."

"What? When?"

"Sadly, not soon enough to make up for all the flowers that we ordered. I've been selling those off, and some varieties will stay fresh longer in the cooler than others. And at least we got the money back from the caterer, less the deposit. In the grand scheme of things, we're not out as much as we could be. Anyway, they're wanting to come in three weeks for a ceremony and reception. They've already filed the relevant paperwork. They've just been trying to find a venue. It's not a huge group. Only around fifty people. So small, intimate. We can easily pull that off. I've made a lot of notations already about options for the ceremony."

"That all sounds great, and we should definitely go over all of it. How much did you quote them?"

Sophie grinned. "That is the best part." She named a figure that was far higher than Kyla had thought they could command on such short notice and would definitely go a long way toward making up for the expense of everything they'd lost over the wedding that wasn't. "And they've already signed the contract."

"Even better. Things are looking up, indeed."

Arm-in-arm, they headed to the great hall to go over plans, discuss options, and divide up the labor so that the upcoming wedding wouldn't overtax either of them. The upside of having just done all this for her brother meant that they both knew the routine and who needed to be contacted about what.

By the time Sophie went home, Kyla was feeling downright cheerful. She'd missed dinner, so she raided the fridge and heated a bowl of leftover soup to go with some of the crusty brown bread Angus had made earlier in the day. Snagging a bottle of beer for the dinner tray, she carried the lot of it up to her room to call David and give him the update.

This part of the castle had no cell service, so she relied on the old land line. The phone itself was ancient, the handset tethered to the base with a curly cord. She secretly liked that cord. Liked being able to fidget with it while she talked. It reminded her of being a teenager, talking for hours with Sophie about some boy or other. With that image in mind, she was smiling as she dialed David's number.

He answered on the second ring. "Hey."

"I have wonderful news."

"What's that?"

"Sophie was able to book a wedding and reception here in three weeks. It should make up for the lion's share of what we lost on Connor's wedding."

"That is excellent news."

"Aaaand." She drew the word out like a delicious piece of caramel. "Raleigh Beaumont has agreed to sell me Lochmara."

In the face of the very, very long pause, Kyla automatically tangled her fingers in the phone cord. "Don't be so effusive."

David sighed. "Kyla…"

"You have to have good news for me."

"I wish I did. I can't get you the money. The estate already carries such a burden of debt, there is no one who's willing to take a risk on you. Not for that kind of money."

She sank down on the edge of the bed. "There has to be someone, somewhere."

"There is no one that I would trust, whose terms I could, in good conscience, encourage you to agree to. With the debt that your father left—"

The last thing she needed was a reminder of that weight on her back. "So that's it?" Were her hopes to be dashed this fast because of father's recklessness?

"I wish I had better news."

Just minutes ago, she'd been flying so high. Certain everything would work out. And now? "What am I supposed to do? Say goodbye to you and potentially marry a stranger? Is that what you want?"

"Of course not. I love you. There has to be another solution."

"The only other option involves us losing everything. I don't see another way out of this."

"I'm sorry, Kyla. I know what this means to you."

But she wasn't sure he did. Oh, he was supportive. But he didn't have the kind of legacy she carried. He couldn't know what losing this place would do to her. Tears burned her eyes, spilling down her cheeks.

"There is one other way." The hesitation in his voice told her she wouldn't like it. "You could sell part of your land. You know there are at least three development groups champing at the bit. Any of them would pay top dollar for it. You could prospectively make some kind of deal with Beaumont that you'll take the proceeds from that sale to pay him for part, and agree to pay the balance later."

"With what money? You've just said no one will take a chance on us. It would hardly be a sensible business decision on his part. He deserves fair market value for the property. Which leaves us, in a word, fucked."

"Have some faith that something will appear."

"You'll forgive me if I don't have a tremendous amount of that left."

"Something has to show up, because I don't want to lose you."

But neither of them was struck with any sudden bolts of inspiration, and by the end of the call, Kyla was left with a profound sense of hopelessness instead of the comfort David usually provided.

It wasn't his fault. He didn't make the lending rules. But how much loss was she expected to endure in her lifetime? She'd already lost both her parents. Her father had lost all the money meant to run the estate for generations to come. And now it looked as if she was going to lose either the man she loved or the home that meant everything to her.

She didn't see any alternative where she got to keep both.

SEVEN

"It'll take me a few days, but I should have a complete appraisal for you by Monday morning. I do think you'll be well pleased."

"Thank you, Mrs. Morton." Raleigh shook the appraiser's hand. "I appreciate you getting to this so quickly."

"Of course." She beamed a smile as he walked her out to her little Peugeot. "I confess, I've always wanted a look at the place. I'm grateful for the opportunity to see what few ever have."

"Glad you enjoyed the tour. I saw stuff I hadn't seen yet, myself."

As he waved her into her car, Raleigh reflected on how weird it was that he technically owned a houseful of stuff that marked the family history of someone he barely knew. If he were staying, he'd have made arrangements to pack up Afton's things and store them until she was ready to face what she'd left behind. That seemed like the right thing to do. But now, with everything going to the MacKeans, he wasn't sure what the right protocol was. He made a mental note to talk to Kyla about it when she contacted him about the sale.

Speak of the devil.

He spotted her car ahead of Hamish's coming up the drive. It had only been a couple of days since their agreement, and he hadn't expected to see her so soon. But she'd been eager, so maybe she was here to iron out the specifics of the sale before he had a chance to change his mind.

Kyla climbed out first, dressed in jeans and hiking boots that looked like they'd seen quite a few seasons. He liked that she hadn't reverted to the formality of the suit for this meeting. It made her seem less like the enemy and more like a real person. Had she been out tromping her own lands this morning? The gorgeous weather certainly begged for it, with highs barely hitting sixty in June. Could she even do that on a weekday? It occurred to him he had no idea what sort of work she did. Was her time purely wrapped up in the running of Ardinmuir, or did she have some other occupation?

Hamish's voice interrupted his musings. "Sorry to drop in on you unannounced."

Raleigh pulled his attention to the lawyer. "It's fine. I figure we've got plenty to talk about. That was the appraiser who just left. She should have a figure on fair market value by Monday."

Hamish and Kyla exchanged a look he couldn't entirely read for the sunglasses she wore.

"I'm guessing we've hit a snag."

"You could say that," Hamish conceded.

"Well, come on in and let's talk about it." It felt strange to invite people in, as if this was home. But what else could he do? For all intents and purposes, until he moved on, this *was* home.

They trailed him inside, and Raleigh realized, as Hamish hung up his coat, that both of them probably knew the place better than he did.

"Can I get y'all something to drink? Water? Iced tea?"

Sunglasses in hand, Kyla blinked at him in confusion. "Iced tea?"

Raleigh shrugged. "I'm Southern. That's how we drink it. Iced and sweet. I've got a pitcher in the fridge."

She pulled a face.

"Hey now, don't knock it 'til you've tried it on a hot day."

Her lips twitched. "We don't get too many of those here. At least not what I imagine you'd consider hot, being from Texas."

"You may want something rather stronger for this conversation," Hamish warned.

"Oh, it's gonna be one of those talks." Yeah, he'd been afraid of that. "Come on, then." He led them back to one of the rooms in the house he'd felt like claiming. The study was full of dark wood, leather furniture, and books. With its view of the estate, it reminded him a little of the study at the ranch.

As he fully absorbed their sober expressions, he had a feeling he'd better not get too attached. Whatever news they brought, it wasn't good.

Hamish remained standing, while Kyla took a seat on one end of the leather sofa, not quite meeting his gaze. The sunlight slanting through the window illuminated her pale face, highlighting the slight puffiness around her eyes. Had she been crying?

Because he didn't like wondering whether this was real or some other manipulation tactic, his voice was a little more brusque than he intended. "Well, spit it out. That shoe leather isn't gonna get any less tough if you keep chewing on it."

She laced her fingers and addressed a spot on the rug somewhere around his feet. "The long and the short of it is that I can't get the money. I cannot afford to buy Lochmara."

"Uh huh." The idea of getting out of here with the value of this place in his bank account had seemed a little too good to be true, even as he'd been willing to entertain the idea. "That is a problem. Are you here to try talking me into a lower offer?"

Kyla's head snapped up, insult whipping color into her cheeks. "No."

Raleigh tipped his head in apology. "All right."

Curling his hands on the back of a chair, Hamish remained ramrod straight. "I owe you an apology for not explaining all of this to you sooner. It's a complex situation, and none of us expected Afton to do... well... this."

Raleigh waved that away. "That doesn't matter. It is what it is. But give it to me straight, right now. If I'm not mistaken, our options are to get married or we both lose everything with absolutely no compensation. Is that pretty much it?"

Kyla nodded, clearly miserable.

"That sums it up," Hamish agreed.

No wonder she'd been crying. If she was half as attached to Ardinmuir as he was to his family ranch, the idea of losing it would be devastating. Raleigh knew exactly what that felt like and wouldn't wish it on anyone. And he wasn't keen on going back to the States with nothing himself.

"Well, what are the divorce laws here like?"

Kyla's head snapped up, her eyes wide. Even Hamish was staring at him like he'd sprouted a second head.

"You can't tell me you never thought of getting divorced. Is there something in the pact prohibiting that?"

"Well, no," Hamish admitted. "The expectation is that the marriage would be final and consummated. The assumption by the authors of the pact itself would have been that children would come from the marriage, thus solidifying the alliance between the two families. Divorce wasn't expressly forbidden because, at the time, it simply wasn't done. Especially once children were involved."

Kids. Jesus. "Are children required?"

"No." A thoughtful expression replaced the initial shock as Hamish seemed to turn over the question. "So, to obtain a divorce here, the couple has to prove an irretrievable breakdown of the marriage. The grounds for such include unreasonable behavior, adultery, or you both agree to the divorce and you've lived separate lives for at least a year, or one of you doesn't agree and you've lived separate lives for at least two years."

Raleigh considered. "I'm assuming unreasonable behavior is stuff like abuse?"

"Yes."

"Maybe I'm oversimplifying, but it seems to me like basically we just have to get married, get divorced, and all this goes away."

"I mean, technically, I think it would probably satisfy the terms laid out. And if the Crown contested, I believe a modern court would find in favor of the defendants for doing what had to be done to satisfy the terms of a pact that should never have been allowed to continue to stand."

Well, that was something.

"Why didn't Afton and Connor just do that?" It seemed a lot less extreme than gambling away a heritage. Although given her remarks about the weight of the responsibility, perhaps there was more to it than simply escaping a marriage she didn't want.

"My brother doesn't believe in divorce," Kyla murmured.

"Do you?"

She opened her mouth. Closed it again and swallowed. "It's never come up before. I don't have the same objections he does, no."

A plan was starting to coalesce in Raleigh's head. He shifted his attention back to Hamish. "When would this marriage need to happen by?"

"The formal filing of the marriage notice form would require at least one month, but you've got a window of up to three before you'd be required to refile the paperwork. There may be some additional paperwork you'd need to file, being an American. I'd need to check."

"Alright then. Hamish, can you excuse us? I think this is something that Kyla and I need to discuss privately."

"Of course. I'll just go have a word with Malcolm." He stepped out, shutting the door behind him with a quiet snick.

When Raleigh had thought about marriage, he'd had some hazy, romantic notion of finding The One and doing the whole song and dance of getting down on one knee, presenting his grandmother's ring. Not that he'd had any contenders for that honor. He'd enjoyed casual relationships over the years, and had had a couple of semi-serious ones back in college and grad school, but he'd been married to the ranch. He certainly hadn't planned on proposing to a proud, prickly Scot who'd gone a little green during the course of the conversation. But he hadn't expected to get screwed out of his rightful legacy, so he was learning how to pivot.

Because Kyla looked scared to death, Raleigh eased toward her slowly, as if she were a horse liable to spook.

"Are you out of your mind?" she whispered.

He sank slowly down on the opposite end of the sofa. "No. I'm just looking at our limited options. Why don't we consider this a business arrangement? We get married to satisfy the terms of the pact. Then, after sufficient time to figure out we don't like each other, so far as the courts would be concerned—say a month or so—we separate to begin the year apart and seek divorce."

"Why not sooner?"

"Because I don't think either of us will fall under the heading of unreasonable behavior, and I'm not committing adultery. Are you? Do you really want that on record as a thing you've done, even against a fake husband?"

She swallowed. "No, but there's the matter of consummation. There's nothing fake about that."

He didn't take her obvious discomfort personally. Being forced to bed a relative stranger wasn't at the top of his list of things to do either, no matter how attractive she might be. "Look, Kyla, you've already told me you're involved with somebody else. This is literally a business arrangement. And regardless of when this damn thing was drafted, I don't think any modern legal body can force us to show our sheets after the wedding night to prove that anything did or didn't happen. I have no problem lying about it if you don't."

She searched his face. "You'd really do this? Marry a virtual stranger?"

"The alternative seems to be that we're both out on our asses with nothing. The fact of it is, I don't want you to lose your home. And I don't want to lose mine again."

Something flickered in her eyes when he said "again," and Raleigh pushed on before she could ask about it. "So why don't you go talk to your boyfriend? See if this is something he can live with. And let me know. If he wants to come up here and talk to me, that's more than fine and fair." Raleigh wondered if her guy was open-minded enough to consider this lunacy. He couldn't honestly say what he'd do in that position, but that wasn't his problem.

Slowly, Kyla nodded. "I'll speak to David."

As he watched her go, it occurred to him that if this was really gonna happen, he should really call Charlotte and loop her in. His second mama would be certain to have opinions on the subject. Probably none of them would be good.

Maybe he'd wait until it was a done deal to tell her.

———

Kyla paced the castle, wandering the rooms, mentally cataloging the history in each one as a reminder of what she was protecting. David was on his way up from Edinburgh. She'd called and begged him to come in person. This certainly wasn't a conversation to be had over the phone. The important ones never were.

She loved this place so much. Every room held memories. The chaos of Christmases in the big Victorian parlor, when their father had set up the antique trains that ran the perimeter of the room. The summer she and Connor had tried to escape an unseasonable heat wave and gotten locked in the tower of the castle. No one had found them for nearly twenty-four hours and the entire estate had been in an uproar, searching. The impassioned Romeo and Juliet recitations she and Sophie had done from the balcony off the addition, before they'd been old enough to understand how utterly foolish the pair had been.

Even when she felt as if she were drowning from the responsibility that had landed on her so young, she'd never wanted to walk away from it. Oh, there might have been moments—low points after she discovered exactly what state their father had left them in—when she'd cursed the entire MacKean legacy. But at the end of the day, this was her place. Her home. Her heart.

"Kyla."

She turned toward David's voice, but she didn't rush into his arms. Perhaps a part of her was already pulling back in expectation of how this conversation would go. If he made her choose between him and this one option to save Ardinmuir, she knew what her choice would be. There was no stopping the innate grief attached to that, so she offered him a hesitant smile instead.

"Thank you for coming."

David closed the distance between them, skimming his hands from her shoulders down her arms as he studied her face. "You've made a decision."

"I've been given an option I hadn't considered before. But I need your input, as this affects both of us."

"Alright."

"Let's sit." Taking his hand in hers, she pulled him to a sofa and tugged him down. "I went to see Raleigh Beaumont today to let him know that I couldn't amass the funds to buy Lochmara. He presented another alternative. A business arrangement. A literal marriage of convenience."

David's face hardened. "You're going to marry him?"

Kyla tightened her hold on his hand. "In name only. He's got no interest in me. I have no interest in him." If a soft, wicked voice called her a liar, she ignored it. A chemical attraction played no role here. "Essentially, we'd marry, stay in the same house for a month, in the name of seeming to give it a solid try, then separate. After a year, we'd file for divorce and go our separate ways."

He said nothing, and she could only hope he was taking it all in.

"I know it's not ideal. But it's the only way we both get to keep our properties. I'm aware it's asking a lot of you. That's a long time to wait for me. And maybe you don't think I'm worth it—"

His kiss stemmed her words and gave her hope. She leaned into it, cupping his cheek and absorbing the familiar taste and feel of him.

His hand tangled in her hair as he eased back. "Of course, you're worth it. This would eliminate the pact entirely and allow Ardinmuir to be free and clear of the whole thing?"

"Yes."

"And what about the actual marriage part of marriage?"

"It wouldn't be real. Neither of us has any intention of this being anything other than a business arrangement."

His brows drew together. "But consummation is expected, isn't it?"

She shrugged. "We just won't and say we did. Raleigh's okay with that." They hadn't sorted out the specifics of where they'd live and keeping separate rooms, but those were all details that could wait until this was fully agreed to.

"Then I say you do it."

Something in her released at his words. "You're really okay with this?"

"I mean, it's not wonderful. It's certainly not what I'd choose. And obviously, I'll have to keep my distance for a while, so things don't appear untoward. But it would only be for a little while, and then you'd be separated. I think you're right. This is the only solution that will work for you both."

With the heaviness of a gallows walk, she realized she was actually going to have to go through with this. She was actually going to marry a stranger. Even the prospect of knowing it was temporary and that Ardinmuir would be safe didn't make this any easier.

"Then I guess we're agreed."

David brushed at the tears tracking down her cheeks. "Here now, it's a month—maybe two at the outside—before you're separated again and things can go back to the way they used to be. We've gone longer than that without seeing each other. It'll be fine. I'm surprised no one thought of this sooner as an option."

There seemed little point in bringing up the fact that her brother had deep objections to the concept of divorce and hadn't been willing to entertain the notion.

Shoving down the tears, she wiped her own face. "All right. I'll let him know. But later. Where's your bag?"

He leaned back. "I actually didn't bring one because I can't stay the night. And, actually, now especially, I shouldn't stay the night. I'm going to head back to the city."

"So late?"

"I've got some important meetings tomorrow that I couldn't miss."

"Oh." Kyla squashed her disappointment. "Thank you for coming so far to see me."

"Of course I did."

She rose when he did, already missing him. "There's just one more thing."

"What?"

"No one but you, me, and Raleigh will know that this is fake. We don't want anyone to have reason to contest it."

"Understood." He pulled her in for a hug and pressed a chaste kiss to her temple. "I'll see myself out."

It wasn't the parting she'd wanted, but she supposed he was right. For now, they needed to keep their distance.

After he'd gone, she wandered down to the kitchen to find her brother and uncle. They were gathered around the table with Hamish, noshing on crisps and drinking beer, while something simmered on the stove.

"Is David putting his stuff upstairs?" Connor asked.

"David's gone."

"What? Why?"

"Because I'm marrying Raleigh Beaumont."

The crisp Connor held fell out of his hand. "You're what?"

"It's not meant to be forever. I don't have the objections to divorce that you do. This is what's necessary to save our home, so this is what I'm doing."

Angus frowned. "And Raleigh is okay with this?"

"It was his idea." Hamish rose from his seat, circling around to take her by the shoulders. "Are you really okay with this, Kyla?"

"I have to be. As you're well aware, I have no other choice." Because he looked almost as miserable as she did, she patted his cheek. "Stop feeling guilty. It's not as if this is your fault. Now, if you'll excuse me, I've got to go speak to my husband-to-be. It seems we've a wedding to plan."

EIGHT

The monkey was giving Raleigh some serious side eye. It sat upon a stone wall, several feet away from its brethren, not looking particularly threatening, but he'd heard stories of the roving bands of Barbary macaques occasionally attacking unsuspecting tourists, so he kept his distance.

Yeah, I feel you, buddy. I think it's surreal, too.

He was getting married tomorrow.

Rather than going through the hassle of having him request a marriage visa in Scotland, they'd elected to fly to Gibraltar, which didn't require one for Americans. Hamish and Connor had come along as their two required witnesses. All the necessary paperwork had been filed with the registry office this morning. Hamish had taken care of all the other details, opting for a no-frills civil ceremony, which made sense, as this was hardly a case of love at first sight.

Then the four of them had taken the day to do a little sightseeing. But not even the famed Rock of Gibraltar itself, or its monkeys, could hold Raleigh's attention. He was too focused on watching his intended bride. She'd been quiet and withdrawn since they'd boarded the plane. With every hour that passed, she grew grimmer and more resolute. Despite the fact that she'd agreed to this scheme, it was obvious this was costing her.

Once Kyla had dropped the act she'd put on that first day he'd met her, Raleigh had come to understand that his first impression of her as being like his bitch of a stepmother had been entirely wrong. She didn't actually want his land. She was simply a woman caught between a rock and a hard place, and he didn't want to make this situation any harder on her than it already was. He hoped he hadn't made a mistake with what he'd set in motion with a phone call a few hours before.

Connor swung away from the view at the top. "I dinna know about the rest of you, but I'm fair starving."

"I could eat," Hamish acknowledged.

Kyla said nothing, just moved toward the trail that would take them back down the mountain.

Raleigh leapt forward, snagging her hand. "Hey."

Startled, she looked at their joined hands before lifting her eyes to his. "What?"

He could feel the fine tremors running through her and had to resist the urge to pull her in for a hug. It sure as hell seemed like she could use one. "Why don't we take the cable car down? It's been a long day, and you don't want to risk twisting an ankle before tomorrow."

She blinked at him, clearly searching for some ulterior motive.

He took a step closer and lowered his voice. "We could get dinner, just us. Have a chance to talk."

Some of the tension melted out of her shoulders. "I think that's a good idea. But I'd like to go back to the hotel first to clean up."

Raleigh just nodded and turned to Connor and Hamish. "We're going on back to the hotel and grabbing a bite without you two. We'll see you tomorrow at the registry office."

Connor opened his mouth, then closed it again when Raleigh just stared him down. He glanced back at his sister. "I'm here if you need me."

"I'm fine. See you tomorrow."

Not until they were in the gondola did she slip her hand from his. Raleigh felt oddly bereft at the loss of contact. Which was ridiculous. This wasn't going to be a real marriage. Shrugging off the sensation, he joined her at the railing, watching the mountain as they descended.

"Thank you."

He glanced down, but she wasn't looking at him. "For what?"

"I needed the break from them. From keeping up appearances."

"They're not under some delusion we're in love with each other."

"No, but they'll be making some assumptions nevertheless. So will everyone else. Lying is... uncomfortable."

"I'd probably think less of you if this were easy."

Those bluebonnet eyes met his. "Nothing about this is easy."

"I know it's not what you want. But it doesn't have to be awful. I figure a big part of why you're struggling is that you don't know me. Not like Connor knew Afton."

"You're not wrong."

"So have dinner with me tonight. Get to know me. Let me get to know you. Maybe we'll surprise ourselves and come out of this whole thing as friends. Because starting tomorrow, for better or worse, we're in this together. At least for the next year."

When she said nothing, Raleigh figured he'd be finding his own food and facing a long night to think about his choices. Her silence lasted until they debarked from the cable car and had made it back to their hotel.

She turned to face him fully, offering her hand. "All right. Dinner. Meet you in the lobby in, say, forty-five minutes?"

He took her hand again, noting how small it felt in his as he gave it a shake. "I'll be there."

A little over an hour later, they'd settled in at a tiny corner table of a cafe a few blocks from the hotel. The waiter had taken their order and left them with wine. Raleigh would have given a lot for a Shinerbock, but he could drink wine when the occasion called for it.

He leaned back in his chair. "What do you want to know?"

"The other day—when you proposed... all of this—you said you didn't want to lose your home again. What did you mean by that?"

Of course, she'd go there first. But it wasn't as if it was a secret.

"My family's ranch, Rosewood, was established in 1851 and was passed down through my mama's family for six generations. It was supposed to come down to me as the seventh, but I was only sixteen when she passed. Way too young to take over the running of it. So everything went to my dad. He remarried not long after. His wife and I... well, we didn't get on."

"Evil stepmother type?"

"Can't really call her a stepmother when she wasn't even a decade older than me. I never thought she'd last. She hated ranch life. But he loved it, and she allegedly loved him. I think she just loved the lifestyle being married to him afforded her. Anyway, he died of a heart attack—well, hell, I guess it's only been about two and a half weeks now."

Kyla's eyes widened, and she reached out to lay her hand over his. "Jesus, Raleigh. I'm so sorry."

Why should that small sign of compassion feel so nice? Maybe it was that he'd felt pretty isolated since he started his Scottish adventure. Or maybe it was just another sign of the thaw of the ice mask he had a feeling she was forced to wear far too often.

"Me, too. But not for the reasons you're thinking. See, the thing is, my daddy was a son of a bitch. He left everything to his second wife. The house. The land. The animals. The equipment. Everything that was mine by right. By birth. And she turned around and sold the entire place to developers."

The hand over his squeezed. "That's awful."

Just thinking of it had him wanting to rage again. But that wasn't what she needed, so he swallowed it down. "Wasn't great. That's why I was in Vegas. I wasn't in a great headspace, and one of my best friends thought it prudent to get me the hell out of town before I could do something I might regret. Which was a near thing when I found out she'd sold my horse."

"That bitch."

The vehemence in Kyla's tone wrangled a little smile from his lips. "Yep. The night I met Afton, she told me I sounded like a walking country song."

Kyla sat back, breaking the physical connection. "How did you meet her?"

"At the bar, actually. I hadn't gone there to gamble. I hadn't gone there for anything in particular. I was trying to get away from all the people, and she sat down next to me. I guess she sensed a kindred spirit of somebody trying to run away from their problems. Anyway, we got to talking, and I told her what had happened to me. That was when she invited me to a private poker game. Just me. I think, right or wrong, she picked me. She didn't want Lochmara to go to just anybody. She wanted somebody who was gonna take care of the land. Take care of the people. Not that she told me any of that. I didn't know what we were gambling for. She said she'd taken care of the buy-in for us both. When I won, I didn't really believe her. Even after talking to Hamish, having my attorney look into things, I don't think I really believed it until I got here."

"It's definitely not the sort of thing that's the norm."

He leaned forward. "The thing is, winning Lochmara, having this chance to do over here what I didn't get a chance to do at home, kind of gave me a renewed sense of purpose. Somewhere to build a new home. So that's why I agreed to this little arrangement of ours. Because she trusted me with her legacy, and I intend to do right by it." This time, he laid his hand over hers. "I intend to do right by you, too. I think, maybe, we got off on the wrong foot that first day. Legacy and history and heritage is something you and I both understand and respect, and I think that's a decent enough starting place for a friendship."

With her free hand, she lifted her glass of wine. "I can work with that. To friendship."

He gently tapped his glass to hers.

She drank, watching him over the rim. "So, it seems it's my turn. What do you want to know about me?"

He thought of what Flora and Hugh had said about how Kyla's parents had been killed. "Do you have more family? Aside from Connor and Angus? Somebody mentioned you'd lost your folks. I'm sorry."

A flicker of pain darkened her eyes. "We've quite a few cousins, once and twice removed. But Connor and Uncle Angus are my only direct family."

"You're the glue. The one who's had to hold everything together."

She seemed surprised at the observation. "Aye, I have. I'm the oldest. Connor always had the duty of marriage, so I guess I sort of took on everything else. On some level, that seemed fair. But now..."

"Now it's your life on the line." He sipped at his wine. "If you weren't stuck in this situation, bound to take care of your family, to marry me, what would you want to do? Is there some dream you've put off because of duty to the family legacy?"

Kyla scooped up her wineglass, staring into the bowl as if it held the answers. "No. No, I never wanted to do anything else. Be anywhere else. Ardinmuir is home."

"You don't feel like it's a burden?"

"The marriage pact is the burden. The rest is a privilege. Even when trying to make things work is sometimes a headache."

His lips curved. "That's a sentiment I appreciate. It's exactly how I felt about Rosewood. I don't think Afton felt like that."

"I expect we're in the minority. Keeping estates like ours running and even remotely profitable is... difficult. Lots of hard decisions to be made. I often feel like we're robbing Peter to pay Paul. To outsiders, it looks as if we must have loads of money, but really, we're land rich."

"I'm sure keeping a six-hundred-year-old castle up and running costs a pretty penny."

She sighed, but there was as much affection as exasperation in the sound. "There's *so* much restoration that needs doing. Parts of the castle have to be shut off because we can't afford to deal with them. I'm hoping that once the threat of losing the place entirely is dealt with, I can turn my attention to new means of generating income to help with that."

"Well, at least that worry will be over tomorrow. I'm only just starting to dig into the finances at Lochmara, but I get the impression it's a similar situation—minus the six-hundred-year-old castle part. Maybe we can help each other think outside the box for new and innovative ways to keep the wolf from the door."

Her lips curved into a warm smile that lit up her eyes, and she lifted her glass again. "I'll drink to that."

As they toasted again, Raleigh thought he just might learn to like his future wife.

———

"Where is he?" Kyla paced a restless circuit of the registry office lobby.

Their appointment for the ceremony was in fifteen minutes, and her groom wasn't here. He wasn't in his room at the hotel, and he hadn't answered his phone.

Christ, had he changed his mind? Was he running? Leaving the same way that Afton had? They weren't that far from places he could gamble.

Connor stepped into her path, grabbing her by the shoulders. "Calm down. He'll be here."

After last night, she would have sworn the same. But he was clearly nowhere to be found.

"How did you stand this?"

"Well, it was different for Afton and me. At least we knew we were going to do this from the time we were wee bairns. We weren't strangers. I'm honestly impressed as hell that you're willing to go through with this."

She and Raleigh had agreed that this was a marriage in name only. It wasn't exactly what her brother imagined. "Aye, well, he has to show up for me to do my duty."

The registry office door opened, and Raleigh stepped inside. "Sorry I'm late."

Kyla took three steps toward him before she stopped herself. "Where have you been?" Fueled by relief, the words spilled out in a rush. But before he could answer, she spotted a second man entering behind him. The dark gray cowboy hat, in a similar style to Raleigh's, told her he'd come with her groom. "Who is this?"

"Sorry. I had to make a run to the airport. You have your witnesses. I have mine. Everybody, I'd like to introduce you to Ezekiel Shaw. Zeke, this is Kyla, her brother, Connor, and their friend, Hamish."

Zeke stepped forward with a broad smile and the same easy, loping grace Raleigh had. He offered his hand. "Ma'am."

Oh, God. There's another one. Why did a Southern drawl make her all fluttery?

"Um, hello."

"I also stopped to get you these." Raleigh thrust a bouquet of colorful flowers into her hands. At her questioning look, his freshly shaved cheeks colored a little, and he shifted on booted feet. "I know we're doing the no-frills thing, but it didn't seem right, you not having flowers."

Moved by his thoughtfulness, she instinctively buried her nose in the blooms, inhaling their delicate scent. "Thank you."

"MacKean and Beaumont?"

Kyla pressed a hand to the stomach that jumped. It was time.

Raleigh offered his arm. On a fortifying breath, she slipped her hand into the crook of his elbow. Holy hell, was that his *muscle* she felt under there?

Doesn't matter. You are not going to feel up your new fake husband.

He escorted her into the registry office, with Connor, Hamish, and Zeke trailing behind.

The officiant, an older gentleman with thinning gray hair and glasses, beamed a smile. "Are you ready?"

"Yes, sir," Raleigh told him.

The man gestured for them to stand in front of his desk and picked up a book. The other men took up positions around them. Zeke pulled out a cell phone and winked at her.

"Let us begin. I would like to welcome you both to this very special day. You have come all the way from the UK to marry in our beautiful Gibraltar, and I wish you all the very best in your future life together." He pushed his glasses up his nose. "First off, I shall be reading what the law of Gibraltar says about marriage. These are special words, and I would like you to give them some thought. Before you are joined in matrimony, I have to remind you of the solemn and binding character of the vows which you are about to make. Marriage, according to the law of Gibraltar, is the union between two people, voluntarily entered into for life to the exclusion of all others."

Oh God.

Kyla started shaking. This was really happening. She was really about to marry a man she'd known for less than a week.

"Sir, if you'd like to repeat after me, 'I do solemnly declare.'"

Raleigh's big warm palm settled over hers where it tucked through his arm, and he squeezed. "I do solemnly declare."

His rich, warm voice rang out. How could he sound so confident?

"That I know not of—"

"That I know not of—"

"Any lawful impediment—"

"Any lawful impediment—"

"Why I, Raleigh Andrew Beaumont—"

"Why I, Raleigh Andrew Beaumont—"

"Should not be joined in matrimony to Kyla Elizabeth MacKean, here present."

"Should not be joined in matrimony to Kyla Elizabeth MacK-ean, here present."

"Very good. Kyla, please repeat after me. I do solemnly declare—"

Praying she didn't look as sick as she felt, she repeated the words. Her voice shook, but she couldn't stop it. The marriage they had planned was fake, but there was nothing false about these vows.

"Okay, so now we come to the main part of the ceremony. Please face each other and join hands."

Kyla handed off her flowers to Hamish. Raleigh shifted toward her, taking both her hands in his.

Her panic must've showed because he stroked his thumbs across her knuckles and whispered, "You've got this."

As she stared into his golden-brown eyes, his calm seemed to leech into her, quieting the cacophony of anxious thoughts. As long as she held that gaze, she could breathe.

"Raleigh, repeat after me. 'I call upon these persons here present—'"

Kyla barely heard the officiant, but Raleigh's voice was clear as he finished it out.

Then it was her turn. "I call upon these persons here present to witness that I, Kyla Elizabeth MacKean, do take thee, Raleigh Andrew Beaumont, to be my lawful wedded husband."

"Wonderful! And with these words, I can now say that you are husband and wife. Sir, you may kiss your lovely bride."

Wait, what? It had been two minutes. They couldn't be married after only two minutes.

As her husband—her *husband?*—stared down at her, Kyla's pulse spiked. They hadn't talked about this. He moved slow and easy, the same way he had with Titania the first time she'd seen him. She'd wondered then how those rough hands would feel on her skin. The pads of his fingers brushed her cheek in a gossamer touch, stroking back her hair before settling against her jaw. Gooseflesh erupted down her neck and arms at the contact, even as her heart threatened to beat straight out of her chest when he tipped her face up.

His lips settled over hers. The chill she'd felt melted into heat as something sparked between them. There was nothing of ease or comfort about this kiss. This was fire. Or the potential for it. Everything in her felt like tinder just waiting for one more spark, and she was shaking again as he pulled back. The gold of his eyes had been swallowed up with black, and she was gratified to hear him release his own shaky breath. At least she wasn't the only one affected.

"And now the rings!"

Rings? She hadn't thought about that. They hadn't even discussed it. And wasn't this out of order? Didn't the rings come before the pronouncement? But Raleigh had turned toward Zeke, holding out his hand. His friend dug into his pocket and produced a small box. He opened it, and Raleigh plucked something from the velvet.

"This was my grandmother's. That's why Zeke's here. I had him bring it to me."

It was another step toward making today feel like a real wedding and less like a business arrangement. It was thoughtful and sweet. But this was a family heirloom. Surely it was something he wanted to hang onto for his real wife. Not that she could say that in front of their audience. But she tried to communicate it with her eyes.

Raleigh just offered a reassuring smile and took her hand.

The officiant jumped in again. "Repeat after me. Kyla, take this ring as a token of our union and a symbol of our love."

Raleigh's fingers were warm as he dutifully repeated the words and slid the ring onto her finger. It settled against her skin, as if it had been sized just for her.

Connor tapped her shoulder and handed over another ring. She glanced down and recognized one of their family pieces. Well, at least everyone else had thought about this part.

She gripped Raleigh's larger hand and slid on the band.

"Raleigh, take this ring as a token of our union and a symbol of our love."

Oh hey, look at that. She'd made it through the last bit and didn't vomit.

"Fantastic." The officiant set his book aside and nudged the marriage register forward. "Okay, so you sit down, and please sign here."

It was self-preservation at that point to cling to her new husband's hand while they signed their names. After that, Zeke insisted on making them pose for more pictures. As Raleigh tucked her comfortably against his side, and she tipped her head to his shoulder and worked up a smile, she wondered if Raleigh had told Zeke the truth, or if he was under the delusion that they'd fallen into some whirlwind courtship. Would anyone believe that?

She thought back to that kiss. Maybe they would, because she certainly hadn't counted on having real chemistry with her fake husband. Maybe they should have a conversation about that, redefining the parameters of their marriage. They'd agreed there'd be no consummation. This kiss was part and parcel of the whole wedding ceremony. That should be the end of it, right? There was no more reason for public displays of affection.

They'd be fine. After all, it was just for a month.

NINE

Kyla hadn't expected to be moving. That was just one thing in a long list of details that she and Raleigh hadn't had a chance to work out before their wedding. But after Hamish, Connor, and Zeke had left them in Gibraltar for their twenty-four-hour "honeymoon," they'd finally sat down to hash out the details. She couldn't fault his logic that it would be far easier to sell the fiction of their marriage from Lochmara. No one else was in residence to know that they were sleeping in separate bedrooms, and they'd be more free to be themselves without her brother's or uncle's potentially prying eyes.

If she felt a bit of a pang packing her things and leaving Ardinmuir, it wasn't as if she wouldn't be back daily to continue the business of running the estate and preparing for the upcoming wedding Sophie had booked. She hadn't packed everything. When Connor questioned her about it, she'd put him off, saying that she'd migrate things slowly, as she needed them. Really, she didn't see the sense in taking all of her stuff for only a month. So, she'd packed several bags of clothes, her toiletries, and only a few small boxes of personal items like pictures and books.

Raleigh swung through the door to her room and scooped up a waiting duffel bag. "Is this the last of it?"

His presence filled the space, making the massive room seem somehow smaller. Kyla was suddenly very aware of the big cushy bed that had, no doubt, at some point in her family history, been host to the consummation of more than one marriage. Finding herself attracted to her new husband was incredibly disconcerting, all things considered. It didn't mean anything. It was probably just gratitude toward him for going through this charade. Thanks to him, her home was safe. The marriage pact was fulfilled. Finally.

She picked up the last box. "Aye, that's it. If I decide there's something else I can't live without, I can come get it easily enough."

"Alright then. Let's head home."

At his *after you* gesture, she stepped into the hall. "I don't know if that's ever going to stop feeling strange."

"Have you ever lived anywhere else but here?"

"I did when I was away at uni in Edinburgh. But not beyond that."

That big hand fell to her shoulder and squeezed. She'd come to appreciate those grounding touches. The reminders that she wasn't in this alone, and it wasn't forever.

"I expect we'll both be in an adjustment period for a while."

"What about you? Did you ever live anywhere besides Rosewood?"

"I left for university, same as you. But I've never lived outside of Texas. This whole new country thing is... something. I like it, though. You Scots aren't all that different from Southerners. Which makes sense. Scots were a huge proportion of who settled the American South, so that culture and a lot of those traditions got carried on."

Connor was coming in as they brought the last of it out. "Is there more?"

"Not right now." Kyla shoved her box into the backseat of her car.

"I can't believe this is all you're taking."

"I'm moving down the road, not to another country. There's no reason to stress myself over this part."

Angus hurried to meet them, a cake carrier in hand. "You can't be leaving without a housewarming present. I made you a Victoria sponge to take with you."

Raleigh took the carrier and peered through the clear plastic dome at the dessert inside. "I'm just gonna go on record and say that I will be happy to volunteer as tribute for any other baked goods you wanna send my way."

Angus grinned. "Have you a sweet tooth, lad?"

"Yes, sir. I'm not ashamed to admit it."

"Then you'll come to poker night. They're my favorite guinea pigs for testing recipes. Connor will text you the details."

Raleigh blinked, obviously surprised by the invitation, but his smile was warm. "I'd like that. Thank you."

Kyla wrapped her uncle in a tight hug. "You're going to take care of yourself. I'm going to check your pill boxes to make sure you're taking your meds. Connor, you'd best keep a close eye on him."

"We bachelors will be just fine without you," her brother declared. "We might even run around in our skivvies."

"Speak for yourself, laddie. I've no interest in freezing my bollocks off."

"I'm sure I'll see you tomorrow. Please be dressed."

"You're barely wed. Take some time, lass. No one's expecting you to get back to work so fast."

"There are a million-and-one things to do to get ready for the reception this weekend and the wedding Sophie booked the weekend after. I don't have time to loll about."

Raleigh slipped an arm around her shoulders, steering her toward the driver's side of her car. "I'll see she puts her feet up for at least a little while every day."

"Good luck with that," Connor called. "She never listens to us."

Mature woman that she was, Kyla stuck her tongue out at him. He crossed his eyes and stuck his out in return.

"Okay," Raleigh drawled. "Time to go."

Over the short drive to Lochmara, her mood dipped, thinking of all the household things she managed that Connor would now need to take over. It wasn't that she didn't trust her brother, but he wasn't the most responsible man. It was natural to worry. They'd never had to do without her for longer than a week.

And they won't have to do without you for even that long. You can see them every day, if you want. This is only for a month.

At Lochmara, she parked behind Raleigh and got out of the car.

He opened the front door. "Pick any room you like. I haven't really settled on anywhere. You're going to need storage space regardless, since these places weren't built with closets. So if somebody asks, that's why your stuff is in a different room than mine."

"Okay."

Raleigh frowned at her. "Kyla?"

"What?"

"Don't take this the wrong way."

"Don't take wha—"

But he just closed the distance between them and wrapped her in a big bear hug. "You really look like you could use one of these."

Oh God, she so could.

On a sigh, she burrowed in, wrapping her arms around his waist. He was a big man, taller than David by several inches, with broad shoulders and long arms that meant he could really enfold her. It felt good to be held, and she was way too damned tired from everything that had happened to talk herself out of taking this gesture of comfort. And they'd talked about becoming friends. Friends hugged. This was fine. It was more than fine. With every second that ticked by, she felt more of the stress and strain and worry slip away.

When was the last time she'd felt like this? As if she didn't stand alone?

She kept expecting him to pull away, but he just held on until she lifted her head. "Thank you. I really did need that." Feeling her cheeks heat, she stepped back, out of his embrace. "You give really good hugs."

"Thanks. I credit my mama for that. She always said you should never be the first person to let go in a hug because the other person might need it more."

"Your mother sounds like a wise woman."

"She was. She'd have liked you."

Uncertain what to do with that, Kyla turned toward her car. "Well, I guess we should start unloading."

They each grabbed a couple of bags and made their way inside and up the stairs, leaving the door open behind them. Unlike Ardinmuir, Lochmara had been built more or less all in one go, so the floor plan made considerably more sense. The stairway turned left at the landing leading up to the residential wing of the house. There were, she knew, eight bedrooms across the second floor. At the top, she hesitated.

"I don't know which room to choose. I've been in this house a thousand times. I ran tame here as a child. It's odd to be here and still see all the things Afton and her family always had, but to know she isn't here."

"Yeah, it does feel weird. Some of the pieces feel like they go with the house. Then other stuff feels really personal. I'm not planning on making big sweeping changes right yet. Not only because I sure can't afford to furnish a house this size from top to bottom, but because I'd rather give her the chance to settle wherever she's gonna settle and come back to get the things she wants."

Kyla glanced at him. "Even though you technically own it?"

"You and I both know she didn't really want to give up everything. She just felt backed into a corner. I have no reason to hold on to her stuff, but I also don't have a reason to sell it. I'm still waiting on all mine to get shipped from the States. Zeke was supposed to be making arrangements for that, actually. I should check on that."

"Did you tell him the truth? About us?"

"He's the one who took me to Vegas, so he knew about the poker game. I gave him the gist that we had to get married because of the pact, but I didn't take it further than that."

She looked down at the ring on her finger, a lovely diamond solitaire framed in antique filigree of rose gold. "But you had him bring this."

"Yeah. It seemed like the right thing to do. You and I are in this together, and my grandmama would have really gotten into this whole thing. She and my granddaddy eloped after a week, too."

"Really?"

He nodded. "Yep. Of course, they did it because they were in love with each other."

"How long were they together?"

"Fifty-two years. They passed within six months of each other. They had a good life. She would've appreciated the lengths that we're willing to go to in order to save these places, so I thought bringing in something of her might give a little good luck to the venture."

"Thank you."

It struck her, in the moment, that he was entirely alone over here. He'd left his home, his friends, and it seemed like there was no more family. For now, he had her, but they were time-limited, and she should do whatever she could to facilitate his settling in and really feeling like this was a home.

"Did Zeke go straight back to the States?"

"No. He's kicking around Europe some, since he was already over here."

"You should invite him to come visit, if he can. Our reception for the formal presentation of us as a couple is this weekend. He should come to the party. In fact, is there anyone else you want to invite? We haven't talked about any of that."

"Well, as a matter of fact, there is somebody I really ought to talk to—"

"Raleigh Andrew Beaumont!" The Southern woman's voice was no nonsense as it rang up from the foyer. "You get your butt down here right now."

His shoulders immediately hunched toward his ears, and he lost a shade or two of color. "Oh, shit. I'm in trouble."

———

Raleigh bolted downstairs to find Charlotte in the foyer, hands on hips, looking perturbed.

Yep, definitely in trouble.

To put off the inevitable scolding, he scooped her up into a huge hug, because it truly was great to see her. "What are you doing here?"

Her arms came around him in a tight squeeze. "Put me down. What do you mean, what am I doing here? Did you really think that you were going to send Zeke to go pick up your grandmother's ring, and I wasn't going to know about it?"

He had actually thought his buddy could pull that off. His mistake. Zeke was losing his touch.

As he tried to come up with some answer that wouldn't dig this hole any deeper, Charlotte leaned past him, spotting Kyla, who stood on the stairs, eyes uncertain. Kyla offered a little finger wave.

Okay, he really needed to do some damage control before this got out of hand.

All the sternness melted out of Charlotte's expression as she stepped around him and made a beeline for Kyla. His bride extended her hand to shake, but in typical Charlotte fashion, she bypassed it entirely and pulled Kyla in. "Nope, sorry. I'm a hugger."

After only a brief hesitation, Kyla squeezed her back. "Hello."

Charlotte pulled back and beamed as she lifted Kyla's left

hand. "You're obviously Raleigh's wife. It's incredibly nice to meet you. I'm going to have to tan his hide because I haven't heard a thing about you."

Kyla's lips twitched. "Same."

They both turned to look at him, and Raleigh felt his ears go hot.

He rubbed at the back of his neck. "Kyla, I'd like you to meet Charlotte Vasquez, my second mama. Charlotte, this is my wife, Kyla MacKean."

It felt strange to claim her like this in front of someone who was such an important part of his life. There was a subtle sense of pride at the statement, and he had to remind himself that their marriage wasn't real. Not like that.

Still, he watched Kyla turn on host mode. "It's wonderful to meet you, Charlotte."

"How long are you here?" As soon as the words were out, Raleigh winced. He hoped they didn't sound unwelcoming.

"Well, I don't entirely know, but I brought all of your stuff. It's out in the rental van."

"You brought everything?"

"Zeke said you wanted it all, so yes."

He hadn't been prepared for that. At least not yet. "Well, we're a little chaotic around here. Kyla's still in the process of moving in. We just got back yesterday, but there's certainly space. Obviously, you'll stay here." He shot a look at Kyla, trying to communicate apology for the imposition without consulting her.

Full of gracious smiles, Kyla jerked a head toward the stairs. "Why don't I go make sure one of the guest rooms is made up?"

"That'd be great, darlin'. Thanks." Putting an arm around Charlotte, he steered her toward the kitchen. "You came a long way. Why don't you let me serve you, for once?"

"Well, I've missed taking care of my boy, but I won't say no."

He automatically filled the kettle to make a fresh pitcher of iced tea.

"So, are you going to tell me now what's going on?"

Raleigh busied his hands pulling out tea bags and sugar, keeping his back to her as he considered what to say. The full truth wasn't an option. Charlotte had very firm opinions on the sanctity of marriage, and she'd no doubt think this entire situation was a terrible idea. He had to play on her inherent romanticism.

"I won this estate in a poker game."

"A poker game?" On the surface, her tone was neutral, but Raleigh knew her and heard the disapproval underneath.

"Yeah. While I was in Vegas with Zeke. I've checked with the attorneys. It's a done deal. All of this is mine." And it would stay that way now, thanks to Kyla.

Remembering what he'd told Charlotte on the day of the reading of the will, he turned around. "Look, I told you you'd always have a place wherever I land. And I meant it. I know neither of us expected that to be in another country, but if you want it, you have a home here."

"I appreciate it. I need to think about that. It would be a big change."

That was the God's honest truth. And maybe she was secretly relieved to finally be free to live her own life again. Raleigh certainly couldn't blame her for that.

She interrupted his thoughts with a smile. "I've never had a chance to come to Europe before, so I'd certainly like to hang around for a visit, at the very least. But I don't want to step on your newlywed toes. And don't think I didn't notice you haven't said a word about how that all came about."

"That's complicated, and everything's been kind of a whirlwind."

"Clearly. I never would have believed you'd be like your granddaddy."

He relaxed a little. This he could let her roll with because it explained things in a way she could accept. But it also added a complication. If she stayed here in the house, she'd expect him to be sharing a room with his wife, as married people did.

"Well, you're welcome to stay as long as you want. It's a huge house. There's plenty of space for all of us." The electric kettle kicked off, and he poured boiling water over the waiting tea bags, leaving it to steep. "I'll be right back. I just want to check with Kyla. See where she's putting you."

He didn't even have to look to feel the Mom stare she was aiming in his direction as he made his escape. Sprinting upstairs, he found Kyla making up a bed at the far end of the hall from his.

Stepping inside, he shut the door. "Okay, we have a little problem."

She tossed a fresh pillow on the bed. "This clearly isn't the stepmonster."

"No. No. Charlotte was my mama's best friend. She stepped in to raise me after Mama died. Stayed on as housekeeper at the ranch all those years after, so I wouldn't be without allies in that house. She truly is my second mother."

"Okay. So what's the problem?"

"She's gonna stay for a bit. Well, that's not exactly the problem. The thing is, I can't tell her the real truth about the status of our marriage."

"If she's here for any length of time, someone is bound to tell her about the marriage pact. I don't think we can hide that part."

"No, you're right. But the business arrangement and the fact that we're planning to get divorced from the outset. She... wouldn't take that well."

"What are you proposing we tell her?"

"Well, she's assuming this is one of those lightning strike, love at first sight sort of deals like my grandparents had. I didn't correct her."

Kyla went brows up. "So now I'm supposed to be in love with you?"

Raleigh appreciated that she didn't sound utterly appalled at the idea. "I'm not telling you how to behave. If she comments on the lack of PDA, I'll just say you're reserved in front of people you don't know. But the thing is... she's gonna expect us to be sharing a room."

Kyla's eyes widened. Even as she opened her mouth to protest, he lifted his hands to stay her.

"I have a solution. The room next to mine is adjoining. There's a door in between. We put all your stuff in there, and so long as the bed's made every day, there's no reason for her to notice if you just come and go from my room. She'll just assume we're sharing a bed."

"All right. That seems logical."

"I'll help move your stuff." It would be fine. They'd just be a little more on top of each other than they originally planned. It didn't have to change anything about their arrangement.

Kyla joined him when he went back downstairs.

Charlotte had finished making the tea and had clearly been investigating the kitchen. "This kitchen is amazing. Can you imagine all the empanadas I could make at that countertop?"

Before anyone could answer, the back door banged open, and Malcolm strode inside. "Who's the lummox who left a van in the middle of the bloody driveway?"

Charlotte's eyes widened at the sight of him, though whether it was from the overwhelming grumpy attitude or the kilt, Raleigh couldn't say. Maybe some of both. She balled her fists on her hips. "I expect that lummox would be me."

Malcolm's head jerked toward her, and he went stock still, his bushy brows drawing down further. "Who are you?"

"Charlotte Vasquez. Who are you?"

He seemed taken aback by the question.

Raleigh waded in. "This is Malcolm Niall, my estate manager. Malcolm, this is my second mother. She's brought my stuff from the States and will be staying here for a while."

Malcolm grunted something that might have been meant as a greeting or might simply have been disgust. "Move the bloody van. You're blocking the road to the south pasture." Then he turned on his heel and stalked out.

As the door shut behind him hard enough to rattle the pictures on the walls, Raleigh flinched. If there was one thing Charlotte had never tolerated, it was door slams.

Hands still on her hips, she swung around. "Well, that's a grade-A, hundred percent grump. He needs a few lessons in manners."

"He's a bit rough around the edges, but he's very good at what he does."

"Lord, I hope so. You better not be picking up any of his bad habits. I raised you better than that."

"No, ma'am. I know better."

Kyla slid into the silence. "We've got your room made up. And despite Malcolm's less than cheery greeting, of course, you're absolutely welcome to stay as long as you like. I look forward to getting to know some of Raleigh's family."

"That's so sweet of you."

"Either way, I do hope you'll be here through the weekend so you can come to our wedding reception. Since we decided to elope, we're having a big party to celebrate with everyone now that we're home."

Charlotte beamed at the two of them. "I wouldn't miss it for the world."

TEN

"The great hall is full of guests. It's almost time for your presentation." Sophie pointedly looked around. "Where's Raleigh?"

"Connor took him off to see that his Highland dress was put on correctly." Which shouldn't be taking this long. She hoped there wasn't a problem with the fit. They'd sent off his measurements to the kilt hire company earlier in the week.

Footsteps clattered outside the library, and Connor swung through the door, handsome in the MacKean dress tartan, with a dark blue argyle jacket and waistcoat. "Well, I did my best. He wasnae exactly cooperative."

"I had to draw the line somewhere." Raleigh's drawl preceded him into the room.

At the sight of him, Kyla's mouth fell open. He'd worn the kilt, having chosen the red Hepburn tartan from his mother's side. A dark waistcoat and argyle jacket topped a crisp white dress shirt. A traditional belt and sporran circled his waist. But instead of the kilt hose and ghillie brogues, he'd worn cowboy boots polished to a gleam. A black Stetson topped off the outfit. He looked magnificent, and for a moment, all she could think about was peeling him out of all those layers to find the man beneath.

Sophie nudged her shoulder and murmured, "Careful there. You're about to drool."

Kyla quietly shut her mouth.

"Look, you can take the man out of Texas, but you can't take all the Texas out of the man." Raleigh tugged at his bowtie. "This damned thing is gonna choke me."

"No, don't. It'll... unravel." Connor sighed with disgust. "I told you to leave it be."

Swallowing down the inconvenient blast of lust, Kyla moved into Raleigh, automatically reaching up to retie his bowtie. "Here now, I'll get it sorted."

He fidgeted as she worked. "Is this a problem? Am I gonna embarrass you like this?"

She paused, meeting his worried gaze and seeing an uncertainty she wasn't accustomed to from him. "You're anything but an embarrassment. And you've a right to be yourself."

He'd asked for little enough in relation to this reception, easily bowing to the original plan they'd mapped out for Connor and Afton. The only concession he'd asked for was for permission to include some proper Texas-style barbeque on the menu. He and Zeke had been smoking meat for two days. Was it unconventional to have brisket shooters? Yes. But the scent of the beef had permeated the entire house, and she couldn't wait to dig in. It was a damned good thing she wasn't wearing white.

Sophie clapped her hands. "Okay, you two. It's time to make your entrance. Connor, go on with you. Make sure Angus is ready with the quaich."

Eyes still on Raleigh, Kyla waved her friend away. "We'll be along in a minute."

"Take your time. It's not like we can start this party without you."

When they were alone, his gaze slid over her. "In case I forget to mention it later, you look beautiful."

"Thank you." She'd opted for a long satin dress that picked up the blue in his tartan. She loved the contrast of the color with her hair, and how the cut accentuated her curves. Because he seemed to expect it, she gave a little twirl so the skirt of her dress belled.

He worked up a smile, but it was a poor man's imitation of his usual grin.

"Your Scots forebears would be proud." Stepping into him again, Kyla skimmed her hands across his shoulders and down his arms, feeling the tension there. "Are you alright?"

He looked like he wanted to tug at the tie again, but refrained. "This is probably not the best time to mention I'm not great with crowds."

She'd noticed his uneasiness in the airport on the way to Gibraltar, but she'd attributed it to anxiety about the wedding. And they'd both been so consumed with the planning on the return leg, she supposed he'd been distracted. But he wasn't distracted now, and his face was a little too pale.

"Is it the number of people in a space or the need to converse with them?"

"Some of both. More the crush of them. Which makes the talking part harder. I'm not real keen on being the focus of all that attention, either."

All through the past week, he'd been there for her, grounding her, reminding her she wasn't in this alone. Seeing his unease, she wanted to return the favor. She curled her hands around his. "Okay, well, I'm fantastic with crowds, so you can let me do all the talking, if you want. Just remember, you're not out there by yourself. I'm right there by your side. Charlotte's here. Zeke's somewhere."

"Guarding the barbeque."

She laughed a little. "As he should. I've been wanting to steal some since yesterday. But either way, it's going to be okay. We just have to get through this formal presentation, and then if we want to find a quiet corner to stick to ourselves, everyone will just think we're being newlyweds."

She purposely didn't think about how appealing an option that was.

"I know there's more to all this than that. We've gotta mingle, and I've gotta meet people. I'll be okay. I just might need a break here and there to step outside, away from everybody."

"If you need a break, just squeeze my hand to let me know. I'll cover for you if need be. Or better yet, I'll make excuses, and we can slip away. One of the benefits of a six-hundred-year-old castle is that there are lots of places to hide."

That earned her the barest flash of dimples.

"That's a plan." He sucked in a bracing breath. "Shall we?"

"Let's do this."

Keeping his hand in hers, she led him through the labyrinthine corridors to the doors of the great hall. Sophie was waiting for them. She said something into her headset, no doubt communicating with the couple of extra staffers they'd hired for the event. The muffled sounds of a male voice she knew was Angus sounded on the other side of the doors, giving some sort of introductory speech. Then the doors opened on a swell of bagpipes.

Raleigh's arm tensed under her hand. She squeezed, and he laid his free hand over hers as they began to process into the room, down the aisle between all the tables, toward the dais, where her uncle waited in front of the ceilidh band. A sense of unreality settled over Kyla as they drew nearer, because this felt far more like a wedding than the hurried ceremony in Gibraltar. She could feel every eye on the two of them, sense the intense curiosity of those gathered here to celebrate. How would this marriage between strangers go? What kind of man had taken over the helm of Lochmara? What had happened to Kyla's beau? As Raleigh helped her up the short stairs, onto the raised platform, she prayed no one would ask.

As the echo of pipe music faded, they turned toward the crowd. Seeing the open curiosity on all those faces drove her closer to her husband, the feel of his strong, tall frame against her side grounding her against whatever they'd be facing. Instinctively, she understood that if she needed it, regardless of his own discomfort, he'd shield her. They were, as he'd repeatedly reminded her, in this together.

Angus still had the microphone and the attention of the guests. "Our happy couple have chosen to kick off this celebration, and symbolize their union in marriage and the joining of their families, in the old Scottish tradition of drinking from a Quaich. The Quaich, otherwise known as the loving cup, originated here in the Highlands many, many years ago, and has long been used as a cup of welcome and farewell. By its shape, you need to use both hands to drink from it, thus reassuring clansman that the other clan weren't hiding a weapon behind their back. It's considered a sign of openness, offering a hand in friendship and trust, which we can all agree are equally good traits in a marriage."

Raleigh had offered her all that in agreeing to marry her, and as she turned to face him, she was overwhelmed with a profound sense of gratitude.

"The bride's brother will now fill the Quaich."

As Connor added a healthy pour of whisky to the shining silver cup, Angus continued, "The whisky in this Quaich is sweet —symbolic of happiness, joy, hope, peace, love, and delight. That same whisky is also a wee bit bitter—symbolic of life's trials and tribulations. Together, these represent love's journey and all the experiences that are inherent to it. As you share the whisky from this Quaich, you're symbolizing your commitment to sharing everything in life and sealing the bond between you, whilst signifying the blending of your families."

Her brother stepped up between them, uncharacteristically serious as he handed her the Quaich. She shook a little as she reached for it, hating that she had to let go of Raleigh to take it between both hands.

Her uncle kept going with the ceremony. "You undertake to share all that the future may bring. All the sweetness life may hold for each of you will be the sweeter because you drink it together, and whatever challenges it may contain will be less difficult because you share them. When you drink now from this cup, you will acknowledge to one another that your lives have now become one."

Eyes on Raleigh's, Kyla lifted the Quaich and drank deep of the whisky, the burn of it torching through some of the nerves. As she handed the cup over, his fingers brushed hers, and sparks danced down her arms. She couldn't think about those sparks and what they might mean. He lifted the cup to his lips, his eyes dilating as they looked into hers.

"By the way, it's tradition to drink the Quaich dry, kiss the bottom, and turn it upside down on your heid."

Raleigh had a mouthful of whisky as he jerked his attention to Angus, who laughed.

"I just made that bit up."

Raleigh held up a finger and drained the cup, to the hoots and hollers of the assembly. He swept off his hat and doffed the Quaich in its place with a grin. Everyone laughed, including Kyla. He swapped back to his hat and handed the cup to Connor before taking her hand again.

Once Angus got himself under control, he managed to finish. "As you have both shared the drink from this Quaich, so may you share your lives. May you explore life's mysteries together and find life's joys heightened, its bitterness sweetened, and all of life enriched by the love of family and friends."

The applause and cheers were deafening. Under the cover of the noise, Kyla rose to her toes to get closer to Raleigh's ear. "Are you a little better now?"

He leaned down, and his lips brushed the shell of her ear. She was so distracted by the feel of it, and the fires it lit from her ear down her spine, she nearly missed his reply.

"I might need to get a few more of those in me to qualify as better."

Hoping he didn't notice the flush in her cheeks, she cleared her throat. "Let's get some food first, so you don't wind up under the table."

"Sounds like a plan."

———

The press of people hemmed Raleigh in on all sides. He'd lost track of names and faces and the number of hands he'd shaken as Kyla made introductions. It seemed she knew everyone. Which made sense. This was her place; these were her people. Because he hoped they'd become his, too, and because he felt his mama sitting on his shoulder reminding him to be polite, he put forth an effort to charm. But his battery was draining fast, and he was already considering calling in that lifeline Kyla had offered and dragging her off to one of those hiding places she mentioned. The only reason he hadn't was because his mind seemed determined to play a reel of suggestions about what he could do there with his new wife, none of which was on the table. Whatever open gestures of affection she made were performative. Despite his name on their marriage certificate, she wasn't really his. He needed to remember that.

"Dude, taste this." Zeke materialized from somewhere and thrust a napkin at Raleigh.

Blinking, he took it. "What am I tasting?"

"Just stuff it in your face."

Figuring Zeke wasn't about to prank him in front of all these people, he bit into the small, whitish square. A smooth, creamy, salty yeastiness burst on his tongue. Cheese. It was some kind of cheese. And it was fantastic.

Instinctively, he turned to Kyla and offered her the last bite. "Try this."

Her brows winged up, but she leaned in to nip the piece from his hand. He didn't think about the intimacy of the gesture until her pretty, painted lips brushed his fingers. Her little hum of pleasure had the blood draining out of his head.

Down, boy.

Deliberately tearing his focus away from her, he tuned in to the cheerful chaos of the guests and Zeke's expectant stare. "What is this?"

"That, my friend, is gold. Or should be. It's artisan cheese being made right under your nose." Zeke reached back, sliding an arm behind the shoulders of a curvy woman with a riot of dark curls to urge her forward. "You need to meet Pippa Wallace, the genius behind what you just ate. She's one of your crofters."

Pippa's brown eyes widened behind her glasses. "Oh, I... um. Hello."

Recognizing someone else as uncomfortable in crowds as he was, Raleigh offered a warm smile. "It's nice to meet you, Pippa. Your cheese is delicious."

"Thank you." Her tawny cheeks darkened with a flush, and she dropped her gaze. "It's just a hobby."

"It should absolutely be more. I'm telling you, this would win awards," Zeke insisted.

"Actually, it has won awards," Kyla added. "That's part of why Sophie and I wanted to feature it at the reception tonight. We're trying to utilize as much local fare as possible with the events we'll be hosting."

"I certainly appreciate the exposure."

Zeke popped another piece into his mouth, moaning in blatant appreciation. "Everybody needs to know about this cheese."

Pippa's gaze darted to him, then away again. "There's only so much of it to go around. My entire operation is small. As I said, it's a hobby. Even if there was more than just me, I'm limited by the size of my herd. Their welfare comes first."

"As it should," Raleigh agreed. "Let's set up time for a conversation later. I'd like to learn more about your setup and process. Maybe there's something I can do to help facilitate things, if for no other reason than to get on the short list for what cheese there is." He was hoping he'd be able to do more than that, if it was something Pippa wanted. Malcolm had told him about all sorts of cottage industries his crofters were engaged in to make ends meet. He wanted to learn more about all of them and find ways to invest in the people affiliated with Lochmara. It was partly about wanting to facilitate trust, but also because he understood that the ultimate route to prosperity for the whole was funneling funds where they'd do the most good. That was something his father had never understood.

Pippa blinked in surprise. "Alright."

Someone thumped a microphone. Angus's voice rang out. "If we can round up the bride and groom, it's time for the first dance."

Kyla linked her arm through his again with a smile. "We're being summoned. It was good to see you, Pippa."

"And you. Oh, and congratulations?"

Raleigh couldn't fault the question at the end. It was one thing for the entire village to be prepared for an arranged marriage expected for years. They likely didn't know what to think about him and Kyla. Nobody was under some delusion that they'd known each other before. He wouldn't be surprised if there were folks betting on how long they'd last. For some reason, the idea of that bothered him, even though he'd gone into this with a clear exit strategy and expiration date. Somehow, it just didn't feel so cut and dried now.

They took their position in the cleared space in front of the band. Over the past week, they'd gotten more physically comfortable with each other, so it no longer felt strange to pull Kyla into his arms as a solo guitar kicked things off. Raleigh didn't recognize the melody or the lyrics when they started. He expected something saccharine and wholly ill-suited to their situation. But the song was all about being surprised and finding home in the last place you expected. He knew she hadn't picked it herself. Probably Sophie was behind the choice. But it didn't change the fact that, in the moment, it felt like a message. One he desperately wanted to be true. Maybe it was because he'd lost his home, lost his family. Or maybe it was the woman herself, who'd turned out to be so much more than he'd thought.

Kyla wasn't unaffected. As they slowly circled to the music, the blue of her eyes was swallowed by the dark of her dilated pupils. He couldn't stop himself from pulling her a little bit closer. Her fingers flexed on his shoulder, tightening on his hand, and she edged closer. The guests, the responsibilities, and the rules they were bound by simply faded, until nothing was left but the two of them beneath the strands of cafe lights, dancing. Dancing. When her face tipped up toward his, Raleigh couldn't stop himself from bowing down, closing the distance between them to take her mouth. The taste of her seeped into him, heady and rich, and he wanted to drown in it. Drown in her. It would be so easy to lose himself. To fall headfirst into this unexpected attraction. Maybe there was more of his grandfather in him than he'd first believed.

At the applause and whoops, they broke apart, the spell of the dance broken. Color streaked across Kyla's cheeks, and her throat worked as she swallowed. Whatever that had been wasn't for the sake of appearances. However much that gratified him, Raleigh knew it didn't matter. That wasn't the agreement they'd made. Their marriage couldn't be real, and they both needed to remember that.

He just wished his fool heart would get the memo, because catching real feelings for his temporary wife was a supremely bad idea.

Eleven

Joints popped as Kyla stretched her arms overhead, feeling aches in muscles she'd forgotten she had. She and Sophie had been working practically round the clock to get everything ready for their first official booked wedding, and the day was almost upon them. Everything was set up, save for the flowers Sophie would bring in tomorrow morning and the food the caterers were preparing off site. There was tons more work to make sure things went off without a hitch. Then there'd be teardown. And, God willing, there'd be more bookings soon that would require them to do it all over again.

Even the idea of it had her whimpering.

"I know." Sophie sighed. "I was considering just curling up under one of the tables."

"It'll get easier, right?"

"In the sense that eventually we'll make a name for ourselves so that we can hire more than help just on the day of, so that we're not working ourselves ragged? Yes. I have faith it will." She looped her arm through Kyla's. "And thanks to you, we have the time to do all of that."

Kyla hummed a noncommittal note.

"How's all that going, anyway?"

"Fine."

Sophie just stared in that quiet way of hers.

"What do you want me to say, Soph?"

"That you don't regret marrying a stranger. That you're okay. I know what you gave up to do this."

Except she hadn't given David up. Not the way everyone thought. As they'd discussed, he was keeping his distance, so she hadn't spoken to him or even exchanged texts or emails since the night he'd left to go back to Edinburgh. But they only had a few more weeks until that changed.

Rather than answer any of her implied questions, Kyla admitted the one truth she could. "Raleigh's a good man, and he's becoming a good friend. We have a lot in common, as it turns out. So yes, I'm okay. Or I will be as soon as I find a horizontal surface to pass out on."

Sophie looked like she wanted to say something more, but held back. Instead, she rose. "You and me both. I'm headed home to crash. Are you staying here for the night?"

She could. She still had plenty of her stuff here, but she found herself shaking her head and moving toward the door. "The clothes I'm wearing tomorrow are at Lochmara, and I don't want to have to drive back out at some point to get them."

It was a flimsy excuse, but Sophie didn't call her on it.

They said goodbye at their cars, and Kyla started the drive home. One of the unexpected benefits of not living where she worked was that the drive to Lochmara gave her an opportunity to unplug and shift gears out of work mode. She'd have to figure out a way to replicate that shift when she moved back to Ardinmuir. But that was a problem for another day.

The house was quiet as she stepped inside. Faint whiffs of garlic, onion, and spices told her someone had been cooking. Likely Charlotte. Raleigh's second mom couldn't seem to stop herself from caretaking, even though she was technically a guest. Kyla's stomach growled at the scent, and she wondered if there were leftovers. She couldn't remember the last time she'd had food today.

"Raleigh?" She kept her voice quiet, in case he'd already gone to bed. He'd been up and out early this morning, dealing with animals before she'd even made it up.

Footsteps sounded from the lounge, and then his broad shoulders filled the doorway. "Hey. You've had a hell of a long day. Come sit down. Have you eaten?"

She tried to ignore the automatic lift she felt at the sight of him. "I was just trying to remember that."

"Charlotte made tortilla soup for supper. Put your feet up. I'll make you a bowl."

"I won't say no."

As he moved off to the kitchen, she went on into the lounge, toeing off her shoes and dropping onto the sofa. Because he'd told her to, she drew her feet up onto the cushion. She knew immediately that was a mistake. Oversized and covered in well-worn leather, this thing was made for naps. If Raleigh didn't hurry, she was gonna fall asleep right here.

He came back with a big bowl of soup dressed with sour cream and shredded cheese, and a bottle of Modelo.

"You are a god among men."

"You're welcome." He sat down at the opposite end of the sofa. "How's everything going with the wedding?"

"Things are lined up as they're supposed to. It'll be an early day tomorrow, but I think everything should turn out fine. What about you? What did you do today?"

"Malcolm and I went to a stock sale. I picked up some new cattle."

She blew on a bite of soup. "Oh? Are you planning to expand the herds to be a bigger part of the business?"

"I've thought about it. Been doing some studying up on the Highland cattle. They're a hell of a lot more environmentally friendly than what we raised in the States, and their meat quality is considered premium. But there's been a trend toward buyers wanting more affordability, with the economy being what it is. Some folks are doing cross breeding between the Highlands and some other breeds, and I might look into that down the line. But I'd like to study some more and talk to some people who've done it before I make a decision about that. No, this was something else. I had a conversation with Pippa Wallace earlier this week. Got a tour of her setup. She doesn't have room at her place to add to her herd, but I do. So I bought the animals, and I'll be responsible for the feeding and care of them. But she'll take the milk and use it to expand her artisan cheese business, in which I now have a small stake."

Kyla stared at him. She'd heard him make remarks along those lines at their reception last weekend, but she hadn't thought it more than polite conversation. She was coming to understand that Raleigh Beaumont didn't make idle promises. "You impress me."

"Oh?"

"Not many people in your shoes would have acquired this place without planning to come in and make sweeping changes to see that it fulfilled their vision. But you're not doing that. You're paying attention. Listening. Learning. And you're investing in other people."

He shrugged and pulled her feet into his lap, tugging off her socks and beginning to knead in a way that made her want to whimper. "I mean, we're nothing without our people, so it makes sense to support them and whatever their endeavors are. Investing in people was something my mom was really passionate about."

"What is it you ultimately want to do here?"

"I'm not entirely sure yet. I'm still exploring the options and getting a good handle on the finances of the estate, where I stand with all the things. I'm trying to really assess the needs in the area before I do anything big. But helping out my crofters is something I can do now that makes their positions more stable, and means I continue to have people who can pay the rent while I figure it out."

It was a smart way to handle it. He was far more intelligent than that laconic drawl made him seem, and she suspected he cultivated that impression on purpose. The more she got to know him, the more he impressed her.

"Sensible." She continued to eat as he rubbed her feet.

"What about you?"

She lifted another spoonful of soup. "What about me?"

"I know you and Sophie are starting this wedding business. Is that really where your passion lies?"

"My passion lies in restoration. The weddings—and hopefully other events—will give us the funds to do more of it. Right now, the focus is on paying off the costs of the equipment, tables, chairs, and the like that we invested in right off the bat. After that, we've got bigger plans to restore other parts of the castle. Some with events in mind. Others are more personal. Some are both. There's a conservatory from the Victorian period that is in terrible, terrible shape, but it was a clear showpiece in its day. Right now, it's completely cut off because it's not safe. Sophie's dying to bring it back to life. But before we get to any of that, we want to be able to hire someone to help with the grounds, and on a more permanent basis with our events." She flashed a wry smile. "Of course, we have to prove we can consistently book them first."

Raleigh switched to the other foot. "Was this what you went to school for? Event management kind of stuff?"

Kyla chuckled. "Hardly. I was bouncing between art history and photography back in uni."

"Where did you land?"

She sobered. "I was twenty when my parents were killed. Business seemed the most sensible course after that. And even that I finished online."

"That's tough." His eyes were warm and full of compassion and understanding. "You had to take on a lot at a really young age."

With a jerk of her shoulders, she turned her focus to the soup.

"Uncle Angus was here, but Connor was barely eighteen. Who else was going to step up?"

He laid one of those big, broad palms on her shin, and the warmth of the touch soaked into her, making her want to set the soup aside and crawl right on into his lap. She hadn't ever talked about the burden she'd taken on from her parents. Not really. Connor and Angus knew some, but neither of them had dug as deep into the books as she had. They didn't know how close they'd been skating to the edge of losing everything.

After a long moment of silence, Raleigh resumed his foot rub. "What about the thousands of other acres of woodlands at Ardinmuir? I know during the season we host guided hunts here. Malcolm's told me about it. But what is it y'all do with all of your land?"

"We used to do hunts, too. But those stopped about five years ago. I was contacted by some university researchers. They gave us a stipend to cease hunting so they could study a variety of native species. That ran out last year, but we'd already had to pull back on a lot of things because we didn't have the staff to manage maintenance. So, right now, it's just being allowed to run wild. I filed it under the heading of things we'd figure out later, after we were certain we wouldn't lose the land."

"Makes sense. Don't spread yourself too thin. I get the sense you've been doing that for a while."

"You aren't wrong." Finished with the soup, she set it aside and reached for the beer.

Raleigh dragged his thumbs down the arch of her foot, and Kyla moaned as the tension lodged there eased. The sound was unabashedly erotic, and heat immediately rushed to her cheeks.

She tipped back the beer to wet her suddenly dry throat.

They'd had a lot of these little intimacies. She'd just considered them a natural byproduct of being married, being housemates, and generally trying to convince Charlotte that they were closer than they were. It was a sort of Stockholm Syndrome caused by forced proximity. All of this would fade when they went their separate ways.

Still, she carefully pulled her feet from his hands and rose. "I'm gonna head on to bed. It's early start tomorrow. Thanks for... everything."

"Night, Kyla."

Ducking her head, she muttered, "Goodnight," and headed for the stairs, trying not to think about how much she truly liked her husband.

———

"What are you doing?"

At the sound of Charlotte's voice, Raleigh straightened from the fridge, a wedge of Pippa's cheese in hand. "I thought I'd throw together a little picnic lunch. Kyla's been working her ass off since we got back, and I'm planning to steal her away today to make sure she takes a break for a couple of hours."

Charlotte's face softened, and she patted his cheek. "You're a good boy. I think a little time away for the day will be good for you both. I'll pull this together. You go sweet talk your girl. That one doesn't seem to know how to stop unless you put a wall in front of her."

His girl. The sound of it rolled around in his head as he climbed the stairs. He liked it too damned much for something that wasn't actually true. Not beyond what was officially on paper. They were attracted to each other, but that didn't change the agreement they'd made at the outset. Kyla intended to remain faithful to David, and Raleigh wouldn't push her on that. The two kisses they'd shared had been initiated by him. They'd been necessary under the circumstances. A public statement. One, his brain seemed determined to remind him, that she'd been entirely into. But he didn't have the right to push that in private. No matter how much he wanted to get his mouth on her again.

Still, that didn't mean he couldn't help make her life easier while he was in it.

She was in her room, hunched over the desk, entering figures into a spreadsheet on her laptop. For a moment, he propped himself in the doorway of his adjoining room and watched her. Dark-framed glasses perched on her nose, adding a sexy librarian vibe he totally didn't need in his list of fantasies. Her red hair was pulled into a messy tail that trailed down her back. His fingers itched to comb through it and massage her scalp until those little worry lines around her eyes relaxed. Not an option. But he'd try the next-best thing.

"You're coming with me today."

Her head came up like some kind of startled bird. "What?"

"You need a break."

Those auburn brows drew together. "But I need to—"

Already anticipating her protests, he stepped into the room. "Nope. I've already called Sophie and Connor to tell them I'm kidnapping you. You're taking the day off. Everything's covered. There's nothing you have to do except come with me."

Kyla opened her mouth as if to object again, but Raleigh just rolled right over her.

"Look, you've been busting your ass from the day we met. I'm sure you were working it off long before that. You deserve a day to play."

"But—"

"Do you ride?" That was definitely something he should know about his wife.

"Yes. But—"

"Then close that laptop, change into jeans and boots, and meet me at the stables. You'll feel better being out in nature, away from all the shit you have to do."

Her sigh spoke of concession.

Thinking of what she'd told him the other night, he added, "Bring your camera."

He backed out of the room before she could say no, but he'd

seen her face light up at the prospect of getting to indulge her love of photography.

Downstairs, Charlotte held out a thermos and picnic hamper. Where the hell had she found that? "This should do you."

He kissed her cheek. "You're a goddess."

"Don't I know it. You two have fun. And don't forget extra blankets."

"Extra blankets?"

She went brows up. "If I've gotta tell you what to do with those, you really need to work on that whole honeymoon phase."

Raleigh did an abrupt about face, feeling the burn of embarrassment racing across his cheeks. "I'm gonna pretend I didn't hear that."

Charlotte's rich laughter followed him out the door.

He had Titania and one of the geldings, a sweet-tempered chestnut named Icarus, saddled and ready to go by the time Kyla came down, a small backpack slung cross-body from her shoulder.

She turned her face up to the gorgeous expanse of blue sky. "It's sunny."

He wondered what work she'd been so immersed in that she hadn't even noticed what was right outside her window. "Hence, a day to be outside. Need a leg up?"

"As it's been a minute, I'll say yes."

Raleigh moved in, trying—and failing—not to notice the floral scent of her shampoo or the feel of her leg beneath his hands as he gave her a leg up. As soon as she was astride Icarus, he focused on the business of adjusting her stirrups, then swung into his own saddle. Titania danced, eager to run.

"Settle down, darlin'. You'll get your chance to fly. Let's warm up a bit first."

They set off at a fast walk, following the stone fence that marked the edge of the south pasture. Day by day, Raleigh had explored the property, both by vehicle and by horseback. He still hadn't seen all of it, and there was a sense of adventure setting out with Kyla to see whatever there was to see. Maybe it was the prospect of having someone to share it with. Particularly someone who seemed to understand how he felt about being of service to the land and the people on it. After years of being dismissed by his father for that perspective, it was refreshing to be respected for it.

He didn't speak, sensing the quiet needed to work on Kyla for a while to unbend whatever was snarled up inside her. Long rides were good for that. He did some of his best thinking checking fences. She'd talk when she was ready. So he led her from pasture to forest and enjoyed the fine weather and the mare he'd fallen head over heels for. Simple, uncomplicated joys.

From time to time, he heard the click of the shutter behind him. That, too, was a simple, uncomplicated joy. One he suspected Kyla engaged in only rarely. She'd been carrying such a heavy weight on her shoulders for so many years, and she'd clearly relegated that love to the realm of impractical and not worth her time. He understood that inclination and had his mama and Charlotte to thank for not going too far in that direction himself. If he could help Kyla find her way back to putting her own happiness on that never-ending list of hers, he'd consider that a worthy accomplishment of their brief marriage.

As they wound out of the woods, the ground sloped up. Raleigh gave Titania her head and let her prance her way to the crest. At the top, he signaled her to stop and stared out at the gorgeous expanse below as he waited for Kyla and Icarus to join them. If his memory of the topographical maps of the area was correct, the river snaking through the glen wound through that pass to the west and around to feed the loch for which the property was named. It was as perfect and peaceful a spot as he could imagine, and evidently he wasn't the only one to think so. At the far end, near a small copse of trees, he spotted white walls and a slate roof.

As Kyla crested the hill, he jerked a head toward the building. "What's that?"

She scanned the valley herself. "Old crofter's cabin, probably."

"Malcolm hasn't introduced me to who lives there."

"Probably because no one does."

"Huh. It didn't occur to me that there were empty ones."

She folded her hands across her pommel. "Oh, aye. Between the two estates, I'm sure there are quite a few that have been abandoned over time because there was nobody to live in them and keep them up. Once they reached a certain degree of disrepair, they just kind of got let go."

"That's a damned shame. Seems like there's a lot of history in them."

Kyla hummed a noncommittal noise as she raised her camera and framed in a shot. "It's a beautiful spot."

"That it is. Let's go take a closer look. You up for a little speed?"

She laughed. "Probably not quite as much as you, but Icarus and I will manage. Go ahead. I know Titania's dying to run."

"See you down there."

He nudged the mare with his heels and felt her explode beneath him, leaping forward into a gallop. Clamping a hand on his hat to hold it in place, he whooped and held on for the ride as she flew down the hillside. This had always been freedom for him. From expectations. From worries. From anything but the glory of the moment and the feel of the wind in his face. By the time they made it to the river, Raleigh was grinning ear to ear.

Kyla and Icarus followed at a more sedate canter. He watched them descend, automatically analyzing her form. Her arms were a little sloppy, but she kept a good seat. Not bad for someone who didn't ride often. She looked worlds lighter as she reined the gelding in beside the water.

"That was fun."

"Nothing like it. Hungry? I figure this is a good spot for our picnic."

"Picnic?"

"You didn't think I'd bring you all the way out here without food, did you? C'mon."

They cooled the horses down and dismounted near the little house. From this close, it was obvious the place was, in fact, abandoned. Several tiles were missing from the roof, and greenery had grown up to choke one wall. It was bigger than it had first appeared. Raleigh itched to check it out, but decided it could wait until after food. He untied the blanket from his saddle—he'd only brought the one—and spread it out on the grass so they could take in the view. Then he grabbed the hamper and knelt to unpack the spread Charlotte had prepared for them.

Kyla's brows rose with every container he pulled out. "Wow. You really take this picnic thing seriously."

"Can't take credit. If it had been left up to me, we'd have probably ended up with peanut butter crackers, Pippa's cheese, and a jar of olives or something. Charlotte took over."

And she'd made them a feast of dried meats, cheese, crackers, the olives, sliced peppers, and dried fruits. What he'd thought was a thermos turned out to be an insulated wine carrier with a bottle of champagne.

Raleigh eyed the label. "Bless her romantic heart. We don't have to drink it if you don't want."

Kyla took the bottle from him. "And disappoint her? Not on your life. She went to a lot of trouble to put this together. We're going to enjoy it."

She untwisted the wire basket and released the cork with a cheerful *pop!*

"Well, all right then." He fished out the glasses from the set and held them out for her to fill.

After she'd rearranged herself on the blanket, he handed her one. "What should we toast to?"

"To the beautiful weather, the end of the pact, and unexpected partnerships."

Raleigh nodded. "To all that." He clinked his glass to hers and drank. "Less of a kick than what we had from the Quaich."

"Suitable for a quieter occasion." She began to layer meat and cheese on a cracker. "Thank you for kidnapping me. You were right. I needed a break."

He popped an apricot in his mouth, considering as he chewed. "You certainly don't have to talk about what's worrying you, but if you want to, I'm a relatively unbiased ear. I kinda thought you'd relax some once the issue of the pact was resolved."

"That's only one layer of a much bigger whole. It was the most pressing problem, but not the biggest." She didn't meet his eyes as she reached for another cracker.

"I'd like to help, if I can."

Her lips curved. "You've a good heart, Raleigh. But you can't fix everything."

She wasn't ready to let him in on whatever was gnawing at her. Maybe she wouldn't ever be. The idea of that shouldn't sting this much. They had an expiration date, so why would she include him in her worries for real?

"Fair enough. But offer stands, if you change your mind. You never know when you just need a different perspective to give you a new answer."

"Noted." She handed him a cracker loaded with salami and some of Pippa's cheese as an obvious peace offering. "And you have helped, bringing me out here and getting me out of my own head."

Letting go of more serious conversation, they ate and drank and laughed, talking of nothing and everything. When the containers were empty and his belly was full, Raleigh stretched out on the blanket and closed his eyes to soak up the rare sun.

At the sound of a shutter clicking, he cracked an eye to find Kyla's camera aimed at him. "Taking blackmail shots?"

"You looked like a piece of art there in the sun. 'Cowboy in Repose.'"

He tried not to let the compliment go to his head. "Not something y'all see a lot of around here." Closing his eyes again, he stretched out his arms and relaxed into the ground. "There are worse places for a nap. You should totally stretch out. Enjoy the peace and quiet for a bit."

After a long moment, she shifted, and Raleigh was shocked when she stretched out beside him, using his arm as a pillow. He didn't dare move or comment on it, even as his mind spun, trying to decide if it meant something.

"See now? Isn't this nice?" He could just barely feel the brush of her body from shoulder to hip, and yeah, it was more than nice.

She hummed her agreement. "Enjoy it. We don't get many days like this."

Degree by degree, he sensed her relax, as the birds chirped and the river gurgled by. They lay there until time lost meaning, and he began to drowse.

He only heard the sound because the wind died down, and he'd sat up before he even fully registered what it was.

Kyla sat up with him, evidently also hearing the noise. "What is that?"

"Problem. Maybe." He listened and heard it again. "Sounds like a cow. This is well outside the common grazing areas. There shouldn't be any cattle up here."

"Maybe there's an escapee?"

"Maybe. I need to find it and get it home, one way or the other. Will you pack this stuff up while I look around?"

"Of course."

She'd finished and joined in the search before he'd done more than narrow down the direction. Between the two of them, it took nearly twenty minutes to track the source, and when he spotted it, he muttered a curse.

The calf couldn't have been more than a week old. It was snarled up in some brush along a narrow, rocky track leading into the glen. The foliage had blocked it from view. On her knees, the poor thing looked exhausted. Raleigh scrambled over the brush to get a closer look. At the sight of him, the calf began to struggle anew, flailing against the rocks and getting nowhere as she lowed in distress.

"Easy. Easy, baby." Raleigh kept his voice low as he moved in, wrapping his arms around the calf to keep it from hurting itself further.

Kyla scrambled down beside him. "Poor baby's foot is caught in a crevice."

"If I hold her still, do you think you can get her free?"

"I'll certainly try."

Raleigh carefully tightened his hold and lifted. The calf bellowed her displeasure right in his ear.

Kyla crouched low. "Just a... There's a rock. If I can get it shifted... There!"

The calf began to thrash as Raleigh stood up with her. "Hold on there, girl. You're okay. You're okay." He continued to croon to her until she settled, resting her furry head against his shoulder. "There now. You're gonna be just fine."

Slowly, he began to stride back toward where they'd left the horses.

"Where's her mother?"

"I don't know. But if she's not with this little gal, I'd say chances are something happened to her. My guess is it's been at least a day or two since she's had anything to eat. I'll have to check with my people, see if anybody's missing one. In the meantime, priority one is getting this sweet girl home."

———

"Get the door."

Kyla rushed ahead of Raleigh to open the door into the kitchen. He followed her inside, carrying the calf like a giant furry baby, wrapped in their picnic blanket. She wasn't sure about the idea of bringing livestock into the house, but at least the stone floors in here would be easy to clean.

"Charlotte!" The calf stirred at Raleigh's bellow, rubbing her head against his shoulder as if to protest the noise. It was the most movement she'd made since he'd gotten in the saddle with her.

"Back already? How was y'all's—Oh, my God." Charlotte stopped dead in the door from the foyer. "What do you need?"

Raleigh carefully lowered to his knees, easing his bundle down to the floor in front of the empty fireplace. "Let's get the first aid kit. Somebody needs to go get Malcolm and see if we've got any bottles. If we don't, he'll know who has some. This poor baby absolutely needs milk. It's been at least a day or two since she's had any."

Before Kyla could volunteer for anything, Charlotte had already grabbed the kit from one of the cupboards and had bolted out the door. Having lived on the ranch with Raleigh for years, she'd probably dealt with something like this before and understood the urgency. Kyla felt helpless and useless. She knew nothing of cows. Livestock wasn't something her family had ever dealt directly in. That was all the purview of their crofters, so she felt entirely out of her depth.

"Come here."

At Raleigh's summons, she immediately crossed over to where he crouched on the floor.

"Sit down by her head. I need you to love on her some and keep her distracted while I get a better look at this leg."

Kyla sat cross-legged and began to stroke the calf's head. "This is as close as I've ever been to a heilan' coo. She's softer than I imagined."

"Hasn't had that weather proof topcoat grow in yet." He moved around to check the leg that had been caught.

The baby blinked huge dark eyes up at Kyla and offered a plaintive little moo.

"Here now, aren't you a love?" Kyla scratched her head and laughed as that little tongue darted out. "You're hungry. We're gonna sort you out. You'll see."

She kept talking and crooning as Raleigh did his exam. The sound of tromping boots announced Malcolm's arrival, with Charlotte close on his heels.

"How is she?"

"Not as bad as she might be. The leg's not broken. A little bruised. She's got a bit of a cut just above her hoof, but it's not bad. I disinfected it. Biggest priority is she's starving. We need milk."

"I brought a bottle, but I dinna have any fresh milk or milk replacer powder."

"Pippa will. Can you call her?"

"Aye." He whipped out his cell phone and stepped outside to make the call.

"We've got a partial gallon in the fridge. I'll put it on to warm." Pans banged as Charlotte set about preparing the bottle.

It wasn't so different from prepping to feed a human baby. As everyone continued to move around the kitchen, Kyla stayed where she was, stroking the calf's head and talking to her in a low voice, as Raleigh had out in the glen.

"Here we go. This will get her started."

Kyla stared at the bottle Charlotte offered. "What am I supposed to do with this?"

"Feed her." Raleigh scooted in close. "Here, hold it like this." He showed her what to do.

She took the bottle and tried to get the calf to take the nipple. "Come on, wee darlin'. Drink some milk for us."

The calf turned her furry head away, settling it in Kyla's lap.

"Seems she's more interested in a cuddle. Come on, sweet girl. You know you're hungry." Raleigh stroked along her side.

Kyla tried shaking the bottle, so a little of the milk squirted on the calf's tongue. That seemed to get her interest. "Here we go. Have some more of that."

Little cow lips wrapped around the rubber nipple and began to suckle.

"She's drinking!" Kyla grinned up at Raleigh and found him very, very close.

Those golden eyes were warm as he grinned back. "She sure is."

It was odd to feel such a moment of connection over an orphaned calf, but there it was.

This man was such a caretaker. Kyla had seen so much proof of that in so many ways. He'd seen that she needed a break and made sure she took one. He'd done it in a quiet sort of way, without any real pressure to talk about everything weighing on her mind. And she'd appreciated that. Instinct told her she could trust him, and she'd been about to tell him everything when they'd heard the calf crying.

Once they'd found her, he'd leapt in, doing what needed to be done to help her. No question. No quibble.

David would never have done this. He might try to help, but it would've been by calling someone else, not getting down and dirty and doing what needed doing himself. She immediately felt guilty for the uncharitable thought. David certainly had a lot of other positive qualities, or she'd never have been with him for the past two years.

But taking care of business was simply what Raleigh Beaumont did. He was a man of action who took care of anything and anyone who fell under his wide mental umbrella of what he considered his. Right now, apparently, he'd decided that included her. He was a big-hearted softy of a man, and every day she found him more and more appealing.

The calf had sucked down most of what they'd put in the bottle by the time Pippa arrived with more. She passed the containers of milk off to Charlotte and came over to inspect their charge.

She stroked a hand down the calf's flank. "Oh, the poor, wee beastie. Where's her mother?"

Raleigh shook his head. "We don't know. Didn't see any sign of her while we were out riding. Malcolm, have you heard of anybody missing any cattle?"

"Not that I've heard, but I'll put the word out."

"Good. In the meantime, we'll keep her here. Do we have any, like, dog beds in the barn or somewhere that we can bring in for her to lie on while we keep her corralled in here?"

Kyla jerked toward him. "In here?"

"Well, yeah. She's gotta be fed three or four times a day. We can't leave her alone right now. Somebody needs to keep an eye on her for the next little while until we find out whether someone claims her, or we manage to get her bonded with a surrogate. And, well, it won't be too long."

She heard, too, what he didn't say. That it would only be for another couple of weeks.

It was a sobering reminder that this arrangement of theirs, where she lived here with him under this roof, was drawing to a close. The idea of walking away from the calm she'd found here, and the stability he'd given her, was more than a little unsettling. And she found she hated the idea of not seeing him every day.

The very fact that such a thought even entered her mind was proof enough this needed to wrap as soon as possible so she could get back to her normal. Reconnect with David and start the clock on their year's separation before the divorce.

But for right now, she'd focus on the calf. One thing at a time.

"Well, if she's going to live inside like a pet, I think she needs a name."

Raleigh's smile spread slow as golden syrup. "What do you think about Mabel?"

TWELVE

"I appreciate y'all being willing to move poker night over here. Mabel's not really where we can leave her alone too long right now." Raleigh stepped back as Angus, Connor, and his cousin, Ewan McBride, who owned The Stag's Head Pub in Glenlaig, stepped into the kitchen, trailed by a fourth guy Raleigh hadn't met.

"Raleigh, Toby Byrne. Toby. Raleigh Beaumont," Connor said, by way of introduction to the lanky guy in a navy t-shirt and kilt.

Toby grinned. "The Texan with the magic touch. Hugh hasnae stopped talking about how you fixed his tractor." At Raleigh's blank look, he continued. "I'm the village mechanic. You saved me an afternoon's pain in the arse."

"Happy to help. And nice to meet you."

Ewan glanced over at the pallet of blankets by the empty fireplace. "I cannae quite believe it's true that you're keeping a cow in the house."

"She's being bottle fed three or four times a day, so we're keeping her close. Ultimately, we're hoping to bond her to a surrogate so she can learn how to be a cow, but for now, she's playing Queen of the castle."

"And a most adorable queen she is." Kyla stepped over the baby gate they were using to keep Mabel corralled to the kitchen and bent to press a kiss to the calf's nose.

She wriggled with pleasure, rubbing her head against Kyla's legs. Raleigh grinned at the pair of them. For all her reluctance, his wife was absolutely besotted with their little fur baby. They were both adorable.

Kyla paused to hug her uncle and pass a faux-serious look over the assembly. "Behave yourselves."

Connor flashed a cheeky grin. "Where's the fun in that?"

"Are you sure you dinna want to stay, lass? I made apple strudel."

She kissed his cheek. "Save me a piece. Sophie and I have work to do to lay out the details for this next wedding." Her gaze slid to Raleigh. "I'll probably be late getting back."

But she did plan to come back. Raleigh tried not to read too much into that. She'd had multiple opportunities where it probably would have been more convenient to stay the night at Ardinmuir, but she kept returning to Lochmara. It was hard not to think she was coming back to him.

"Drive safe." He itched to touch her, but stayed where he was on the other side of the kitchen island.

"Take care of my girl." She gave Mabel one last ear scritch before heading for the door with a wave. "Oh, hello, Malcolm."

The estate manager muttered a greeting and tromped inside past her. Raleigh could tell from the look on his face that he had some kind of news. Somehow, over the past few weeks, he'd learned to read some of the subtleties in the other man's scowls.

"What is it?"

"We finally found Mabel's mother." Malcolm shook his head in regret. "Looks like she slipped in a ravine and rolled onto her back. Couldnae right herself, poor beastie."

Raleigh had suspected it would turn out to be something like that. "Who'd she belong to?"

"I dinna ken. There wasnae a tag on her ear."

Raleigh released a breath he hadn't realized he'd been holding. He and Kyla were both attached. He hadn't relished the idea of giving the calf up. "Unless or until someone proves ownership, Mabel is staying here."

Hearing her name, Mabel trotted over to him, butting his legs for attention. He obliged with a good scratch around her ears and under her chin. She leaned into the touch, sticking her tongue out with pleasure.

"She's like a big dog." At the sound of Connor's voice, she abandoned Raleigh and wandered over to where he'd sat at the kitchen table, flashing her big, liquid brown eyes at him.

"Traitor," Raleigh muttered, without heat.

"I think she's more interested in my crisps than me."

"Don't you dare give her any," Raleigh warned. "She's only two weeks old and her stomach isn't ready for more than milk. My wife will kill me if she has any accidents in the house."

There was a beat of silence before Angus began shuffling cards. "You two seem to be getting on well."

"We're settling into a groove." A groove that would be ending in a week.

Raleigh didn't want to think about how much he was dreading the day Kyla moved out to start their separation. He'd gotten used to having her as part of his day. Used to talking over ideas for the estate and sharing meals. Even with Charlotte off exploring more of the country this week, they hadn't changed the routine they'd established. They were still acting married, even without an audience. Part of his dread was around the fact that she'd be leaving about the same time Charlotte did. Raleigh didn't want to be alone again. But part of it was Kyla herself. He liked her. And he had a healthy respect for what she'd accomplished.

But none of that gave him any reason to delay things. Neither did the fact that he felt more than a passing attraction to her. One he was pretty sure she returned. It might have been proximity and not about him at all. Certainly, his ego didn't like the idea of that. Maybe there was more of his granddaddy in him than he thought, because he wanted to believe they'd found a real connection. But if they had, she was the one who had to change the deal they'd made. He wondered what kind of man David Murray was, and what kind of relationship they had.

Raleigh considered asking, but though Angus and Connor knew about the plan for divorce, he didn't know if Ewan and Malcolm did, and certainly Toby had no reason to be aware of the situation. Raleigh didn't want to make it weird. Could he satisfy his curiosity either way?

As they all took their seats at the table, Angus began to deal. "Where's the lovely Charlotte?"

"I think she's hitting up Skye today. She's been using us as a base for shorter jaunts since she got here, but this last week she wants to go a bit further field."

"She's going home soon?" Malcolm didn't look up from his cards.

Raleigh couldn't tell whether there was disappointment or relief in his tone. Charlotte and Malcolm annoyed each other, no question. But Raleigh wasn't sure if that was true annoyance or if it was something else.

"I believe she's planning to fly home next week."

Malcolm merely grunted.

Not getting involved.

If there was something between his second mama and his estate manager, it was none of his business.

Snacks were passed as they played through the first couple of hands. And still, the question of Kyla's relationship with David Murray circled in the back of Raleigh's brain. When else might he get the opportunity to ask about the other man? He didn't feel right posing the question to Kyla herself.

"Can I ask y'all something?"

All eyes turned to him, expectant.

"I'll caveat this by saying if y'all aren't comfortable disclosing any of this, that's totally understandable, and I'll take my curiosity and shove it."

Connor angled his head. "You want to know about David."

Was he that transparent? Maybe so. "Can you blame me? Kyla doesn't talk about him, and I don't want to pressure her about it. I figure it's got to be a sensitive subject. But I'm curious."

Connor and his uncle exchanged a glance. "Well, I, for one, never cared for him."

"Why?"

"I mean, he's... fine. Banker in Edinburgh. They dated long distance for a couple of years. But they never made sense to me."

"How so?"

"All our lives, Kyla's been invested in Ardinmuir. It's all she ever wanted, and I dinna think David ever really understood that. I think that, if Afton had stuck around and married me, and Kyla never got pulled into things on that level, David was under some delusion she'd be willing to move her life to him. Maybe she would have tried, but I dinna think she'd have been happy doing that."

Kyla would *hate* moving her life somewhere else. Raleigh knew that, down to his bones. Her heart was, and always would be, tied to Ardinmuir. She was wired so much like him. Giving up her legacy and family history would be akin to walking away from herself. Surely, she knew that. Understood it. Nothing she'd ever said to him had indicated she intended to walk away from Ardinmuir, even if they didn't stay married.

His mind stopped. Divorce had been their plan from the beginning, but... what if it didn't have to be? What would she say if he said he wanted to give their marriage a real shot? Did he want that?

Raleigh filed it away to think about later.

"David's a good enough lad," Angus put in. "But he's not right for our Kyla."

Which begged the question of whether they thought Raleigh was. He couldn't ask. Wouldn't. Their opinions on the subject weren't important. Hers was the only one that mattered.

"Are we gonna braid each other's hair next?" Ewan demanded. "I came for poker."

"I'm here for the beer," Toby added.

"I'm here for the sweets," Raleigh admitted, reaching for another slice of strudel.

"Not for the gambling?" Connor asked.

"I'm not much of a gambler."

They stared at him.

"What?"

"Are you saying it was just luck that you won this estate from Afton?" Connor asked. "Because the woman's a cardsharp. We banned her from poker night because she kept taking all our money. Malcolm taught her too well."

"Sorry. Not sorry."

Raleigh thought back to Vegas. "I'm saying she lost deliberately. It takes skill to lose that spectacularly. She picked me for this." It was flattering. Fortunate.

But now he wondered if she'd chosen him only because he seemed like he'd honor her legacy and take care of the land and its people, or if she'd chosen him on purpose for Kyla, too.

———

Kyla watched as Mabel enthusiastically nursed from the sleepy-looking surrogate, her heart sinking. "I know it's what's best for her, but I can't help feeling sad. She's our wee furry bairn."

Raleigh draped an arm over her shoulders. "I know. We both got attached. But she's gotta learn how to be a cow, not just a spoiled house pet. Lord knows, she's not gonna fit in the house in a couple of months. But we can still come see her. She's not gonna forget us."

Needing the comfort, Kyla leaned into him on a sigh. "It won't be the same."

Nothing would. In just three days, she was scheduled to move back home to Ardinmuir to begin their year of separation. The idea of it upset her more than she wanted to admit. She was so conflicted about the whole thing. This past month with Raleigh had been so much better than she could have expected. They'd formed a true friendship. Then there was that damnable attraction she'd been trying to deny.

On his own sigh, he pressed a kiss to her temple. An innocent brush of lips. A sign of affection. It had her thinking of their wedding, their reception. Of how he'd tasted. How his body had felt against hers. She hadn't been able to forget it, and more than one long night had stretched out with her knowing just one paneled door separated her from his bed. One paneled door and the honor of the man who'd made vows to her.

And if, in those dark, lonely hours, she considered climbing into that bed, she blamed it on a longing for intimacy. Even before she'd been subject to the marriage pact, it had been a while. Hectic and conflicting schedules with David had seen to that. But beyond that yearning for physical closeness, somehow, in the past few weeks, Raleigh was the one who'd come to mean comfort. Maybe it was just because he was the one who'd been there. Not just physically present, but engaged and interested in every aspect of her life. He was so solid and steady, such a natural caretaker. After a lifetime of taking care of everyone else, that was beyond appealing.

Raleigh had her questioning everything about her life, her plan. She'd never expected to develop real feelings for her supposed-to-be-fake husband. Kyla knew she needed to do a lot of thinking and self-reflection. But it could wait until she returned to Ardinmuir, when she was no longer seeing him every day. How could she truly assess how she felt with Raleigh in such close proximity, distracting her with that heady combination of caretaking cowboy hotness? That wouldn't be fair to either man.

A whistle from the house had them both turning.

Raleigh dropped his arm. "That'll be Charlotte saying dinner's ready."

Already missing his touch, Kyla began walking back. "I can't believe she opted to cook her own going away dinner."

"Well, she's not thinking of it that way. She just wants to cook a family dinner since she knows she won't get a chance for a while after she flies home tomorrow."

Raleigh fell into step beside her, close enough that the back of his hand occasionally brushed hers. Kyla knew she could reach out and take that hand, twine her fingers with his. He wouldn't reject it. Instead, she curled her fingers in on themselves.

"I think you get your caretaker habits from her."

His chuckle was like a verbal caress. "It'd be hard not to. She comes by it very naturally and passed all those lessons on over the years. But I get it from my mama, too."

When he lapsed into silence, Kyla looked up, seeing the sadness on his face. "What is it?"

"I'm just really gonna miss her when she goes. It's gonna be real damned quiet around here."

Because, of course, Kyla was supposed to leave, too. Should she put it off? Give him a little more time to settle in after Charlotte flew home? If she stayed, would it be for him or for her? Because she was a little afraid of the answer, she redirected. "Do you wish she'd stay?"

"Well, I'd love for her to be nearby, because she's family. But I don't want to hold her back if there's something else she wants to do. She's rearranged half her adult life for me, and it's not fair for me to expect or ask her to do it all again. But I have been thinking about a proposition that might make her want to."

"Oh? What's that?"

"Well, before Mama got sick, Charlotte worked in the hospitality industry. She was an exec in a major hotel chain back in Texas."

"Charlotte worked corporate?" Kyla couldn't keep the shock from her tone.

"I know, right? You wouldn't think it. But she did, until she took a leave of absence to take care of Mama, and then finally quit to take care of me. She gave up a lot for my family, and I want to pay that back, if I can."

"Do you think she wants to go back to that sort of work?"

"No. I've asked her that before, and she said there are more important things in life, and nothing about that job really made her happy. But I've been thinking about how I've got this big ass house that I don't really want to live in all by myself. I was wondering what it would take to turn it into a B and B."

"Oh." The thought hadn't ever crossed Kyla's mind. "You'd want to have guests in and out all the time?"

"I mean, *I* don't want to live in a B and B or run one, but I was thinking she might. She enjoys taking care of people, making them feel at home. So it's been on my list of things to talk to her about tonight, before she leaves. What do you think? Is that a terrible idea?"

What did it say that Kyla immediately thought of how such a venture would dovetail with her own business? How many more people might be inclined to book Ardinmuir for their wedding if there was more lodging to be had locally?

This isn't about you, and that's getting far ahead of things.

"It's certainly something that seems like it would suit her care-taking bent. The house would be perfect for it, and it's definitely a business that could help support the estate. People would love to stay on this kind of property. There are certainly more considerations to bringing people in—legalities and the like, but it's worth talking to her about."

"All right. I'll see what she thinks."

"But what if she does want to do it? You just said you don't want to live in a B and B."

"There are other empty houses on the property. I could fix one of them up to live in. It's only me. I don't need much."

Only him. Because she was moving out. Damn it, there went that twinge around her heart again.

Charlotte was already filling plates when they stepped into the kitchen. Despite the bright smile she'd pasted on, there was no missing the faint air of sadness around her. If Kyla were a betting woman, she'd lay odds that Charlotte didn't want to leave Raleigh either.

She nudged him. "Go ahead and ask her."

"Ask me what?"

"Well, I've been doing some thinking." Raleigh went into his spiel, laying out the personal and the logical.

Kyla couldn't help but smile as she watched the change come over Charlotte's face, the excitement lighting her dark eyes. She was going to say yes, and Raleigh would still have someone here for him. No matter what else happened, Kyla would be glad of that. He needed family.

The phone in her pocket began to ring. She fished it out, seeing her brother's name flash across the screen. For just a moment, she considered letting it go to voicemail. Dinner was ready, after all. But she could let him know she'd call him back after.

"Hey, Con. Can I—"

"Kyla." Her name was a croak that set her instantly on edge.

Her fingers tightened around the phone. "What is it?"

At the sound of alarm in her voice, Raleigh broke off, turning toward her, those leonine eyes meeting hers.

Connor took a deep breath. "Angus had a heart attack."

THIRTEEN

Any news?

Raleigh glanced up from Charlotte's text, taking in their group. Connor paced a restless circuit in front of the windows. Ewan sat across the hospital waiting room, knee bouncing, fingers tapping the arm of his chair. Kyla hunched, pale-faced and shaking, next to Sophie, who murmured quiet assurances. And her hand was clamped around his like a vise.

With his free hand, Raleigh managed to tap out a reply. *Not yet. Angus is still in surgery.*

Because he'd needed a bypass.

Charlotte's reply popped up a minute later. *How are you doing?*

It was a fair question and no one else here would think to ask. Raleigh hated hospitals. The scents and sounds of them always made him think about those final months, watching his mother slowly wither away as the cancer continued its unstoppable march through her body. But he wouldn't mention it. They all had enough to worry about. So long as he kept his focus on them, he'd be fine.

Raleigh: *I'm okay.*

He couldn't say the same for his wife.

Kyla had been crying off and on since she got the call, all through the harrowing drive to the hospital and during the seemingly endless wait. Raleigh wondered what memories hospitals might bring up for her. He didn't know whether either of their parents had survived the plane crash long enough to make it this far. Asking would only make things worse, and they were bad enough on their own. It was enough to know that, other than her brother, Angus was the last direct family she had. There was nothing Raleigh could do for her but be here to make her feel supported and less alone.

The death grip she had on his hand told him she appreciated his presence, at least a little bit.

The three dots began to bounce again, stopping and starting more than once before her next text came through. *I cancelled my flight. Here as long as you need me. Do you want me to pack y'all a bag? I can send Malcolm with some fresh clothes and toiletries. Or borrow one of the estate cars and come myself.*

Raleigh: *Not yet. Kyla isn't gonna go anywhere until we know something. Will keep you posted.*

He slipped the phone into his pocket and met Sophie's gaze over Kyla's head.

She offered a bolstering smile. "I'm gonna go see if I can find some tea that doesn't taste like arse. I'll be back."

Kyla jerked a nod of acknowledgment. A fresh tremor pulsed through her as Sophie walked away, and Raleigh couldn't stop himself from detangling his hand to put his arm around her. She burrowed in, pressing her face against his throat.

"I'm so bloody scared."

"I know." Wanting to offer what comfort he could, Raleigh pressed his lips to her brow and squeezed tighter. "But Connor got Angus here fast. He did everything he was supposed to."

"I should have been there."

Hearing the self-blame in her voice, he tipped her face up. "No. Don't you go down that road. You're not God, and you're allowed to live your life. Don't get stuck churning on what ifs."

Her red-rimmed eyes were miserable. "It's hard not to."

He brushed a tear away with his thumb and wished there was anything he could say or do to make this easier on her. "I know. But Angus wouldn't want that. Positive thoughts, alright?"

Kyla nodded and settled back against him with a sniff.

Raleigh wondered if he should find a way to get in touch with David. If she'd feel better with him. But she hadn't asked for that, and for the moment, at least, she seemed comfortable leaning on Raleigh. The last thing he wanted was to leave her in the middle of this. These people might not be his family, but they were hers, and until a judge declared otherwise, she was his to look out for.

The thump of rapid footfalls had them all looking up. An older gentleman with thinning silver hair that stood out in stark relief against his olive skin rushed into the waiting room. "Has there been any news?"

Kyla straightened. "Munro? What are you doing here?"

"Connor called me."

She turned her attention to her brother. "Angus will be furious with you."

Connor crossed his arms with clear belligerence. "Good. Then it'll give him a reason to wake the fuck up so he can shout at me."

Pain lanced across the new man's face. "Is Angus..." Munro cut himself off, scrubbing a hand down his face. "Is he going to be all right?"

"We don't know yet." Kyla shoved up from the chair and crossed to wrap him in a hug. "It's good to see you, even under the circumstances."

Munro hugged her back with easy affection and a familiarity that told Raleigh he'd been a part of her life at some point, even if he wasn't now. Connor moved in next, repeating the hug.

"Thanks for calling me, lad. I know things didn't end well with Angus and me, but you're right that I wanted to be here."

Connor squeezed Munro's shoulder. "Maybe we'll be lucky and the whole thing will show him he made a mistake."

The older man's smile was sad around the edges. "We both know that's not likely. I doubt he'll see me. But I'll be glad to know he's okay."

Ewan gestured to the empty row of chairs beside him. "Grab a seat."

Munro sank into a chair. "I don't suppose you're hiding a flask somewhere?"

The corner of Ewan's mouth twitched. "I did, but we already emptied it. Sorry."

"Ah, well, it was worth asking."

As Kyla resumed her seat beside Raleigh, automatically reaching for his hand, Munro's attention turned to them. "And who's this, then?"

"Oh, Munro, this is my husband, Raleigh Beaumont."

Her claiming of him had a warmth spreading in Raleigh's chest.

Munro's dark eyes widened. "Husband. I didn't realize you'd married. Congratulations."

"It's... still new."

Well, that was one way of putting it.

Raleigh inclined his head. "Nice to meet you, sir."

"A Yank?"

"A Texan, actually."

Munro smiled a little. "I visited Texas once, many years ago. Delicious food. I'm Munro Sinclair. An old... friend of the family."

It was obvious to Raleigh that there'd been more between Munro and Angus than friendship, just as it was clear Munro still very much cared. He wondered what had happened between the two men, and whether this would present an opportunity for some kind of reconciliation. Perhaps the only occasional silver lining to medical emergencies was a reevaluation of priorities in favor of the things that were truly important.

"MacKean?"

They all shot to their feet and moved toward the doctor, a slim woman with glossy black hair pulled back into a tail.

"How is he?" Connor demanded.

"I'm Dr. Lee. I'm pleased to report that Mr. MacKean came through surgery just fine. He had a blockage in one of his valves, which has been repaired.

Kyla's hand tightened on Raleigh's arm. "Is he awake?"

"Not yet. It'll be another hour or two before he comes around and can have visitors."

Her fingers flexed. "What's the prognosis?"

"He'll be ready to go home in a few days. All things considered, he was very lucky. You got him in quickly, and that made all the difference. We have no reason to believe that he won't make a full recovery."

Kyla sucked in a breath. "Oh, thank God." Then she promptly turned into Raleigh's chest and burst into tears.

He held her tight as she let loose all the fear and worry of the past hours and knew he couldn't walk away. Not yet. She needed support to handle what was coming with Angus's recovery. The start of their official separation would just have to wait.

Six-hundred-year-old castles were not designed for convalescence. Kyla fretted over the fact that there was no way Angus could get to and from his room in his current condition. The cardiologist had been clear that he wouldn't be able to climb stairs for a while. So they'd converted one of the rooms off the kitchen that had, at some point in the past, technically been servants quarters. The space was small, but Raleigh and Connor had emptied it out and wrestled in a bed, Angus's favorite chair, and a little writing desk with just enough room for a TV so he could watch his favorite cookery programs. Sophie had brought flowers, and Kyla had dug up as many comfortable pillows and blankets as she could find to cozy it up.

But it wasn't his space, so she worried.

She didn't like the pallor of his skin by the time he settled in the chair. He was breathing so hard, after so little effort. The doctor had warned them, but she worried about that, too. She'd have sworn he'd lost at least ten pounds in the hospital. He looked so frail in the wingback chair, and for once she had no trouble remembering he was in his eighties. It terrified her. She'd been operating one step below panic for days and couldn't seem to stop. Her only recourse had been to keep *doing* things, so she didn't go mad.

"Can I get you anything? A cuppa? Something to eat?" As soon as the words were out of her mouth, Kyla realized she hadn't done the shopping. She didn't even know what they had in the house.

"I'm fine."

Her hands knit together. "You had a heart attack."

"A minor one."

"They had to do heart surgery!" Mortified by the fresh tears, she struggled to pull her rioting emotions back.

Raleigh stroked a hand down her back. "And he came through like a champ." His voice was low, soothing. The tone he used on the horses. He'd been using it a lot on her the past few days, and it did help some.

But it didn't stop the dozens of what-if scenarios spilling through her mind. "I'm sorry. I just... I don't want to lose you." She couldn't lose anyone else she loved.

Angus sighed and reached out for her hand. "Kyla, love, I'm going to be okay. I'm doing everything the doctor said. I love you, but go away. I want to rest." He softened the dismissal with a squeeze of her fingers. "Go rest yourself. I know you haven't."

It was true enough. She'd split her time between the hospital and working with Sophie to continue planning for the next wedding they had booked. Sophie was taking the lion's share there, which was hardly fair, but it was unavoidable. Kyla vowed to make it up to her. When she was less exhausted.

"All right. But if you need anything—"

"If he needs anything, he's got the walkie, and I'm taking the other," Connor interrupted. "Go rest."

"But—"

"Kyla, honey, come on." Raleigh wrapped an arm around her shoulders, steering her out of the room.

Charlotte was in the kitchen folding up some kind of tote bags. "He all settled?"

Raleigh nodded. "Yeah. I think he'll be down pretty soon. Us, too. We're all pretty wiped."

"Well, I'll get out of your hair. The fridge and freezer are loaded up with heart-healthy soups and casseroles, and I did a grocery run for basics, so you shouldn't need to think about food for a couple of weeks."

Kyla stared at her. "You did all that?"

"Baby, this is what Southerners do. We show our love and support through food."

Tears of gratitude spilled down her cheeks. Before Kyla could stop herself, she wrapped Charlotte in a tight hug. "Thank you. That was incredibly kind."

The other woman squeezed back. "Of course. Y'all are family."

She meant it. Kyla didn't quite know what to do with that. They'd been just the three of them for so long.

Charlotte stepped back. "You're about dead on your feet. Go rest. Connor already took y'all's bags up to your room."

Of course, she'd assume that Raleigh would be staying here and in her room. Kyla could've argued that he had things to tend to back at Lochmara, but the truth was, she was glad to have him here. Aside from the fact that he was someone else who could physically lift Angus if anything went wrong, he'd just been such a rock for her through this whole ordeal.

He placed a hand on the small of her back, giving a little nudge toward the door. "Go on up. I'll see Charlotte out and be up in a bit."

Relieved of responsibilities for the moment, Kyla didn't object. As she climbed the stairs to her room, she realized she was down-to-the-bone exhausted. Someone—Connor, probably—had left on a lamp. Their bags were piled at the foot of the bed. She had no idea what Charlotte had packed her—and didn't much care. It was one less thing she had to do herself.

Though she'd been gone for only a month, it felt strange to be here. Not only because a huge proportion of her things were still at Lochmara, but because she wasn't the same woman who'd left. The thought startled her. It was just the sleep deprivation talking. She eyed the bed, with its thick duvet and mountain of pillows. In a dozen steps, she could be falling face-first onto it. But there were probably things she needed to attend to first.

She felt Raleigh before he spoke.

"Nobody would blame you if you went to bed early. You haven't slept properly in days."

"Don't think I'm not considering it."

He edged around her and crossed to pick up his bag. "Where do you want me? I didn't want to bring it up downstairs."

Here.

For a moment, Kyla pressed her lips together, at war with herself. Charlotte wasn't here, necessitating the fiction of their marriage. Everyone in this house knew they planned to get a divorce. Their separation was meant to begin days ago. But she didn't know how to face all her fears in the dark, and she'd learned that he could keep the thought monsters away.

"Will you stay with me? I don't really want to be alone right now."

"Of course."

His easy acquiescence broke her paralysis. She picked up her own bag and opened it to find bagged toiletries neatly placed on top. "Charlotte is a godsend."

"Yeah, she is. Why don't you take the bathroom first?"

There was comfort in falling into routine, even if it wasn't routine to be doing it here. Kyla washed her face and brushed her teeth and decided that would do. It wasn't as if she was out to seduce anybody. She didn't have the energy for it, even if that had been on the table.

One step out of the bathroom proved her a liar.

Raleigh had stripped out of his jeans and shirt and was just tugging up some light cotton pyjama bottoms. She caught the barest fraction of his backside before he settled them into place and turned.

For all they'd been living in relatively close quarters for the past month, she'd never seen him shirtless. She'd known, objectively, that he was a muscular man. He'd hugged her often, so she'd been pressed close enough against him to notice. But a fully clothed hug was about comfort. Affection. This was different. A light smattering of sandy hair covered his pecs, narrowing to a trail that disappeared into the waistband of those pants. She didn't allow her eyes to slip lower because lust was already curling through her like smoke.

"All clear?"

Of course they weren't all clear. There were a million and one reasons why this was a terrible idea.

Then Kyla realized he was asking about the bathroom. "Sure. Of course."

If he noticed the blush burning in her cheeks, he didn't comment. He did grab a t-shirt and tugged it on as he went to brush his own teeth. As if that would do anything to erase the image of his shirtless torso that was now irrevocably burned into her brain.

She changed into her own pajamas, and before she could talk herself out of it, turned back the covers and slid into bed. As the familiar mattress enveloped her, she sighed. There was nothing like your own bed.

Raleigh emerged from the bathroom. "Got everything you need?"

Because she didn't trust herself to speak, Kyla merely hummed an assent. He switched off the light and crawled in on the other side. The bed dipped under his weight, rolling her toward him. His arms came around her, pulling her in. She didn't fight it. This was why she'd asked him to stay. Because he'd hold her and keep her grounded enough that she could maybe sleep.

She'd thought it would be weird, sharing a bed with him. But it just felt like an extension of all the hugs and casual touches they'd shared. His broad, callused palm slid beneath her hair to stroke her nape. She knew it was meant to soothe her to sleep. Instead, it just made her wonder what that hand would feel like on the rest of her.

What would he do if she kissed him right now? If she turned to him for more than simply being held?

Raleigh shifted, pressing a kiss to her brow. "Stop thinking so hard. You need rest. Go to sleep."

"My brain doesn't want to turn off." Not a lie.

"I could lecture you on tractor engine specs. That's sure to make you nod off."

She laughed softly. That was definitely not the option she'd been thinking of for taking her brain offline.

Sobering, she settled her head against his shoulder and made a confession that only felt safe in the dark. "I'm really glad you're here."

He settled his cheek against her hair. "I'm here as long as you want me."

It was a dangerous promise, because Kyla wasn't sure she'd ever stop wanting him.

With that damning thought ringing through her head, she slid into sleep.

FOURTEEN

Raleigh woke slowly, arms full of woman, his body humming in anticipation of pleasure. On a contented sigh, he settled closer, nestling his erection more firmly against the curve of her perfect ass, tightening his hand on the breast in his palm. As his thumb brushed one beaded nipple, she groaned, pressing into his hand and back into his groin. It would take so little effort to shimmy down their sleep pants and slide into her tight, wet—

Brain finally coming awake, he froze.

Oh, God. Not a dream.

As he lay there, hardly daring to breathe, Kyla settled again, her breath evening out. Raleigh felt the rise and fall of it against his palm because, sometime in the night, his hand had crept up beneath her sleep shirt and laid claim to that breast as if he had a right to it. Horrified, he carefully began to extricate himself. This was not what she'd asked for last night. She hadn't wanted to be left alone. She'd only wanted to be held. This was absolutely not what she'd meant, and his sleeping self was a horny, opportunistic asshole.

Moving as if she were a bomb that could detonate at any

moment, he unwound himself and slid out of bed. She rolled into the warm spot he vacated, but otherwise didn't stir. Loosing a slow breath, he dragged on clothes. She needed more sleep, and he needed to get the hell away from her until he was sure he had himself under control.

His inconvenient morning wood had faded by the time he found another bathroom and headed downstairs. In his semi-conscious state, he took a wrong turn that landed him in a room of what looked like a wonderland of castoff furniture that would have Charlotte salivating. Backtracking, he finally located the right staircase and made his way toward what he hoped was the kitchen.

Please God, let there be coffee.

The sound of banging pots alerted him that at least someone was up. Connor turned from the stove when Raleigh stepped into the room.

"You look like the dog's dinner. Coffee's on." He jerked his head toward a pot on the counter.

Raleigh shot him a wry smile and headed for the coffeemaker. "Thanks."

"Trouble sleeping?" Angus asked.

He'd slept like a damned baby all wrapped up with his wife, and that was a problem. Taking a page out of Malcolm's book, Raleigh just grunted and poured himself a steaming cup that blessedly didn't smell like battery acid. Leaning back against the counter, he took his first sip and looked Angus over.

His face had more color this morning. It was clear he'd rested better at home. That was probably on Connor. Left to her own devices, Kyla would probably have checked on him every hour, just like the nurses at the hospital, which wouldn't have done either of them any good.

Connor slid a bowl of oatmeal in front of his uncle and turned to Raleigh. "What are your plans for the day?"

"Well, Malcolm's taking care of everything back home, so I'm here to do whatever needs doing."

"Great. I need to run. I've got some work to do this morning, and I didn't want to leave himself here alone."

Angus scowled at his nephew and glared at the oatmeal, which was probably plain. "I dinna need a babysitter."

"How about just some company? It'll maybe help Kyla come down off DEFCON Magenta."

The old man sighed. "Fair point."

"Good. Great. We're all in agreement, then. I'm off before something else comes up. I've got my mobile if you need anything." Connor was out the door before either of them could say another word.

"Well, okay then." Raleigh carried his coffee to the table and sat. "What is it he does for a living, anyway? Kyla's never said."

"He does a lot of what Malcolm does. Interfaces with tenants, manages the boots-on-the ground part of the estate, where Kyla handles the business. Picks up some odd jobs on top of that. And, in the normal course of things, he hires out and gives tours of various areas of Scotland."

"Ah." Raleigh sipped and decided that his fallback career could be barista. He made damned good coffee.

"So, how is your lovely bride this morning?"

"Still sleeping, for now. She needs it, so I'm hoping she'll be down for a while longer."

Angus added some golden syrup to his oatmeal from the little green tin on the table.

Raleigh arched a brow. "Are you supposed to be eating that?"

Angus managed a tired facsimile of his usual twinkle. "I won't tell, if you won't."

"You expect me to keep secrets from my wife?"

"If you ever want another Victoria sponge, I do. I'm only having a wee dab. You cannae expect me to eat it with nothing."

Yeah, plain oatmeal didn't appeal to Raleigh either. "Baby steps. But I'm watching you. If you keel over again, Kyla's absolutely gonna lose it. She's had enough stress the last couple of months to last a lifetime."

"You care for her."

Uncomfortable with the truth of it, he jerked a shrug. "Yeah, of course, I do."

Angus huffed a laugh. "Come now, lad. There's no 'of course' to it. You jumped in and married a stranger. That disnae always lead to affection."

"She's not a stranger now." Aware he was walking through a minefield, Raleigh sipped his coffee and weighed his words. "She matters to me. By extension, so do y'all."

"Will you allow an old man to be nosy?"

Knowing he couldn't very well stop the guy from asking his questions, Raleigh shrugged. "You did just have a heart attack, so I guess you get a little extra latitude. Doesn't mean I'll answer."

Angus didn't laugh. "Connor was right in what he said at poker night. All Kyla has ever thought about is her duty to this place, to the family. Not in the same way Connor did, but she never wanted anything else. She hasnae been able to admit it to herself, but she's not going to be happy somewhere else. David will never have a life here. She'd have figured that out on her own, eventually. But then you came along."

Fighting not to shift under those sharp blue eyes, Raleigh just sipped again. "I don't hear a question in there."

"David walked away without a fight. To me, that says one of two things: Either he disnae care enough to try, or he knew this marriage between you and Kyla was meant to be temporary, and he's just biding his time."

Raleigh said nothing, not wanting to incriminate either of them.

Angus stirred his oatmeal. "That's okay. I don't need confirmation of what was decided behind closed doors. But if I can offer some unsolicited advice—you're the one who made vows to her. You're the one who's been here. Who's supported her every step of the way, through all this crazy and beyond. You share her passions and have actually asked about her dreams. If, over the past month, you've come to care deeply for her—and from my perspective, it seems you have—then dinna let her go."

It was so much in line with what he'd been wrestling with himself. And yet that wasn't the agreement they'd made.

As if reading his mind, Angus continued. "You're an honorable man, Raleigh, so I'm thinking you need someone who will give you permission and reassure you it is well within your rights as her husband—her real, legal husband—to try to woo her. And if she walks away in the end, well, then she does. But if she disnae..." He trailed off, but Raleigh could fill in the blanks himself.

If she didn't walk away, could they have a real marriage? A glimmer of what his grandparents had found? After the shit example of his parents, he'd never thought to find a match like that. But Kyla was... so much more than he'd imagined. And he found he wanted to try.

"Do you really think I stand a shot?" The words slipped out before he could think better of them.

An all-knowing smile softened that wrinkled face. "Oh lad, if you could see the way she looks at you. She disnae know what to do about it yet, and that's probably going to take her a while to wrap her head around. But I think, if you put your full effort toward wooing her, it wouldnae take long for her to fall."

He definitely needed more coffee before he thought about that. Rising, he headed back to the pot to fill his mug.

Kyla stumbled in, still in pajamas, eyes heavy from sleep. "I can't believe you didn't wake me."

"You needed the sleep. Coffee or tea?" Raleigh asked.

"Tea. Strong enough to make the spoon stand up."

"On it." He filled the electric kettle as she wandered over to her uncle.

"You look better this morning." She bent to kiss his cheek.

"A good night's sleep will do wonders."

They fell into easy familial patter as Raleigh measured leaves and filled the infuser with the blend he knew was her favorite. He'd watched her make it often enough, he felt sure he could do it correctly.

When it had steeped, he doctored it with half-and-half and sugar, as she liked, and carried the mug over to where she'd sat. He couldn't quite resist laying a hand on her shoulder as he set the mug on the table. "See how this works for you."

Kyla sipped, closing her eyes on a hum of bliss and tipping her head against his arm. "Perfect."

Angus shot him an I-told-you-so smile.

Maybe it wasn't flowers and poetry, but a properly made cup of caffeine was a start. He had a lot more work to do if he was going to properly court his wife.

———

It didn't matter how much Kyla played with the numbers in her spreadsheet. Without some kind of miracle by the end of the year, the income from the wedding business wouldn't be enough to keep the wolf from the door. They were, in a word, fucked.

Heartsick and weary to the bone, she slipped off her reading glasses and rubbed at her eyes. She wanted to believe an answer was out there somewhere, but she was out of ideas. She'd carried this burden for years, never letting on how terrible things really were. It had always felt like a problem for the future, after the marriage pact had been satisfied. That had been Connor's part, and she hadn't wanted to burden him further. They'd lived life in a form of constant triage. Now she'd been the one to resolve the pact, and she couldn't see how she could avoid telling her brother the truth. But she didn't want to add to the stress and strain of the household while Angus was recovering. She didn't want him to know at all.

"I come bearing tea and dessert. It's not one of Angus's cakes, but Charlotte makes a damned tasty apple pie."

Kyla straightened, but didn't manage to neutralize her expression before Raleigh saw her. She should've expected him. This was the routine they'd established over the past month at Lochmara, meeting over dinner or dessert to talk about anything and everything. Of course, he'd assume they'd do the same here. It was part of his promise to make sure she actually slowed down for a little bit each day.

He set a steaming mug and a plate on the desk beside her, his golden eyes searching her face. "I'm thinking I should've gone for the a la mode. What's wrong? Problem with the wedding?"

"No. All that's on track, mostly thanks to Sophie picking up the slack while we've dealt with Angus."

"That's part of the point of having business partners. So there's somebody to carry the ball when you can't." He snagged a chair and dragged it over to the desk, sitting beside her. "What's going on, darlin'?"

He'd more than proven she could trust him. She'd already nearly told him everything on the day of their picnic. Would have, if they hadn't gotten derailed by Mabel's rescue. Maybe as an outsider to the situation, he'd have some insight she lacked. And even if he didn't, she needed to tell someone. Who better than the man who was keeping her other secrets?

Kyla pivoted to face him, close enough that their knees brushed. A frisson of... something shot up her leg to more sensitive parts, reminding her of this morning, when he'd been wrapped around her. Even hours later, she could still feel the imprint of his work-roughened hand on her breast and the heat of his erection against her backside. Just the thought of it caused a pull low in her belly. She'd liked having him in her bed, liked having his hands on her. And a part of her was disappointed he'd pulled away. Which just went to prove that, of the two of them, he was the more noble. It was hard to hang on to her resolve now that he wasn't a stranger anymore. He'd been her partner in so many ways she hadn't expected, and that was just as seductive as the chemistry that had taken them by surprise.

She should really find him another room tonight. Or at least erect a wall of pillows or something.

"Kyla?"

She jolted, realizing she'd been staring at him. "Sorry." Heat streaked across her cheeks as she reached for the pie. Fortification with sugar seemed like an excellent plan. She forked up a bite, momentarily distracted by the tart sweet burst of flavor on her tongue. "Mmm. Angus might have some competition in the pie department."

"You should try her peach cobbler. But you're evading. If you'd rather not tell me, just say so."

"No, it's not that. I'm working up to it." She ate two more bites and washed them down with the tea. He'd made it just right again. Another little sign that he paid attention. How long had it taken David to learn how she took her tea?

Getting off track, MacKean. Focus.

"We're in massive debt. I always knew we were in some degree of it. As I told you early on, keeping a place like this running costs an exorbitant amount of money, and that's not something my family's had for quite some time. But I didn't know how bad it was until I took over the running of the estate on my parents' death." She sipped at the tea to wet her suddenly dry throat. "There was supposed to be enough to keep things running for at least another generation, with conservative management. It was what my grandfather had managed to set up. But when I inherited the books, I found it was almost all gone. My father, it seemed, had a gambling problem. I don't know if he had some goal in mind or if it was purely an addiction. All I know is that he lost whatever little nest egg we had."

Understanding lit his face. "So the fact that I won the estate in a poker game didn't exactly make a positive first impression."

"No. I made assumptions about you. I apologize for my behavior when we first met. I know better now."

Raleigh waved that away. "We're way past that now, sugar. Keep going."

"Connor and I knew nothing until after they died. He still doesn't know the full extent of it, but we've been scrambling ever since to make ends meet and keep our heads above water. Everything we've done has been a Band-aid on what I'm afraid is a mortal wound. The wedding business will help, but that's going to take time to build, and I don't know if we're going to manage to do it fast enough. I've done projections for growth and the necessary investment in staff and equipment we'd have to make for that. Even if we were to book an event every weekend for the rest of the year, it wouldn't be enough."

"Enough for what, exactly?"

"We have a balloon payment coming up at the first of the year. The terms of the loan gave us ten years to pay it off, with less required up front. When I agreed to it after my parents died, that felt like plenty of time to get things sorted. But that's just not how it happened. There was always one more thing. The simple fact is, we need other forms of income. I may have to actually agree to sell part of the land. It's not something I want to do, ever. But it's an option on the table."

"How much is the payment coming due?"

She told him, and he let out a low whistle that made her wince.

"Connor and Angus don't know about this?"

"No. They know there are loans because there have always been loans. But they don't know it's this bad."

"Loans, plural. There are others?"

"None so pressing, but yes. I've tried to find a way to refinance over the years, but our situation is such that no one was willing to let us."

"So, basically, you've been carrying this whole thing on your shoulders, by yourself, since you were twenty?"

"Yes."

"Shit, woman." Raleigh blew out a breath, then leaned forward, plucking the mug from her hands and curling his strong fingers around hers. "First off, *if* you opted to sell part of the land, there's nothing that says you have to sell it to a development group. I'll back you a hundred percent to avoid ever doing that. Second, there are bound to be other avenues you haven't had the time or bandwidth to explore. You said we've got until the first of the year?"

We. The ease with which he said it made her throat tighten. "Two weeks after Christmas."

"Okay. So we have six months. I can work with that."

She could see the wheels turning in his brain. No balking. No judging. Just instantly trying to find a way to help. She didn't know what to do with that. What to do with him.

"Raleigh, you're so..."

His mouth quirked in a wry smile that made one of his dimples pop. "What? Stubborn? Nosy?"

"Good." On a little laugh, she cupped his cheek, feeling the bristle of his beard against her palm. "You are such a good man."

He tipped his head, pressing into her touch. "We said for better or for worse, all right? We'll figure this out together."

Did he have any idea how appealing that was? How appealing *he* was?

Riding on gratitude and relief, she tipped forward, brushing her mouth to his. She only meant it to be a fleeting thing. A gesture of affection. But the warmth of his lips drew her in, made her linger. On a sigh, he brought his hands—those wonderful, gentle hands—up to cradle her face, and her heart stuttered. It would be so easy to get lost in this. Lost in him. To distract them both from the worries that waited. But they'd still be there on the other side of pleasure. And she'd made a promise.

Reluctantly, she eased back. "Sorry."

"For what?" His thumb stroked her cheek, making her shudder.

She pulled back far enough to look into those leonine eyes. "This has gotten... complicated." It seemed only fair she acknowledge that. "I don't know if I can handle complicated."

If he was offended or angry, he didn't show it. All she saw in his face was an understanding that rocked her to the core.

"Fair enough. You've got a lot on your plate. But if you change your mind... I'm here." He pulled away and picked up his pie, kicking back in his chair as if he hadn't just blown her mind. "Now, let's do some brainstorming."

FIFTEEN

Kyla was up and out before Raleigh woke in the morning. He wasn't entirely sure she'd slept at all after the late night they'd spent going over debts and assets. But she hadn't kicked him out to another room, and he had to consider that was a step in the right direction. She felt something for him, beyond just attraction, and while she wasn't comfortable with it, and didn't seem to know what to do about it, she wasn't putting distance between them. That was enough for him, for now.

She was a woman who valued promises, both made and kept, so this deliberate shift beyond the business arrangement they'd originally outlined would take time. Raleigh intended to give it to her. But he also planned to put his all into finding a way to cover the upcoming balloon payment. That would woo his very practical-minded wife more than any romantic gesture. And, freed of the worst of her worries, she'd be more receptive to romance. That was his theory, anyway.

Raleigh wanted to do a more extensive exploration of Ardinmuir today, so he hoped to catch Connor before he left to make arrangements for Angus. The old man was getting understandably perturbed at being babysat, but he wasn't yet entirely in the clear and wouldn't do well stuck in a vehicle for several hours, even if he probably did have valuable insight and stories to share about the estate. If worse came to worst, he could call Charlotte and beg her to pop over for a few hours, but he hated to do that. She'd already done so much. Maybe Ewan could take a shift at some point before he went into the pub.

The murmur of an unfamiliar voice had him picking up his pace to the kitchen. Angus sat with a cup of tea in his usual spot at the table. And beside him was Munro Sinclair. Both men looked up at his arrival.

"Mornin'." Raleigh searched Angus's face for any signs of distress. He still didn't know what had gone wrong between them, and Munro had left the hospital without seeing Angus the day of his surgery, once they'd received the news that he was expected to fully recover.

"Mornin', lad. I believe you've met Munro?"

"I did." He nodded to the other man and moved to the coffeepot. "I'm guessing Connor's already gone?"

"Left for work half an hour ago. Kyla's in town, meeting with Sophie."

"I figured as much. They're putting the pedal to the metal to get things ready for this weekend's wedding." He kicked back against the counter. "Listen, I've got things I need to do today, off premises. If I leave you to your own devices, are you gonna behave yourself?"

Angus made what Raleigh had come to decide was a Scottish noise of insult deep in his throat. "I always behave."

Munro snorted. "That's a lie, that is. I've been watching you get into trouble for more than fifty years."

They exchanged glares that told Raleigh there'd been a deep friendship in addition to whatever else lay between them. "Would you be interested in watching him *not* get into trouble for a while today? I'd feel better if somebody were around to keep our boy here company."

Munro sobered and looked at Angus. "Your call."

A multitude of emotions flickered over his face—amusement,

regret, and maybe some longing. At last, Angus inclined his head. "Stay, if you can. We've a lot to catch up on."

Not wanting to upset whatever reunion was happening, Raleigh poured his coffee into a travel mug and snagged a couple of granola bars for the road. He knew from previous conversations that Ardinmuir was nearly twelve thousand acres that butted up against his own property. The map he'd seen mounted on the wall of the castle library dated back to the nineteenth century. If a more modern one existed, he didn't have it, and he decided it was better to ask forgiveness than permission if he inadvertently trespassed on someone else's land. God knew, everybody around here had probably heard of him, even if they hadn't yet met.

His goal for the day was to get a better grasp of what sort of land resources were part of the MacKean holdings. Business was Kyla's strong suit. Land management was his. He'd been doing some research on his own about various grants and programs, related to a multitude of topics, on offer in Scotland and the broader UK, including wind energy and rewilding. None of them would be fast solutions, but he hoped that familiarizing himself with what they had might spark some new ideas.

He took what he estimated was a peripheral road that led out to what he hoped was the outer edge of the estate. Much like Lochmara, there were several occupied crofts that all seemed to abut a common grazing area. There were the expected sheep, some Highland coos, and even a herd of alpacas. But, in general, it seemed that Ardinmuir had fewer crofts in use. He wondered why as he turned onto a winding track that took him away from the glen and up the mountain. Had Peter Lennox simply been more interested in being a landlord? Was that holdover from the fact that his original ancestor had been a farmer? Maybe it was simply that maintaining those properties, and the leases that went with them, had been too much for Kyla to handle when the weight of the estate fell on her shoulders.

Raleigh filed it away and began to make notes about the location and condition of each of the empty crofts he came across. As Kyla had told him on their picnic, there were many in various states of disrepair. Some had roofs that had caved in. Others had been half swallowed by vines and other greenery. All were clearly very old, something his brain struggled to wrap around. The idea of something out here lasting so long was mind-boggling. Some of these cabins probably predated Rosewood. That was wild.

The morning dragged on toward lunch as he drove into the woods, following yet another rutted track. He had a vague notion of where he was in relation to the castle and was confident he could get back. A couple of miles in, the track opened up to yet another stone structure. It was like coming upon Hansel and Gretel's cottage, all the way down to the plume of smoke curling from the chimney. There was no vehicle.

Curious, Raleigh pulled up in front and parked.

The door opened as he prepared to knock, and a wide-eyed bearded guy, who couldn't be more than about twenty-two, blinked at him. "Hello."

"Hi." Raleigh's gaze slid over the man's shoulder into the interior, noting no sign of furniture. "Do you happen to be aware you're on private property?"

"I didn't, no. It wasn't locked. I thought it was a bothy and stopped in for shelter last night."

"A what now?"

"A bothy. A shelter for hillwalkers. They're scattered all over the Highlands."

He took in the guy's hiking boots. "So, you're hiking through the area?"

"I am."

"Pretty place. The thing is, it's all private property, so unless you got permission from my wife or her brother..."

Confusion flickered. "Scotland has freedom to roam. I can wander anywhere I please, so long as I leave the place the way I found it. I've not caused any damage, I swear."

Well, that sounded like a whole lot of bullshit to Raleigh. The idea of people being able to walk wherever the hell they wanted stepped all over his American sense of boundaries and privacy. But he knew they did things differently here, so he didn't call the guy out. "We appreciate that. So, now you know that this isn't a bothy, be sure that fire's well and truly out before you move on your way, okay?"

"Of course. I'm headed out as soon as I've had lunch."

Raleigh tipped his hat and decided he'd circle back later to check.

He continued his survey into the afternoon, wishing he'd packed some lunch. Maybe he ought to head back and regroup. Even as he thought it, he spotted another curl of smoke in the distance. Too aware of the damage fire would wreak, he turned in that direction. It took three wrong turns and a dead end before he finally pulled up in front of yet another cabin. This one seemed to be in better shape, and he was surprised to see Connor's SUV out front.

What the hell was he doing way out here?

And what the hell was that roar? A wall of sound greeted Raleigh as he climbed out of the driver's seat. As he approached the partly ajar door, he heard a rhythmic clanging, like metal on metal.

Beyond curious, he pushed the door open and stepped inside.

Connor stood in a filthy t-shirt and leather apron, pounding at something on an anvil.

"What the hell, man?"

Connor spun, shoving up safety goggles. "What are you doing here?" His eyes were wild and angry, his gaze shooting past Raleigh's shoulder. "Are you alone?"

"Yeah. What is all this?"

"Nothing."

"Heh, yeah. No. Try again. You have a forge?"

Scowling, his brother-in-law tossed the hammer aside. "Yes, I have a forge."

Raleigh pivoted, taking in the space, noting an assortment of what appeared to be partly completed blades and other decorative elements he couldn't identify, along with a multitude of tools he couldn't identify. "You're a blacksmith. That's damned cool. Why didn't anybody mention it?"

"Nobody knows. And nobody can know."

"Why?"

"It's... personal." Embarrassment seemed to color his anger. "You can't tell Kyla."

"If you want me to lie to your sister, I'm gonna need more."

Connor heaved a sigh and scrubbed a hand over his face, smearing soot on his cheeks. "Because I'm working on something to help with the debt, and I don't know if it will work, and I don't want to get her hopes up."

Raleigh fixed him with a glare. "You're aware of the debt?"

"Of the loan coming due in January. Yes."

Temper kindled on Kyla's behalf. "Do you have any idea of the weight that she's been carrying by herself? She's kept all this to herself, trying to protect you and Angus. And you knew, and didn't tell her?"

Shamefaced, he slumped back against a worktable. "No, I didn't realize. Not until she moved out. I stumbled across some paperwork she left behind and dug in. I'm sure she still knows a lot more than I do."

Well, at least he hadn't known long. Still. "Why didn't you confront her?"

"Well, she ended up taking my role in all of this by marrying you. I thought I'd pick up and take hers."

"Jesus Christ." Raleigh paced a circle. "You two can't communicate, can you?"

"We MacKeans are a stubborn lot."

"You think?"

Connor crossed to a mini-fridge and grabbed two bottles of water, tossing one at Raleigh. "Look, this was something I got into a few years ago as a hobby. It turned out I had an aptitude, and I've managed to generate an audience. I've been taking more orders since I found out, to have more to put toward what's coming due."

"So... the odd jobs and leading tours Angus mentioned? You're not doing those at all?"

"The odd jobs, yes. But the tours, no. Not for several months. This was more profitable and less complicated."

Raleigh wondered how keeping a secret like this was less complicated than tours, but didn't ask. "How long did you think you were gonna be able to hide this?"

"I dinna ken. I wanted to be able to do something for her, after everything she's done for me. Can you understand that?"

"Yeah. I get that. And same."

"Is that why you're still here? Why you moved to Ardinmuir with her and haven't started the necessary separation for a divorce?"

"Are you asking if I'm in love with your sister?"

Connor's brows shot up. "Are you?"

Raleigh didn't know. But if he wasn't, he was sure as hell well on the way. "That's between me and Kyla. But if I said I wanted to give things a real shot, would I have your support?"

"Fuck yes. You're good to her and good for her. Never, over the past couple of years, did I see David Murray do anything to step up and try to ease her burdens by anything more than just distraction."

"All right, then. You don't want me to tell Kyla about all this, I won't. I don't like it, but I think it'll be better coming from you, either way. But you need to decide how you're going to break this to her, because I'm not gonna keep my mouth shut forever. You two need to have a conversation and clear the air, then we need to make a collective plan, because all of these little independent offshoots of ideas are not going to be as effective as all of us being on the same page."

"Agreed. Just let me get through with what I'm doing. I'd like to be able to show her what I'm actually capable of. I just need some more time."

"Fair enough. I'm thinking about some other options myself. I can keep her distracted with those."

"Thank you." He finished draining the water. "I need to get back to work."

"All right. A few questions first, though. I ran into a guy camped out in one of the empty crofter cabins. He mentioned something about a freedom to roam. Is that actually a thing?"

"Yes. Scotland passed a Land Reform Act back in the early 2000s. Hikers and cyclists can have access to anywhere in Scotland, with some restrictions, provided they behave responsibly. We get some hillwalkers from time to time."

Raleigh filed that away. "How many of these empty crofter cabins would you say y'all have?"

"I don't know. Maybe twenty. It may be that there are more. There are quite a few that are uninhabitable."

"Yeah, I've been checking those out today. Is there a map somewhere that has all of them?"

Curiosity replaced the lingering traces of hostility. "I'm sure there is somewhere. Why?"

"I'm thinking about something. I need to noodle on a little bit more. Then I want to talk to your sister about it."

"But you'll keep her away from here?"

"I will. Hell, I'm turned around enough, I think I'd have a hard time finding my way back."

Connor finally cracked a smile. "That was the idea. I'll give you directions back to the castle."

———

"Thank you so much! This wedding was just a dream come true."

Kyla beamed at the gushing bride. "We're so happy you chose to commemorate such an important occasion with us here at Ardinmuir."

The clearly besotted groom hooked an arm around his wife's waist and gently began steering her toward their car.

"I'm telling everyone I know about you!"

Sophie waved. "We appreciate that, Lisa. And if you'd leave us a review, that would be amazing."

"You bet I will." She broke free of her husband and rushed back over, throwing her arms around first Sophie and then Kyla in an enthusiastic hug. "Thank you!"

Warmth bloomed in Kyla's chest at the impulsive show of affection. It was the first time she'd thought much about the joy they could bring to others with this business. Her focus had been so much on the numbers and the dry functionality of the thing. But seeing Lisa and Ben this truly happy was a different kind of validation. One she hadn't realized she needed. For the first time, it occurred to her that this job might actually be fulfilling, not just lucrative.

As the newlyweds finally made it into their car, Sophie linked her arm through Kyla's. "That's a job well done, that."

Kyla tipped her head to her friend's. "It is, indeed. Even my cold, unromantic heart can see that."

"You're not cold. You're just practical. That doesn't mean you're immune to romance. It just might look a little different. Speaking of..."

"What?" Kyla followed her gaze to see Raleigh striding out of the house. Her heart gave a little bump at the sight of those long, jeans-clad legs eating up the ground between them.

He'd been around all week, pitching in wherever needed, as she'd learned was his way. But she hadn't really seen him for any substantial time in days. Not alone, anyway. He'd been off catching up on his own business or keeping an eye on Angus. And at night, he'd shared her bed, keeping respectfully on his side, his breath a quiet anchor in the dark.

"Can I steal you away?"

If her brain sent her down a fantasy rabbit hole that involved him carrying her off into the sunset on horseback, who could blame her? But instead of voicing the *Yes, please,* she stuck to the practical. "We've got all this breakdown that needs to be done."

"Is there another event booked soon enough that this has to be torn down today?"

"No, but we need to get it all in before the rain comes."

Sophie nudged her toward Raleigh. "I've got volunteers lined up to help with teardown. They'll be here shortly. You've earned a little time off."

Kyla dug in her heels. "I'm not leaving you alone with all this. You already handled the lion's share of the planning on this one."

"As I said, I've got help coming. Raleigh, I order you to take her away."

His dimples flashed. "Yes, ma'am. Come on, darlin'."

Feeling more than a little railroaded, Kyla let him lead her over to his 4x4 and tuck her into the passenger seat. As he circled around front, she glanced up at the lowering sky, sending up a quiet prayer of thanks that the rain had held off until the wedding party and guests had departed. It wouldn't hold off that much longer, though.

As Raleigh turned out of the main castle drive and headed away from Glenlaig, Kyla sat forward. "Where are we going?"

"I'm about to kill two birds with one stone. I'm gonna feed you—because I know you haven't sat down long enough to eat more than two bites since breakfast—and while I do, I'm gonna tell you about an idea I had for another revenue stream."

"Another revenue stream?"

"Yep. See, I've spent most of this week driving around Ardinmuir, exploring the estate. Y'all have twenty-two empty crofters cottages. Of those, six could be easily made habitable with some cleaning and minor updates like paint and small repairs to weatherproof. The others need more work to varying degrees, but by my calculations, if we put some real elbow grease into it, we could probably have three or four of them ready for leasing in a couple of weeks."

Kyla absorbed that. "I appreciate your enthusiasm, but I don't think we can find tenants for the crofts that fast."

"No, no. I'm not talking about renting the crofts. I'm talking about turning the houses into AirBnBs. Vacation rentals. Think about it. You're hosting these events. These people are coming in from far and wide and, in some cases, having to drive a pretty significant distance to be in the wedding party or attend as a guest or whatever. If you can offer them the option of accommodation, that gives convenience to them and you a chance to charge a premium. Plus, if they're not being booked in conjunction with events, you can rent them out to tourists."

Her heart began to thrum with excitement, but she held herself back. "It's not a bad idea, in theory, but there would be so much work involved. And the expense of updating and furnishing them is bound to be prohibitive."

"Not as bad as you might think. I've already been looking into some of the details for all of this in relation to Charlotte. AirBnB and VRBO are the easiest way to do this. It isn't a thing you have to manage all the time. You don't need an innkeeper. I mean, you've gotta have somebody to clean it in between guests, but the furnishing isn't a big deal. You've got a castle full of furniture. I feel sure we can manage to kit out a few of them. I'm bringing you out here to show you what I mean."

The sky continued to darken as he wove deeper into the wilderness of the estate, and Raleigh turned on the headlights to cut through the gloom. When those lights swept across the face of a stone cabin, it was like stumbling on something out of a fairy tale. Nature was creeping around every side of the building, such that it seemed to sprout from the ground like a plant itself. Flowers tumbled out of an old wheelbarrow beside the door. That had Sophie written all over it. Some effort had been made to clear the area in front so that there was room to park, but it didn't detract from the overall rustic charm of the place.

As Kyla slid out, Raleigh snagged her hand and pulled her toward the cabin. "C'mon."

He opened the door and tugged her into the darkened house.

"Wait right there." Releasing her, he crossed to some kind of table and struck a match. "The power's still not on, so we're going atmospheric for the evening, but I think this will give you an idea." He touched the match to the wick of an oil lamp and a warm glow began to suffuse the space.

Kyla stood where she was, taking in the scene gradually revealed as he lit three more lamps. The place was a big, open rectangle, but for a corner closed in for the bath. A brass bed took up one wall, made up with a quilt Kyla knew had been made by her granny. A pair of armchairs were positioned in front of the empty fireplace, on either side of an old steamer trunk. On the far wall, a narrow table and chairs stood opposite the range. The table was set for a candlelit dinner, and scents of roasted meat and vegetables had her mouth watering.

"How did you do all this?"

Raleigh lit the candles on the table, then shook out the match. "I had help. Connor said I could use some of the furniture from that storage room in the castle. He and Ewan helped me haul it out here and set it up. Angus coached me through making dinner."

Her gaze shot to his. "You cooked, too?"

She couldn't quite tell in the dim light, but she thought his cheeks flushed.

"I'm not helpless in the kitchen. Though I'm far more comfortable around a grill or smoker." Spreading his hands to encompass the house, he looked at her. "What do you think? I mean, obviously it still needs proper decorating by somebody who knows more about it than I do. But it's cozy, right? Cozy's a selling point for a vacation rental."

A rumble of thunder shook the house, and rain began to drum against the window. Kyla wrapped both arms around herself against the faint chill. "It's impressive what you've pulled together. I concede that."

"Cold?" He strode over to the fireplace and began laying in wood from a basket to the side. "Let's have a fire. Best I can tell, there's no central heat or air in any of these places."

"No, there wouldn't be. We've no need for air conditioning

up here, and these are all old enough they'd have been heated by fireplace or woodstove."

As flames began to lick at the wood he'd stacked, Raleigh rocked back on his heels. "I can't get over the idea of having a fire in summer and not burning up. But it's nice."

Kyla could see the possibilities, but she'd seen possibilities before. "You've put a lot of thought into this."

"I wanted to show you proof of concept." He straightened and crossed over to open a laptop she hadn't noticed on the table. "But it's not just about how it looks. I've run the numbers. I did some research on rental rates across the Highlands for comparable properties. Self-serve vacation rentals have been huge business, especially since the pandemic, because people want to get out and away. There are nightly rates, weekend rates, and even week-long rates. Alladale, the wilderness reserve north of here? They trade on the fact that they're incredibly remote, and they lease their properties by the week for literally thousands of pounds. I broke it down a few different ways in a spreadsheet."

As he turned the screen toward her and began reeling off calculations and projections, Kyla stared at him, her heart beginning to pound. She'd shared her problem with him. And instead of telling her no, instead of telling her it couldn't be done, he'd gone out and found her a real, viable answer that she could live with. And maybe it wouldn't end up working in the grand scheme of things, but he'd tried. He'd taken the time and put himself out there to give her what she needed. Hell, he'd made her a *spreadsheet,* speaking the language of her ever-so-practical heart.

No one had ever done anything like this for her before.

That thrumming heart shot warmth through her chest and her limbs, and she reached up to cup Raleigh's cheek. He stopped speaking mid-sentence and turned toward her, his eyes searching hers.

Bringing her other hand up to frame his face, she murmured, "Thank you," and drew his mouth to hers.

Sixteen

Gratitude tasted a special kind of sweet. As Kyla rose to her toes, pressing her pretty, perfect lips to his, Raleigh wrapped his arms around her and reveled in it. His whole motivation for this scheme was to take some of the weight off her shoulders. Judging by how she was kissing him, he'd succeeded. Maybe even more than he'd expected. She'd initiated, so he didn't hesitate to kiss her back, threading his fingers in her silky hair and glorying in the feel of her body pressed close to his. If she'd made a single move toward retreat, he'd have let her go. Instead, her mouth opened against his, her tongue darting out to taste and explore. Angling his head, he deepened the kiss, wringing a little whimper from her that had his body going from zero to reporting for duty in less than two seconds. He wouldn't take more than she wanted to give, but as long as she was driving this train, he was here for the ride.

Kyla's hands slid from his face to his chest, her palms tracing his muscles. Something had changed here. The restraint he'd felt from her up to this point simply wasn't there—a fact confirmed when she tugged his shirt from the waistband of his jeans.

Oh, hell yes.

The first touch of her hands on his skin lit him up. He'd

wanted to feel her touch for weeks, so he did nothing to stop her exploration. His own hands gently tugged her blouse from the waist of her skirt, sliding beneath to trace the soft, warm skin along her spine. Shuddering, she began shoving his shirt higher in unmistakable demand.

Only then did he pause, reaching for the last shreds of his control. "Are you sure?"

Her bluebonnet eyes were nearly black as they unflinchingly met his. "Yes."

That was all he needed. With one hand, he dragged his shirt up and off, tossing it to the side. She hummed low and possessive in the back of her throat, her eyes going impossibly darker as she moved into him again, stroking his chest and bringing her mouth back to his.

Raleigh dove, letting his desire off its leash and taking her mouth as he'd wanted to for weeks. She rose to meet him, her kiss every bit as hungry as his as they circled toward the bed, touching, taking in a way they hadn't dared before. When the back of his legs bumped against the mattress, he pivoted, putting her against the edge so there was no question where this was headed. Her answer was to strip her own shirt up and off, leaving her in nothing but a pale pink bra, a trim pencil skirt, and heels. Like she'd worn on the first day they'd met.

He knew the woman behind that mask now. Had fallen more than half in love with her loyal, stubborn, gorgeous self. She stood before him, shoulders straight and proud as he took her in. No. His Kyla wouldn't be bashful here.

His.

Testing them both, Raleigh traced a finger over the swell of one breast, at the edge of her bra, watching her eyes drift closed at the touch. She swayed toward him as he moved to her back and unclasped the hook, drawing the cups away. Her fair skin was flushed with desire and firelight. He wanted to touch and take, but this was new for both of them, and they had time.

Gripping her hips, he pulled her to him, capturing her mouth again. Her hands wrapped around his, dragging them up, laying them over her breasts until she arched into the joint touch with a sigh. Understanding it for the permission it was, he shifted his hold, cupping the fullness in his palms and thumbing her nipples until they drew tight.

"These have been driving me crazy." To illustrate the point, he bent to suck one pearled bud into his mouth.

On a strangled whimper, her knees wobbled, and she gripped his shoulders to keep from falling. To solve the issue, he scooped her up, settling her back on the bed and stretching out over her. He continued to worship her breasts until she began to writhe beneath him, her fingers fisting in his hair. Dragging one hand up her bare thigh, he bunched her skirt beneath his hand until his fingers found the edge of her underwear. He couldn't pull them off with one hand at this angle, so he traced the edge to the seam between her thighs, growling at the dampness he found there.

Gasping his name, she arched into his fingers, inviting more.

Lifting his head, he scooted down her body until he found the zipper at the side of the skirt and lowered it. She watched him with heavy-lidded eyes as he slowly dragged the skirt and underwear down, leaving her bare.

He breathed a reverent curse. She was all creamy limbs and copper hair, and he wanted to map every inch of her with his mouth and his hands.

As if reading his mind, she blinked up at him. "What are you waiting for?"

"Darlin', I'm just enjoying the view. You're gorgeous. Better than every fantasy I've tortured myself with these past weeks."

"You fantasized about me?"

He eased back over her so he could look into her eyes. "Hell, yes."

She twined her fingers back into his hair. "Show me."

With a wicked grin, he lowered his mouth to the paradise between her thighs.

Kyla's head dropped back on a gasp. "Oh, God, yes."

They'd been circling around each other for weeks, ignoring this heat between them, so she was more than primed for his ministrations. When she came apart screaming his name, he felt like a god. This was his *wife*, and it was finally, blessedly, time to claim her.

Her eyes were hungry as she watched him slide from the bed, shucking his jeans and boxers before coming back to join her. She reached for him, stroking a hand down his chest and lower to curl around his erection, tracing a thumb around his crown to spread the moisture there.

Raleigh's eyes crossed as he struggled to hold himself still for the touch.

"Mmm, all mine."

The possessive purr had him opening his eyes. "Every rock-hard inch."

She drew him to her, wrapping her legs and arms around him. Not until his shaft nudged the heat of her entrance did he hesitate, one last thread of sanity remaining.

"I'm not... I didn't plan... There's no condom." Christ. How had he not considered this? If he had to stop now, he just might cry.

"It's fine. I'm covered." Framing his face, she brushed her lips to his. "Finish it. Take me."

Needing no further encouragement, pressed forward, sliding into her perfect, wet heat, until they both cried out.

"You okay?" he managed.

"Yes. God. You feel incredible."

"Let's see if we can level up on that." Capturing her mouth again, he began a slow retreat and thrust, until he was fully seated in the cradle of her hips.

Brow pressed to hers, he held there as her body adjusted to his. This felt different from any sex he'd had before. Not only because he was bare, but because this was his wife. It was primal, possessive, and he nearly lost himself in the claiming. But she had to come first, and by God, he was making this worth the wait.

He took his time, experimenting with rhythm, listening and learning her responses to every touch, every angle. She gasped and moaned and clung to him as he drove her up and up, until she was urging him to go deeper and faster. He was staring down at her beautiful, fire-lit face as those blue eyes blurred with pleasure and she shattered. As her body tightened around his, claiming him every bit as much as he claimed her, he slid over the edge and emptied himself inside her, that last bricks of his defenses crumbling to dust.

———

A log collapsed in the fireplace, sending up a shower of sparks. Kyla's whole body felt bathed in them, little pinpricks of light and heat. Surely, if anyone looked at her now, they'd see glitter. Relaxed and wonderfully sated, she lay naked and tangled with Raleigh. Now her husband, in every sense of the word.

A distant part of her brain waited for the guilt. She hadn't planned this. Had, in fact, gone out of her way to avoid this very thing. But how could she feel guilty for this sense of warmth and connection? This man saw her, cared for her. She'd made vows to him. And maybe they hadn't been intended to be more than a business arrangement at the start, but clearly, they'd become more, despite their best intentions. This physical release was just a natural extension of that.

Add to all of that, it had been really stupendous sex.

The broad, work-roughened palm that had settled possessively on her ass began to stroke little patterns on her back. "You're thinking awful hard." His drawl was thicker and deeper after sex, and damn if it didn't make her want him all over again.

Turning her head a scant inch, she kissed whatever part of him she could reach, nestling her cheek against his throat. "I was just thinking there's no more lying. We've well and truly fulfilled the intention of the pact."

His hand stilled. "Are you okay with that?"

Kyla wasn't ready to consider all the ramifications of the question, so she leaned into the light and teasing. "After two spectacular orgasms, I'm struggling to find any reason to complain."

Because he said nothing, she splayed a hand over his heart, feeling the slow thump beneath her palm. "I just want to stay in the moment right now."

"Okay." He pressed a kiss to her brow. "You hungry?"

Relieved he wasn't going to make an issue of what they'd just done, she pushed herself up. "Starving."

Sliding out of bed, she scooped up his shirt and pulled it on, secretly loving being surrounded by his scent.

Raleigh's eyes darkened as he took her in. "That's a good look on you, Red. I like seeing you in my clothes."

Her own gaze slid down his lean, muscled form, lingering on the erection that was already beginning to stiffen again. "I can see that. But you promised to feed me." To remove herself from temptation, she moved to the bathroom. "Get to the kitchen, Cowboy."

"Yes, ma'am."

By the time she came back out, he'd put on his jeans and arranged containers of food on the trunk in front of the fire.

"It's a little cold. I hadn't planned on getting distracted from dinner."

Stepping around him, she sank into one of the chairs and forked up a bite of roasted pork. "Zero complaints. It's delicious."

They fell on the food like ravening beasts, sticking to lighter, easier topics as the fire crackled in the hearth. It was easy to feel like they were in their own little world here. No burdens, no responsibilities. Just the two of them, enjoying the rare intimacy of sharing a meal half naked, as they both pretended not to be thinking about getting fully naked all over again.

By the time she'd inhaled the last bite of raspberry roulade, she realized the drum of rain on the window had ceased. Real life was waiting.

"We should get back."

Raleigh studied her. "Do you want to get back?"

"To be completely honest with you, I was thinking about dragging you straight back to that bed. But we need to get back and check on things. I left Sophie to handle everything, and despite her protests to the contrary, that's not fair."

With a regretful curve of his lips, he nodded. "Fair enough." Leaning across the trunk, he brushed his lips softly over hers. "I feel compelled to remind you we have a bed back at the castle, too. A bigger one."

Kyla grinned. "So we do."

They made quick work of packing up the remains of their dinner, and slower work of changing back into their proper clothes. Kyla stepped back into the bathroom to try to do something with her hair. She looked well and truly rumpled, and felt certain that anyone who laid eyes on her would know exactly what she'd been up to. And what did it matter? Everyone already assumed they'd been sleeping together already. This only confirmed expectations.

Giving up on her hair as a lost cause, she joined Raleigh at the door. Once he confirmed the fire was out, they loaded into the SUV and headed back to Ardinmuir. His hand snaked across the center console to link with hers. The sweet gesture made her more than a little giddy. It seemed now that the wall of denial she'd thrown up had finally begun to collapse, everything he did made her *feel*. Part of her wanted to believe it was simply the product of excellent sex, but a deeper part knew it was more than that. She'd have to figure out what to do with... all of it. For his part, Raleigh didn't ask questions, didn't push, and Kyla was grateful.

They were well into the gloaming by the time they made it back to the castle. In the wake of the storm, the tattered clouds made for a gorgeous watercolor sky. The two of them stood watching for long minutes as day bled into night. When the light had dimmed enough that she couldn't clearly see Raleigh's face, she sighed and turned toward the steps. Time to face the world again.

He caught her hand, tugging her to a stop. "Kyla. Look, I know we didn't plan on this. But in the spirit of full disclosure, I feel like you should know... I want to try this for real. Us. I want a real marriage. Because I think we've proved that we can be pretty fucking great together. And I hope you think so, too."

He wanted her. Not a business arrangement. Not duty to uphold a marriage pact signed by ancestors long gone to dust. He wanted her. Exactly as she was. Exactly *where* she was.

Kyla's throat went thick. Did he have any idea what a gift he was offering?

How the hell had she stumbled into marriage with a man like him? A man who, impossibly, miraculously, understood her? A man who wanted her?

He deserved an answer, but before she could do more than take a step toward him, headlights flashed over the two of them.

She raised her arm to block her eyes, even as Raleigh half stepped in front of her as a shield. The car's engine shut off, and a door opened.

"Kyla."

The lovely post-coital haze she'd been floating in evaporated, replaced by an immediate sense of dread in the pit of her stomach.

"David."

She hadn't expected to see him. She hadn't given him more than a passing thought in weeks. And here was the guilt she'd expected, as she remembered the promise she'd made to him that she'd just very thoroughly broken.

"What are you doing here?"

He looked back and forth between the two of them, definitely not missing their clasped hands. She could only hope the dim light hid the obvious evidence of their earlier activities.

"I came to check on you. I expected to hear from you weeks ago. What is he doing here?"

Beside her, Raleigh straightened and let out a little growl. She squeezed his hand once and let it go. "Can you give us some privacy?"

Her husband gave her a long, measured look before nodding and going inside.

Kyla struggled to pull herself together for a confrontation she hadn't been expecting. She blurted out the first thing that occurred to her. "Angus had a heart attack."

David stepped closer. "Jesus. Is he all right?"

She scooped a hand through her hair. "He had bypass surgery. He's home recovering now, but it was really terrifying. Raleigh's been here helping out while Angus gets back on his feet." It wasn't a lie, but it was so much less than the truth.

"My God. I'm so sorry." He stepped in and wrapped her in a hug.

His embrace felt stilted and awkward, and it took her several seconds to return it. She told herself it was just because they hadn't seen each other in months, and Raleigh was probably watching from the house. She didn't take a full breath until David stepped back. "I'm sorry. I should have let you know, but things have been crazy between the heart attack and Sophie and I getting our business off the ground. Things have just gotten away from me."

"So you haven't started the year of separation yet?"

"No."

David's shoulders slumped. "Well, I can't say I'm not disappointed, but I understand there are extenuating circumstances. You're nothing if not a woman of your word."

God. Did he have to remind her of that in this moment? Shame slid like a sharpened blade into her gut.

"Now that Angus is on the mend, Beaumont will be going back to his place soon. Right?"

Kyla hesitated. She and Raleigh had discussed none of this, and the idea of him leaving now added to the sickness beginning to roil in her belly.

Seeing her hesitation, David sobered. "Have you changed your mind?"

How could she even answer that question? "This whole situation has been a lot more complicated than we expected." It was such a weak, evasive response, but it was all she could manage in the moment.

"I see." He was pulling away. She could feel it, even without being able to clearly see his face.

"No, you don't." And yet, how could she explain it without hurting him?

"No, I suppose I don't. How could I when we haven't talked? I know that's what we agreed, but I'm not sure it was for the best. I'm not sure any of our agreement was for the best."

Panic skittered through her. "What are you saying?"

"I'm saying you need to make a decision. Either he goes, and we pick back up as we intended. Or you need to call this whole thing off. That's your decision to make, and I need an answer. The sooner the better. Because I love you, and if you no longer love me, I deserve the chance to move on."

"That's fair." When she didn't immediately rush to reassure him that she loved him, too, she knew she'd hurt him, anyway. At no point had she ever wanted to do that. "I'm sorry I don't have a ready answer. I need time to think."

A muscle jumped in his jaw. "Okay, I'll give it to you. But it seems like this should be pretty cut and dried. I want an answer by Monday. You should be able to get things straight in your head and know what you want by then. Come to me, ready to start divorce proceedings, or cut me loose."

"Monday," she repeated. Two days to decide the rest of her life. But she couldn't claim it was an unreasonable deadline, so she nodded.

He took a step back. "I've missed you, Kyla. And I really hope to see you soon."

She stood in the dark until long after he'd driven away. All her pleasure in the day had wicked away, replaced by sickness and grief and worry, because no matter what choice she made, she'd hurt someone she cared about.

By some miracle, she avoided running into her brother or

uncle on her way upstairs. Raleigh was in their room, pacing like a caged animal. He looked up as she stepped inside.

Kyla couldn't make herself meet his eyes. "He wants a decision one way or the other by Monday. Obviously, you deserve one, too."

"I see."

"I need to think, and I need to be alone to do it. I think it would best for you to go back to Lochmara for now."

After a long moment, he nodded. "I can respect that."

Quick and quiet, he packed his bag. If he was angry, he didn't show it. The careful control was actually worse. She wished she knew where his head was and whether he'd changed his mind when confronted with the terms they'd originally agreed to.

At the door, he stopped, not looking back. "I know this wasn't what you were expecting. I know this isn't easy. But I just ask that you think about everything that's happened, not just where we were and who we were when we started out. I know promises matter to you. They matter to me, too. And I think it's important for us both to remember that we're the ones who made real vows to each other. To my mind, that supersedes everything else."

Without another word, he shut the door quietly behind him, leaving her alone to make the biggest decision of her life.

SEVENTEEN

Lochmara felt different when Raleigh got back. It wasn't as if he hadn't been to the estate since he'd moved in at Ardinmuir. He'd been by to check on things, meeting with a handful of tenants, spending some time with Mabel and Titania, and checking in with Charlotte. But by and large, he'd let Malcolm continue to handle everything so he could focus on the family in the wake of Angus's heart attack.

Family. He'd come to count all the MacKeans as his over the past couple of months, finding a closeness with them that could only be wrought by surviving extreme circumstances together. But was it all a lie? Was he alone in everything he felt?

Knowing Charlotte was liable to still be up and not wanting to face her yet, Raleigh parked out by the barn and wandered inside. The horses were in for the night. He made his way down the row, scratching ears and rubbing noses. Titania gave him her back when he approached.

"I know I haven't been around much. I'm sorry about that."

The mare gave an irritable twitch of her tail.

"Does it help if I admit I missed you?"

Titania snorted and took a step closer.

"What if I promise a good long ride tomorrow? Just you and me."

She eyed him warily, then finally stepped close enough he could touch, as if deciding his offer was acceptable. Raleigh stroked her nose and reached to scratch the spot she liked under her chin as penance. Twisting her head, she pressed into his touch.

"There we go. That's the spot."

The moment he stopped, she head-butted his chest.

He huffed a laugh. "Understood. My servitude isn't paid off yet."

A happy moo sounded from outside the barn.

"I gotta check in with the little one. I'll see you tomorrow, pretty girl." With one last scratch, he strode down the aisle and outside to the fence where Mabel was calling.

The motion-activated security light had snapped on, bathing her in a bright-white glow. She'd put on good weight and height these past few weeks and had taken to spending more of her time outside with her foster mother, but she still got excited seeing any of her people.

"Hey, baby girl. Did you miss me?"

Tail swishing, she pressed her head through the fence to rub along his legs. Raleigh slid through the bars so he could give her a good rubdown. She wriggled and moaned in ecstasy. Damn, Kyla would be sorry she missed this. For just a moment, he considered snapping a selfie of the two of them and sending it along with a text. *We miss you.*

Which was... ridiculous. He'd just seen his wife. Hell, he'd been inside her mere hours ago.

And there was a very good chance it would be the one and only time.

"What are you doing back so late? Did you and Kyla have a fight?"

Of course, Charlotte would have seen his SUV.

"No." He straightened to face her, knowing the security light would illuminate his face.

Her expression shifted immediately to concern. "Honey, what's wrong?"

On a slow exhale, he admitted the miserable truth. "I fell in love with my wife."

Charlotte tightened her arms over the cardigan she wore and blinked at him. "That's generally the accepted way of things."

Raleigh scrubbed a hand over his face. "No. I wasn't supposed to. It was supposed to be a business arrangement."

"A business arrangement?"

At this point, he might as well come clean about the whole thing, so she'd be prepared for the prospective fallout. "Well, that's a story."

She nodded in that sage, all-knowing way she had. "Why don't you come inside. I'll pour you a whisky and you can tell me."

At least she wasn't offering him tea.

Mabel followed when he headed for the gate.

"Go ahead and bring her. She's still got a bed in the kitchen, and it won't hurt her to have another bottle."

Trailed by the cheerful calf, Raleigh followed Charlotte to the back door and into the kitchen. Mabel wandered straight to the fridge and mooed.

"You need to develop some patience, young lady," Charlotte told her.

Mabel just batted her eyes as if to say, "I am adorable and such rules do not apply."

"You fix the bottle. I'll get the booze."

Having a task to occupy his hands helped. He went about the business of warming the milk and filling the bottle before joining Charlotte at the table where she'd poured them each two small glasses of whisky.

She nudged one at him. "Start talkin', honey."

So, holding the bottle for Mabel, he did, going back to the beginning and explaining everything about how he'd come to marry Kyla.

"I wondered if it was something like that, since you were sleeping in separate rooms."

"You knew?"

Her laughter echoed off the kitchen walls. "Lord, yes. You're no better at sneaking in and out now than you were at seventeen, when you hid Betsy Carmichael in your room."

Raleigh froze in horror, one hand on his whisky glass. "You knew about that?"

"Of course, I did."

Mortification crawled up the back of his neck. He'd been much happier in his ignorance that Charlotte knew he'd lost his virginity with Betsy Carmichael his junior year of high school. "Let's just... not talk about that, okay?"

Her lips twitched in amusement. "Fine with me. Anyway, I knew everything wasn't what you were presenting when I got here, but I could see a spark between you two. I figured, given a sufficient amount of time and a little encouragement, that it could turn into something. I take it that finally happened."

He thought of her soft kiss and the "Thank you," that had changed everything. "Yeah."

"So, what's the problem?"

"The problem is that she is technically, sort of, kinda promised to someone else."

Her amusement faded. "Explain."

When he'd finished, she sat back in her chair, finger tapping against her glass. "Were they engaged?"

"No. Nowhere near it, so far as I know. They'd just been dating long distance for the past couple years."

"Okay, well, that's certainly an unusual arrangement for the three of you. And I can see how that would lead to some complicated feelings—especially on Kyla's part. But I do feel compelled to point out that, no matter what the two of them agreed to, it doesn't supersede the real, legal vows y'all took. You *are* married."

"Yeah, well, she's currently making the decision about whether we're going to stay that way. He showed up tonight and fucked up everything. Gave her an ultimatum and a deadline. She asked for time alone to think, so here I am. Waiting. Because I'm not the one who's gonna pressure her." And he hoped like hell that didn't blow up in his face.

Apparently hearing the misery in his voice, Mabel laid her head in Raleigh's lap. He wrapped an arm around her, absorbing the comfort she offered.

Charlotte laid a hand over his and squeezed. "Do you have any sense of which way she's gonna lean?"

"Before he showed up, I don't think it would have been a question. But now he's reminded her of what she agreed to. She's stubborn and honorable to a fault."

"Sounds like somebody else I know. You two are so alike. You have so much in common, and that's what makes you such a good match. I have to have faith that she's gonna see that."

"God, I hope so. I don't know what I'm going to do if she picks him."

He'd built a family around her, and she could tear them away again. That idea was far more upsetting than he wanted to admit. "I don't know if I can stay here and live a life in this village and not be with her."

Sympathy shone in her dark eyes. "Those are big, heavy things to think about. But I don't think you have to be prepared to leave town next week if things don't go in your favor. It's possible that, if she feels guilty and decides to give the other guy a try, she'll figure out he's not right for her."

"How can you speak to that? You don't even know the guy."

"People talk. Gossip is just as much a currency here as it is back home. Reading between the lines of what people have said and not, he's nothing special. She doesn't light up around him. Or so they say. She does light up with you."

Was Charlotte right? Would Kyla ultimately choose to give them a real chance? If she didn't, what was he prepared to endure in the name of keeping the new home that he'd built?

Kyla's ass had gone to sleep sometime in the past hour she'd been waiting on the front stoop of Sophie's flower shop. That's what she got for camping out on the pavement instead of waiting in her car, but she figured she deserved the discomfort. She knew her best friend would be along at some point this morning to put together an arrangement for the upcoming church service, as she did every week. After the long night she'd just had, she needed a friendly face and a supportive ear.

At the sound of footsteps echoing from around the corner, she unfolded herself, feeling about eighty years old.

Sophie, who was digging around in her purse, looked up and squeaked. "Kyla! You scared the life out of me. What are you doing here?" As she got closer, her face softened. "Oh, it's like that, is it? I'll put on the kettle."

She unlocked the door and let them inside. The front of the shop was small and cluttered, full of the fun and the fanciful as vases and baskets perched on shelves lining the walls, showing off her wares. The cheerful chaos covered up the peeling wallpaper the landlord refused to let her strip. Kyla followed her around the counter and through the door that led to Sophie's private domain.

Here were the worktables and the cooler that held the flowers she so loved. Unlike the front, this space was organized with regimented efficiency, the tools of her trade neatly lined up, waiting for use. It was a strong counterpoint to the sagging ceiling and the water dripping into buckets in two different corners.

"Milligan still hasn't seen to the roof?"

Sophie sighed as she moved to fill the kettle in the little kitchenette. "Of course not."

"Cheap old bastard. Given what he charges you for this place, he ought to have gutted it and renovated the entire thing by now."

"You and I both know he's not going to do more than the bare minimum. It's fine."

"Well, when the business takes off, you'll be able to afford to move to a better space."

"I'll deal with this as long as I have to. You know I'm putting all my spare pence into saving up to move out of my stepmother's house."

Kyla bit back the automatic offer for her to move into Ardinmuir. God knew, they had plenty of room. But she'd made the overture before, repeatedly, and always been shot down. Sophie didn't want charity. She wanted only what she'd worked for. Even if it meant being stuck in the house with the nightmare of a hypochondriac her late father had left her with.

She opened a tin and pulled out two tea bags, plopping them into mismatched mugs. "Now, why are you here looking so glum when you were in such a good mood when you left yesterday afternoon?"

"I didn't sleep last night." The bed had felt too empty and her mind too full.

"What's going on?"

Kyla had come here to unburden herself, so why should this confession feel so hard? "I haven't been honest with you."

Sophie studied her with level gray eyes. "Haven't been honest with me or haven't been honest with yourself?"

Feeling her shoulders hunching up toward her ears, Kyla forced them down. "Maybe some of both."

The kettle kicked off and Sophie doused the tea bags with water, setting a timer.

"When I decided to marry Raleigh, it was just supposed to be a business arrangement. It was his idea. He knew I was involved with David—"

"You've been involved with David these last two months?"

"No." She explained the arrangement. "Raleigh and I were supposed to separate after a month and start the countdown for the year's separation so we could get divorced. Then a month hit, and it just didn't seem like the right time. We put it off. And then Angus had the heart attack, and Raleigh moved back with me to Ardinmuir, and things just got complicated."

Sophie handed over a mug of tea. "I've got eyes in my head. I know it didn't stay a business arrangement. I see how you two look at each other."

Kyla flushed, wondering what others had seen that she hadn't even been able to admit to herself. "I wasn't supposed to develop feelings for him."

Her friend snorted. "Love, if you didn't develop feelings for a man like that, I'd have to check you for a pulse. Not only is he gorgeous, he's kind and helpful. Thoughtful. More to the point, he's here. He's been here for you every single day since he married you."

"Yeah, yeah, I know. And I'm not immune to any of that. I think, if he'd set out to seduce me on purpose, I could have resisted. But this is just who he is."

"So, is that the problem? That you gave into the attraction to your actual husband? Because if that's not where last night ended up after what I helped him set up, I'll be most disappointed in you."

Face flaming, Kyla stared blindly into her tea. "Partly. David showed up at the castle last night."

"Shite. Talk about wiping out the post-coital glow."

"He was understandably upset that I hadn't started the separation as we discussed. I mean, when I explained about Angus, he understood—he's not a monster. But he's not blind, either. He gave me an ultimatum. I have to let him know by tomorrow whether our agreement is still valid, or I have to cut him loose."

Sophie dropped her gaze, her face going very, very neutral, which was a clear tell that she was trying desperately not to express an opinion.

"You think this should be an easy decision."

"It's not for me to say."

"Oh, come on, Sophie. You know I don't come here for you to blow smoke up my arse."

"All right." She sipped at her tea and seemed to take a few moments to gather her thoughts. "I'm the first to admit, I don't really know David. You've been with him for two years, and certainly, I've met him, but he's not truly spent any real time here getting to know the rest of us. He was a distraction. A vacation from your normal life. And as such, it's been kind of hard to take him seriously as someone that you would really consider spending your life with. Then here comes Raleigh, larger than life, in that big Texas way of his, and for all that he was a surprise, he fits. He's made himself fit. He's found ways to integrate in the community. He's found ways to become part of the family. He's gotten to know all of us. None of that sounds like a business arrangement. With Raleigh, you wouldn't have to choose between him and the life here that you love."

"David isn't making me choose between him and Ardinmuir."

Sophie arched one dark brow. "Isn't he? The understanding between the two of you, before all of this, when Connor was still supposed to marry Afton, was that once the marriage pact was settled, you two would start talking about the next phase of things. And I think you need to ask yourself why, when it came down to it, you extended the time with your husband."

"It was because—"

"It's *not* just because of Angus. I think it's because, deep down, you already know the choice that you need to make."

Miserable, Kyla set the mug aside and rubbed her hands on her thighs. "But how can I make that choice? How can I break my word?"

"I'm not saying it's easy or comfortable. I know what promises mean to you. I know how important it is for you to feel aboveboard and like you're beyond reproach. And I know you feel guilty about the feelings that you've developed for Raleigh. But that disnae make them wrong."

"But what if all of this is just a product of proximity? What if this is some kind of weird Stockholm Syndrome?"

Sophie looked askance in her direction. "Do you really think it's that?"

"I don't know. That's why I sent him back to Lochmara last night, so that I could have some time to think away from him and find some clarity."

"And did you? Find clarity?"

All she'd found was a long, empty night that had dragged on for what felt like days.

When Kyla said nothing, Sophie continued in her quiet, tough love sort of way. "I think you found clarity. I think you're just uncomfortable with the truth that clarity has given you. But it's not my choice. My opinion disnae matter. You need to accept the fact that, one way or the other, you will disappoint one of these two men that you care about. That is unavoidable. The decision you have to make, dear girl, is whether you're going to disappoint yourself. Is your conscience and soothing the sting of guilt worth more to you than your heart? Because that's what's really on the line here."

Kyla slumped back onto a stool, unable to summon any arguments against that. "Well, when you put it like that..."

"I think you know what you have to do."

As the certainty of it settled into her bones, Kyla nodded. "Yeah. Yeah, I think I do." She wrapped her friend in a tight hug. "Thanks, Soph. I'll see you later."

EIGHTEEN

There'd been no word from Kyla.

Raleigh told himself he hadn't expected any yet, but a part of him had thought she'd show up this morning like the heroine in a movie, declaring she'd made a terrible mistake and, of course, she loved him. Complete with sunrise backdrop. Possibly that was the part that had fallen asleep while watching *Pride and Prejudice* with Charlotte last night. After three whiskies, it hadn't seemed like such a terrible idea.

But he'd been in such a shit mood when he woke from a restless night's sleep that Charlotte had banished him from the house. So, he spent Sunday putting Titania through her paces. They went out for a long ride, not returning until well after lunch. Usually that kind of ride would clear his head, but he was no more settled by the time he'd cooled the mare down and given her a good grooming. As he was pondering whether he could sneak into his own house to find something to eat, he heard a vehicle pull up. He managed not to run out of the barn. Barely. And a good thing, too, as it wasn't his wife arriving to profess her love and devotion.

Instead, a familiar kilted figure slid out of the driver's seat of the big van with a wave. "Raleigh!"

Squashing his disappointment, he strode over to meet his guest. "Toby. Good to see you, man. What're you doing out here?"

"I had a call over to Lukas Fulton's place, so I was in the neighborhood. Hadn't seen you since poker night last month, so I thought I'd stop by and see if you'd be interested in popping into the village with me for a pint. Unless you've got other plans."

Raleigh wasn't feeling especially social. Hell, even Mabel was avoiding him and his bad mood today. But maybe that was a good enough reason to take Toby up on his offer. The other man could talk the ear off a donkey, so maybe he'd be a good distraction. And it would save him from trying to tiptoe around Charlotte to figure out something to eat.

"Sure. I haven't had lunch yet. I could go for a beer and some fish and chips."

"Brilliant. Follow me in?"

"Let me just wash up, and I'll be right behind you."

Raleigh expected the crowd at The Stag's Head to have thinned at this point in the afternoon, but evidently the post-church crowd had given way to the football crowd. Several clusters of people occupied tables around the three televisions mounted on the walls. He spotted Hugh McGowan nursing a pint with Stephen Ramsay, a sheep farmer who leased grazing rights from Ardinmuir. Theo Gordan stood chatting at the bar with Pippa Wallace. A half-dozen people lifted their hands in a wave and called out a greeting to him by name.

The welcome warmed a little of the cold that had lodged in his chest since last night. He'd found—or made—a place for himself here. People were starting to recognize and accept him. That meant something.

But it didn't stop the gut-level disquiet at the idea that he could just as easily lose it if Kyla chose David. But would he lose it? He hadn't met all of these people through her. Quite a few of them were his own tenants. It wasn't as if they had to choose sides in the divorce.

Positive thinking, Beaumont. You don't even know that there's gonna be a divorce.

Evidently, his inner pep talk didn't do much.

Behind the bar, Ewan eyed him. "You look like shite."

Raleigh shot a bland stare at the former Royal Marine. "The military taught you such excellent manners."

"They didn't pay me to be charmin'. Whisky or beer?"

"Beer. And can I put in an order for fish and chips?"

"Aye." He called the order back to the kitchen and filled a glass with Deuchars IPA.

From across the pub, Toby waved. "Oy! Raleigh! Come over. I've someone I want you to meet."

Scooping up his pint, he wandered over.

"Raleigh, this is Lochlan Reid. I've just been telling him you're a man of horses." Toby jerked a thumb in Raleigh's direction. "Made Afton's Titania fall right in love with him, and you know what a moody thing she is."

"She just wants to be made to feel special. Same as any woman."

Lochlan grinned. "This is why you're married, and Toby here is perpetually single. Good to meet you."

Raleigh shook the other man's hand. "And you. So, you're a fellow horseman?"

"Well, not exactly. I'm looking to acquire some. But as I've never owned any before, I don't quite know what I'm getting into or what I should look for."

Toby gestured toward Raleigh with his own pint. "I figured you'd be the one who could keep him from making a horrible mistake."

"I can certainly give some advice. Tell me about what you're looking for."

As Toby set up a game of darts, they found a table and settled in. Raleigh drank his beer and listened. It was nice to lose himself for a while in discussion of one of his favorite subjects.

"I think, before you go off meeting with any prospective sellers, it'd be good to hit up an auction or two. Get a clearer lay of the land and what's on offer, what prices different animals are going for. I'd be happy to go with you to some."

Lochlan brightened. "Really?"

"I love a good livestock auction."

"That'd be great."

"I can look into it. See what's coming up within an easy drive. We'll find a day that works for us both." And hell, maybe he'd find a few more for his own stable. Or maybe he'd find an appropriate candidate to sire a foal with Titania. It wouldn't make up for losing Zodiac, but he had to move on sometime.

They were exchanging contact information when the door to the pub crashed open. The entire place went suddenly silent, and all eyes turned to the entrance. Connor raced in, white-faced.

Raleigh was on his feet, headed over before his brother-in-law spotted him.

"Thank Christ. Charlotte thought you were here."

Something was wrong. Very, very wrong. "What is it? What happened? Is it Angus?"

"No. It's Kyla. There's been an accident."

The words sucker punched Raleigh hard enough that it took him a moment to draw enough breath to speak. "An accident? What? Where is she?"

"Hospital. Come on. We have to get to Edinburgh."

He stumbled. "Edinburgh?"

"Aye. It happened on the A90, just outside the city."

Raleigh didn't hear anything else for the roaring in his head. He was dimly aware of Ewan shouting that he'd cover the tab. To just go. Connor dragged him from the building toward the waiting Land Rover. And as he got in the passenger seat to go to his wife, his heart cracked clean in two. Because underneath his desperate worry about the woman he loved was the answer he'd dreaded.

She'd chosen his rival.

Two hospitals in as many months. And this time, Raleigh wasn't here to support somebody else. The woman he loved was fighting for her life, in God knew what kind of shape, and he could do nothing.

Because Hamish was local, they'd sent him ahead to find out what he could. It wasn't much. All he'd been able to tell them was that Kyla was in surgery and what floor they should report to on their arrival.

On the entire elevator ride up, Raleigh flexed his hands, needing to move, to do, to act. As soon as the doors slid open, he and Connor spilled off, skirting around an older woman like a couple of border collies on a mission. Following the directions they'd been given, they found the waiting area.

Hamish shot to his feet. "You made it."

Raleigh scrutinized his face, analyzing it for the dread or careful neutrality that signified the worst news. "Has there been any word?"

"No. But it should be soon. How are you holding up?"

How could he even answer that without knowing what state Kyla was in? All he knew was that she'd been coming here to choose someone else. He'd just spent the past several hours wrestling with the idea that he could lose her in a way he hadn't considered before. Death was infinitely worse than divorce. He didn't want to conceive of a world without Kyla in it. Because his mind too readily supplied the dull tone of a flatlining heart monitor, Raleigh turned away and strode to a window to get himself under control.

Dimly, he was aware of Connor speaking behind him, asking what they knew of the accident. Raleigh couldn't think about that. Hell, he didn't want more details to flesh out the nightmare scenarios that had been cycling through his brain for the past few hours. He needed facts. He needed to see her for himself.

"Family of Kyla MacKean?"

Raleigh spun from the window, crossing the space so fast the doctor, a middle-aged man with salt and pepper hair, took a step back. "I'm her husband, Raleigh Beaumont. How is she?"

"She has a concussion, and there was some damage to her shoulder that we've repaired. She'll need some physiotherapy, but there's no reason to think she won't make a full recovery."

Full recovery.

Relief left him all but staggering. She would be fine. No lasting damage. It wouldn't be like losing his mother.

Because his knees weren't entirely steady, he gripped the back of a nearby chair. "When can we see her?"

"She's being moved to a room for recovery. It'll be awhile yet before she wakes up from the anesthesia, and she'll be pretty out of it when she does. But you can go in, one at a time. I'll have a nurse take you."

"Thank you."

As the doctor walked away, Connor muttered, "Thank Christ."

Hamish squeezed his shoulders. "She'll be up and bossing you around before you know it."

She'd be up to all kinds of changes. Because she was going to be okay. Raleigh couldn't let himself move on to the next part of that just yet. He needed to recalibrate before he could deal with the rest.

"Mr. Beaumont? I'm here to take you to your wife."

Raleigh looked to Connor. They hadn't discussed who'd go first.

Connor dropped into a chair. "Go on. I'll see her next."

Jerking a nod, Raleigh followed the nurse to Kyla's room. He braced himself before stepping inside. The slow, steady beat of a heart monitor greeted him as he opened the door, and his gut clenched. Everything smelled of antiseptic and starch. The scent of his nightmares. He pushed himself past the entryway and into the room.

Kyla lay in the bed, small and pale against the sheets, but for the livid bruising on her face and peeking out from the neck of her hospital gown. She probably had bruising along the seatbelt and wherever the airbag hit. Her shoulder was bandaged and immobilized. As he crept closer, he could see an assortment of tiny cuts on her face that had been cleaned and closed with medical glue. The God-forsaken beeping had waves of old memories threatening to drag him under. The last thing she needed was him losing his shit.

Clenching his hands, he circled to the other side of the bed, lowering himself into the lone visitor's chair and taking her uninjured hand. It felt so small and cold in his. Wanting to warm it, he folded both hands around hers.

"You scared the shit out of me." His voice came out in a croak through the tightness in his throat. "I've been making all kinds of deals with God that you just be okay. Doc tells me you will be. I'll be honest, I don't actually know what I agreed to, so the Almighty might have a hell of a tab for me to pay. But that's okay. I'll take it. I'm just glad you're gonna be alright. I really didn't need another reason to hate hospitals. I don't wanna lose anybody else in one."

But he was going to lose her, anyway. There was no avoiding that. He knew the decision hadn't been an easy one for her, and even though he hadn't been the winner, he wanted to reassure her.

"I just need you to know that it's okay. I understand. You've made your choice, and that's absolutely your right. I want you to be happy, and if he makes you happy, I won't stand in the way. I'm not gonna fight you. The fact is, I wasn't supposed to fall in love with you. This wasn't what we agreed to. Neither of us was supposed to catch feelings, so it's not on you that I did. I mean, not beyond the fact that you're amazing."

He kept his gaze on her face, looking for any flicker that what he was saying was getting through, but he saw nothing. Maybe that was for the best. He still needed to finish unburdening himself.

"I want you to know that I love you. I don't know if it would have made a difference if I'd told you that yesterday. Probably wouldn't. I didn't say it because I thought it would freak you out. It's too late now, and that's okay. I don't want you to worry yourself. You just need to put your energy and efforts toward getting better. I'll still be around. It might take me a bit to get okay with us not being married. But maybe, eventually, we can get to where we can be friends. That's what we said we'd be when we started out, anyway."

God, he was babbling. He really ought to wrap this up.

Squeezing her hand, he rose. "I'm gonna let your brother have a turn. He's worried about you. And just so you know, Angus is fine. Munro is staying with him. Between you and me, I think they're at least rekindling their friendship. Maybe something else. Not sure. You'll have to let me know as things go."

Leaning over, he pressed a kiss to her brow. Aware it would probably be the last time, he lingered several seconds, absorbing the feel of her skin, and the faint scent of her floral shampoo. "You get better now, you hear?"

He forced himself to walk out before his resolve shattered and he lowered himself to begging.

Connor shot to his feet when Raleigh came back to the waiting room. "How is she?"

"Sleeping. Go on back."

When he'd disappeared, Raleigh gave in and scrubbed both hands over his face. He just needed to hold his shit together long enough to take care of the rest of this. Then he'd go find somewhere to get blind, stinking drunk.

Hamish settled a hand on his shoulder. "Are you okay?"

"Not even a little bit. Do you know how to get in touch with David Murray?"

Hamish blinked, clearly taken aback by the question. "I do. Why?"

"Because she was coming here to see him."

"Oh." The usually eloquent lawyer had nothing else to say to that, and why should he? It was what it was.

"It's the least I can do to make sure that he's here when she wakes up. Can you get in touch with him for me?" Raleigh figured nobody could blame him for farming that call out.

"Yes, of course, but—"

He didn't want to hear whatever came after that *"but."* "There's one more thing I need you to do, as my lawyer."

"Name it."

"Start the paperwork for our divorce."

NINETEEN

An entire regiment of off-key pipers was warming up in Kyla's head. The discordant drone rang inside her skull, loud enough she wanted to whimper. But that seemed like a lot of work. What the actual fuck had she drunk last night? Had she been drinking last night? As the pain dragged her out of the oblivion of sleep, she became aware of other aches. Namely... everything. Her whole body hurt. Maybe if she rolled over, she could get more comfortable.

Moving turned out to be too much effort, but it roused her enough to notice the warm hand clasping hers.

He came. He's here. Wherever here is.

"Raleigh?" When his arms didn't come around her, she worked her eyes open. The fuzzy vision resolved itself into an unfamiliar room full of grays and whites. In the dim light, she focused on the figure by the bed.

David. Not Raleigh.

What was he doing here?

His face brightened, and he leaned closer. "You're awake. You scared everybody."

Something had clearly gone wrong. "What happened? Where is here?"

"There was an accident. You're in the hospital. You have a concussion."

An accident. She'd been on the road. Coming to see David. But she'd hadn't made it to Edinburgh. Whatever had happened was still a blank in her fuzzy mind. She turned her head, trying to look around, but didn't get far. One of her arms seemed to be immobilized. That couldn't be good.

"I got... hurt?"

He nodded, his face twisting with regret. "When I gave you the ultimatum, I never dreamed something like this would happen on the way to come to me. I'm so sorry, sweetheart."

On the way to come to me.

No, that wasn't right. Kyla shook her head and immediately regretted it. "No. No, I wasn't." It was hard freaking hard to string words together. But she had to clarify. "I was coming to break things off."

When he froze, Kyla cursed herself for her bumbled delivery. Damn it, she'd had a speech prepared before all this bullshit. Not that she could remember it now.

"You... Oh." David struggled to control his expression, and she didn't miss the hurt. "I thought I... Well, it doesn't matter what I thought."

Delivering disappointing news after a concussion should probably be illegal. "I needed to tell you in person. I owed that to you after the last two years."

"So you're... really choosing the cowboy?" He didn't manage to mask the disbelief.

"I love him. I know it doesn't make sense to you, but Raleigh and I fit." She knew she'd had a better explanation than that prepared, but she couldn't find it past the pounding in her skull. "I'm really sorry, David."

"Well, okay, that's—of course, that's not what I wanted to hear, but okay." He looked around the room at anything but her before finally rising to his feet. "I guess I'll go. I'm glad you're going to be okay."

"I'm sorry." It was inadequate to keep repeating it, but what else could she say? "Thank you for coming to check on me."

"Of course." He squeezed her hand once more. "Be well, Kyla." And without another word, he walked out.

This wasn't at all how she'd imagined this would go. She'd expected to see him, break the news, and have time to get home to surprise Raleigh before bed. What time was it, anyway? What day was it? How long had she been here? Did her family even know where she was? Did Raleigh know she'd been hurt?

The door to her room opened again.

"You're awake." Relief filled the familiar voice. Hamish. A friend, but not who she wanted to see.

"Apparently. I feel awful."

"You have a concussion, among other injuries. They had to do surgery on your shoulder, but they say you'll fully recover."

That explained why it seemed to be strapped down. "Good to know. Is there water?"

"Of course. Here." He picked up a cup with a straw and carefully maneuvered it so she could sip.

The cool water felt amazing on her parched throat.

"Was David going to the cafeteria, then?"

Kyla sank back onto her pillows, exhausted by the simple movement. "No, he was leaving for good. We're over."

"Oh, damn." Setting the water aside, Hamish scrubbed a hand over his face. "Kyla, I'm sorry. This is all my fault." His shoulders hunched up to his ears, like a schoolboy caught at mischief that had gotten out of hand, and guilt shone out of his blue eyes.

"How is this your fault?"

"You wouldn't have been dragged into this marriage pact at all if I'd kept my mouth shut."

Was he actually speaking nonsense, or was that the concussion slowing her brain? "What are you talking about?"

"I'm the one who told Afton about the loophole allowing her

to gamble the estate away. I didn't really think she'd do it. She was just so miserable, I couldn't *not* tell her."

Later, after she'd healed, Kyla would have the time and energy to process the implications of his confession. At the moment, only one part of it mattered. With her free hand, she reached for his. "Then thank you."

"What?"

"She sent me the love of my life."

Hamish stared at her. "Raleigh?"

She tried to laugh and regretted it. "Yes, Raleigh. He's perfect for me. Maybe it took me some time to get on board, but I'm in it now."

Hamish tried to blank his face, but she'd known him far too many years for him to pull it off.

"Hamish, where's Raleigh? Doesn't he know I'm here?"

"Aye, he does, but... We can talk about this when you're feeling better."

"No." His evasive behavior was setting off alarm bells, which didn't help the headache. But her injured brain struggled to put the pieces together. "Hamish, why was David here? How did he know to come here?"

"Raleigh had me call him for you. He said David was the reason you were coming to Edinburgh."

"Yes. No..." Her brain struggled to work through what Hamish had said to figure out why it wasn't right. Of course, David was the reason she was coming to Edinburgh, but only to break it off cleanly. "Not the way he thinks. Shite." Panic shot fresh energy into her limbs, and she struggled to sit up.

Hamish leaned over her, hands up like the school crossing patrol. "No, no, no. Stop. You're not in any shape to move."

"I need to talk to Raleigh." God, if he'd brought David here, he had it all wrong. She had to set him straight.

"Okay. I'll call him. Just... don't move, okay?"

Hamish pulled out his phone and dialed. She could hear

voicemail pick up immediately. "Hey Raleigh, this is Hamish. Kyla's awake and asking for you. Call me back."

"If he's got his phone off, he thinks the worst. Damn it. I should have talked to him first. I just wanted to have everything free and clear when I went to him."

Catching his cringe, she felt her stomach dip. "What is it?"

"Aye, he does think the worst. He asked me to draw up your divorce papers."

The beeping she'd been only vaguely aware of until now began going mad. She fought to sit up. "No. Hamish. You have to find him. You have to get me out of here. I have to talk to him."

The door opened, and a nurse rushed in. "What's going on here?" She glared daggers at Hamish.

"Hamish, he can't leave." She managed to jackknife into a sitting position and felt tears on her cheeks, as much from pain as panic.

"Miss, you must lie back down." The nurse began to press her back.

"No!"

"Kyla! What happened?" Connor came skidding to a stop somewhere behind the nurse.

"Find Raleigh. Both of you have to find him. He doesn't know I love him."

Connor and Hamish exchanged a look as another nurse came in with a syringe.

"Don't you fucking dare sedate me," Kyla warned.

"Then lie back and rest," the first nurse insisted.

Reluctantly, she subsided back, seeking her brother's gaze. "Please, Connor. You have to find him."

He jerked a nod. "I've got you."

———

Raleigh was still sober. That definitely wasn't his preferred state, but while there was probably somewhere in Edinburgh he could still find alcohol in the middle of the damned night on a Sunday, getting blind, stinking drunk in a town he didn't know, when he didn't have Zeke or anyone else to watch his back, would be really damned stupid. He thought about just walking, but he didn't know a damned thing about the area of the city he was in. And much as he might welcome a brawl right now as a distraction, he knew that, too, would be foolish. So he'd parked himself in a quiet, empty corner of the cafeteria to wait for morning. Once the sun was up and everything opened for the day, he'd figure out what bus, train, or car would get him back to Lochmara without seeing anybody connected to his life here.

He'd turned his phone off hours ago to avoid any well-intentioned texts from Charlotte. If losing his wife didn't count as a reason for a good brood, he didn't know what did. He knew the pain of loss. Having his mother ripped from his life by degrees far too soon had given him an up-close-and-personal tutorial. But at least she hadn't wanted to leave him. She'd held on as long as she could, fighting an unwinnable fight.

Knowing Kyla had chosen someone else was a whole new level of fresh hell. Because there was rejection bound up in the loss. And maybe that wasn't fair. He'd known going into their marriage that she had feelings for someone else. The more fool him for believing everything had changed for her, too, over the past couple of months. Maybe he'd deluded himself about the whole thing. Maybe, after losing his mom and the ranch and everything he knew, he'd just wanted to cling too hard to where he'd landed and to the woman he'd landed with. But that was doing a disservice to her. Even if Kyla didn't know or care, he owed it to himself to admit that he'd well and truly fallen for her.

Admitting he was at rock bottom—or damned close to it—was the first in what would inevitably be a long road of healing. At the moment, that was the only step he was willing to take.

The hospital PA system crackled to life. There were muffled voices and what sounded like a scuffle of some kind.

"Attention please, Raleigh Beaumont, please return to the

nurse's station on your wife's floor. Raleigh Beaumont, please return to the nurse's station on your wife's floor."

Was that... Connor?

"Sir, you can't—"

There were more sounds, as if someone was trying to take the phone away.

"For everyone else, if you see a man in a black cowboy hat anywhere in or around the hospital, stop him from leaving!"

The last word came from a distance as someone definitely yanked the phone away.

What the actual hell was going on? His first instinct was alarm before his overtired brain pointed out that if there was an actual medical problem, it wouldn't have been Connor breaking God knew how many hospital rules to try to get ahold of him. Pulling out his phone, he tried to power it back on, but apparently it had died at some point. If they'd tried to call him, he certainly wouldn't know about it.

Shoving to his feet, he headed out of the cafeteria. A janitor looked up as he hit the hallway.

"I guess that was you then, lad?"

"Seems like. Where's the nearest stairwell or elevator that'll get me upstairs?" He could probably find it, but he hadn't exactly been paying attention when he'd wandered down here.

The older man shifted his mop handle to one hand. "Oh, well, the lift is — You know what? Never mind. That sounded urgent. The stairs are down that hall, the last door on the right."

"Cheers, man."

Raleigh took off at a lope, finding the stairs with ease and pounding up them. Breathing heavily, he shoved out of the stairwell on the right floor and immediately heard the chaos. Voices were arguing. A cluster of people blocked the hall. A hospital security guard had Connor by the arm, but that didn't seem to be the center of the drama. There seemed to be some kind of standoff.

"I don't care whether it's against medical advice or not. I am not waiting around to let him leave."

The sound of Kyla's furious declaration had a knot loosening in his gut. Whatever was going on, she hadn't fallen victim to some medical emergency like an unexpected blood clot.

He picked up his pace and some of the people shifted where he could see her in a wheelchair, with a blanket across her lap.

"What the hell are you doing? You should be in bed."

She stopped fighting, her gaze snapping to his. "You're here."

"Yeah. I was in the cafeteria." As he got closer, he saw she was crying and cursed himself six ways from Sunday.

"I thought you'd left."

He'd wanted to. Had planned on it. But seeing her like this absolutely tore him up inside. "I thought you wanted me to."

She started sobbing harder. "No, you have it wrong. I should have come to you first. But I wanted to have everything free and clear, and I felt like I owed it to David to break things off in person. But I choose you. I choose us."

Raleigh dropped to his knees in front of the wheelchair, as much because they didn't want to hold him as to get closer to her. He took her hand. "Baby, if you keep crying that hard, you're gonna pop a stitch. Take a breath."

Kyla's hand tightened on his like a vise. "I love you. Please don't go."

Her words flowed into him, filling up all the places that had gone dark with grief and regret when he'd thought he'd lost her. Very gently, he laid his brow against hers, needing to hear confirmation, to make sure he wasn't dreaming. "You love me?"

She hiccuped. "It's kind of impossible not to."

His face actually hurt from the smile of relief that took over his mouth. "Thank Christ. I thought it was just me."

"Not just you. You're it for me, Raleigh Beaumont. Maybe our marriage was the biggest gamble we've ever made, but it came with the biggest reward."

"Are you filming this?" Hamish whispered.

"Of course I am. They'll want this later." Definitely Connor.

"Can you flip him off for me?" Kyla asked. "I don't have a hand free."

On a laugh, Raleigh did as his wife asked, shooting a middle finger up in his brother-in-law's direction as he leaned forward for a brief, gentle kiss.

Applause and whoops broke out all around them.

Somebody other than Kyla sniffed. "I have no idea what just happened here, but that was beautiful."

Reluctantly, Raleigh dropped back to his haunches. "Now that all that's cleared up, will you be a good little patient and go back to bed? Because I guarandamntee this is way more active than you're supposed to be with a concussion and that shoulder."

"Only if you'll stay."

He folded her hand between both of us. "Darlin', there's nowhere else I'd rather be."

Epilogue

"T-Minus one hour until guests arrive. You're on duty for distracting the birthday boy."

Kyla saluted Charlotte, relieved when her shoulder didn't twinge. She still had a few weeks of physical therapy to go, but it was well on its way back to normal. "I'm on it."

"Remember to keep him away from the windows so he doesn't see the setup."

"I promise, he won't even consider looking out the windows."

Charlotte's laughter followed her out the back door.

They'd moved back to Lochmara, now that Angus was definitively on the mend, and, as she hadn't wanted to intrude on their legitimate newlywed toes, Charlotte had moved into the other half of the staff quarters duplex while she, Raleigh, Connor, and a handful of others worked on renovating the rest of the crofters cottages on both their estates. The AirBnB venture had gone exceptionally well, dovetailing with the event planning business exactly as Raleigh had foreseen. There'd been some delays with her accident, and she and Sophie had been forced to take on some paid help earlier than intended, but they were still on track to probably be able to make that balloon payment next January. She'd finally reached a stage where she wasn't actively worried about it all the time. With Raleigh and the rest of their family by their side, they'd find a way to make it.

Life was, in a word, pretty damned perfect, and tonight was a celebration of that for Raleigh's birthday.

He just didn't know it yet.

As she headed out to the barn, Mabel trotted up to the fence for loving. At four months old, she was already over two hundred pounds, but she was still as much of a fuzzy love bug as ever. Kyla slipped through the rails of the fence to give her a good rub over-all, making her low and wriggle in ecstasy. She still stuck her tongue out when she was happy, a fact which never stopped making Kyla laugh.

"Okay, sweet bairn, that's got to do for now. I've got to go see your da." With a final scratch, Kyla slipped back through the fence and went in search of her other half.

She found him in conversation with Malcolm in the barn. "Can I steal my husband away?"

Malcolm, who looked profoundly annoyed, gave a definitive nod. "Please, take him away."

She wasn't sure how much of his attitude was an act and how much was legitimate. He and Raleigh were still finding their footing with each other. Now that Raleigh had been here long enough to see how things were done, he'd moved into the realm of making some decisions about some areas of the estate. Malcolm wasn't exactly keen on change.

Raleigh wrapped an arm around her, tugging her into his side as Malcolm strode away. "What can I do for you, darlin'?"

"I need you to come with me."

She dragged him back to the house and up to their bedroom, closing and locking the door behind them.

Raleigh went brows up. "What's all this?"

"A birthday surprise." She stepped into him, running her hands up his chest.

He grinned, flashing those dimples she loved so much. "Oh?"

"I mean, you would have gotten this surprise this morning, but you were up and out before I managed to wake up."

His hands curved around her hips. "The life of a farmer means rarely sleeping in."

"Well, the life of this farmer is going to make room for a little afternoon delight." She ran a finger inside the waistband of his jeans, feeling his abs contract at the contact.

Her assignment was to distract him, and this was absolutely her favorite way to do it. Fingers working at his shirt buttons, she began to back him toward the bed. "There's just one more thing I wanted to give you."

"Does it involve you wearing my cowboy hat and nothing else?"

Intrigued, and more than a little turned on by the idea, she grinned. "No, but that would make a nice addendum." She paused to pull a hard plastic case out of her back pocket and handed it over.

His brows drew together in confusion. "What is this?"

"Open it."

He cracked it open to reveal the blister pack with her next month of birth control inside. "I'm not sure I get it."

"One of the things that's most important to both of us is family, and I wanted to give you the option to say if you're maybe ready to start one." More than a little nervous when his expression didn't change, she rushed on to the rest. "If you're not, I can go ahead and take it on my regular schedule. But if you are..." she trailed off, wondering if this was a big mistake. Maybe it was too soon.

Raleigh cupped her cheek, tipping her face back up to his. Those golden eyes were soft. "You want to make a family with me?"

"I mean, I know we haven't talked about it, and we've basically done everything backward with our relationship, but... yes. If that's something you want."

He tossed the case over his shoulder and brought his other hand up to frame her face. "Hell yes."

Then his mouth was on hers with a fresh urgency that lit a fire in her blood. She forgot about her mission, about distraction, about everything but him as they stripped each other, kissing, touching, taking. He tumbled her onto the bed, and they rolled, a tangle of naked limbs, fighting to get closer. Then she was sinking down, taking him inside in one slow slide that left her gasping.

"Jesus, how does it get better and better every time?"

"Practice makes... perfect?" Hands gripping her hips, he bucked into her to emphasize the point and hit a delicious pleasure point that had her rocking to find it again.

"Mmm, does this feel different to you?"

"I don't know. Maybe. I really like the idea of making a baby with you. It's like this extra level of turn-on."

"Not just me, then. Thank God." She bent to take his mouth in a long, delicious kiss as she rode him right to the edge of oblivion.

But even as her inner muscles began to quake, he rolled her beneath him, driving deeper. Her orgasm struck like a tsunami, and she wrapped around him, glorying in the feel of his release spilling inside her.

Holy shit.

Raleigh slumped over her, careful to brace enough of his weight on his arms that he didn't crush her. He nuzzled her throat. "So, does this new situation mean I don't have to clean up just yet?"

Kyla hummed with pleasure as aftershocks continued to flutter. "Don't move on my account. You're exactly where I want you." She squeezed her inner muscles and felt his cock twitch.

He laughed and nipped her throat. "Minx."

Drowsy and happy, she traced nonsense shapes on the back of his shoulder. From the reports of other friends, she knew it would probably take a while before a pregnancy actually happened. If conceptual sex was always this good, she was perfectly okay with that. A hundred or so orgasms in pursuit of procreation seemed like a super reasonable price to pay for starting a family.

From somewhere outside came the sound of car doors, reminding Kyla of her whole purpose in distracting him.

Raleigh pushed himself up. "What's that?"

Locking her legs around his waist, she kept him from leaving the bed. "Nothing you need to concern yourself with."

"If somebody's here, I should probably go see about it."

"No, you shouldn't."

When he just stared down at her, one brow arched in expectation, she groaned. "Okay, I had an ulterior motive for dragging you up here."

"You mean apart from getting me naked?"

"Yeah. Apart from that." Kyla bit her lip, wondering how much to say.

His own mouth flattened. "There's a party, isn't there?"

"Don't get mad. Charlotte and I wanted to do something special for your birthday. I'm telling you now because I know you hate surprises. Or at least the crowds. It's not going to be a huge crowd. It's just family and friends."

On a sigh, he settled back over her. "Okay, fine. Should I still act surprised?"

"Yes. Please still act surprised when we go downstairs."

"When are we expected downstairs?"

Twisting her neck, she glanced at the clock. "Not for another half hour."

"Well, in that case, I think we have time for my version of my birthday surprise."

By the time they surfaced again, Kyla had an entirely new appreciation for Raleigh's hat, and they were officially past the party hour.

"We're going to be late to your party."

He tweaked her bare butt. "I'm not supposed to know there is a party, and I say it's well worth it."

"I cannot disagree."

After taking the world's fastest shower, they headed downstairs and outside to where the party had been set up in the formal garden.

A roar of "Surprise!" greeted them as they stepped into the torchlight.

Raleigh took a step back, evidently not having to fake it when their guests stepped forward with applause. Seeing all of them in one place, Kyla considered that maybe it was a bigger group than he'd imagined when she'd told him family and friends. But he'd made a lot of friends over the past few months, and they'd all wanted to celebrate his birthday.

The two of them made the rounds so he could shake hands and accept hugs. Hugh and Flora McGowan. Connor and Sophie. Toby Byrne. Lochlan Reid. Charlotte, of course. Hamish had come up from Edinburgh. Angus and Munro were manning the cake table and the glorious confection of sugar that Angus had made for a birthday cake. Ewan was passing out beers. Pippa Wallace. Behind her was the biggest surprise.

"Zeke!" Raleigh tugged his laughing friend in for a back-slapping hug. "I can't believe you're here!"

Zeke grinned and squeezed Raleigh's shoulder. "Couldn't miss it."

Somebody turned on the music. As he continued to greet the rest of their guests, most of whom were other tenants, she began looking around for Malcolm. He was supposed to be here.

She spotted his tall figure striding away in the shadows, toward his house. Here for the surprise; gone for the party.

Kyla knew this whole thing had to be hard on him. In many ways, this was a subtle acknowledgment that Afton wasn't coming back. None of them had heard from her since her precipitous trip to Vegas. She hadn't even contacted Raleigh to have him send her things. Afton had been something of a surrogate daughter to Malcolm, so her disappearance and lack of contact had to hurt him. He needed time to come to terms with the whole thing, whatever that looked like.

She'd leave him to his brood. She certainly wasn't the one who could heal all those emotional wounds. For her part, tonight was for celebration with the love of her life.

At a piercing whistle, she turned to see Raleigh waving her over. "C'mon, Red. I wanna dance with my wife."

———

The moment consciousness began filtering into Malcolm's brain, he regretted his life choices. His head ached as if someone were playing it like a bodhran drum. Each pulse of pain echoed through his body with terrible familiarity, though it had been twenty years since he'd allowed himself to get this blootered. How much whisky had he put away?

Cracking open his eyes, he made a noise akin to a dying cow at the pain lancing through his eyes.

Definitely regretting life choices.

There was nothing for it but to drag his arse out of bed for an ocean of water and some painkillers.

Feeling fragile as glass, he slowly pushed himself vertical, riding out the storm of vertigo that accompanied the motion. His feet and chest were bare, but he still wore his kilt. Evidently, he'd passed out before managing to undress completely. Shoving to his feet, he cursed every one of his fifty years and stumbled across the hardwood floor to the bathroom.

After emptying his bladder, he fumbled a bottle of aspirin out of the medicine cabinet and shook three into his palm, washing them down with water from the sink. The single swallow made him realize exactly how parched he was, so he bent to drink more straight from the tap. That simple change in altitude made him whimper but didn't stop him from gulping until his throat no longer burned.

Straightening, he gripped the edges of the sink until the room stopped spinning. The man in the mirror was an unwelcome sight. His graying hair stood up at all angles and his eyes were a bloodshot mess. This had once been his everyday. His answer to a grief he hadn't known how to handle. Until Peter Lennox had dragged him out of the bottle and made him an offer he hadn't been able to refuse.

Malcolm hadn't fallen back into that bottle in all this time. Not until last night. But he thought his old friend would grant him some leniency considering it had been the anniversary of the worst day of his life and, for the first time in years, Afton hadn't been here to distract him.

Whisky had seemed an excellent idea in the face of everyone else's revelry for Raleigh's birthday. It was hardly the Yank's fault that his birthday was so ill-timed, but nobody could've expected him to celebrate.

A dim memory of tequila shots swam into his muzzy brain. Which made no sense. Malcolm didn't actually like tequila. He didn't even remember buying any. But if he'd poured that on top of the whisky, it would explain the current state of his head.

He needed food, the greasier the better. Maybe he had the ingredients for a full fry up in the fridge.

Opening the door to the bedroom, his gaze fell on the rumpled bed, and he stopped cold. Because his bed wasn't empty.

As he watched, the tiny lump of a person beneath the covers rolled over and opened long-lashed eyes of the exact shade of the coffee he desperately wanted.

Charlotte's gaze zeroed in on him, and that sassy mouth that drove him nuts curved into a sleepy smile. "Morning."

Oh fuck. What have I done?

Get your Bonus Epilogue

Need another hit of Raleigh and Kyla's happily ever after? I've got you, boo! Get your bonus epilogue here: https://kaitnolan.com/bonus-epilogue-cowboy-in-a-kilt/

CHOOSE YOUR NEXT ROMANCE

Next up in the Kilted Hearts series is, *Grump in a Kilt,* in which Malcolm and Charlotte, his sunshiny nemesis, join forces to give a runaway a home and just might fight a new family along the way.

Meanwhile, if you're looking for more grumpy soft for sunshine romance to tide you over, check out *Someone Like You,* the first book in the Rescue My Heart series. This trilogy is all about a trio of former Army Ranger finding their way in civilian life and falling in love along the way. This first one features a runaway author, an accident-causing bear, and forced proximity because of a Tennessee blizzard. You don't want to miss it.

Other Books By Kait Nolan

A complete and up-to-date list of all my books can be found at https://kaitnolan.com.

Kilted Hearts
Small Town Contemporary Scottish Romance

- *Jilting The Kilt* (prequel)
- *Cowboy in a Kilt* (Raleigh and Kyla): January 13
- *Grump in a Kilt* (Malcolm and Charlotte): March 10
- *Playboy in a Kilt* (Connor and Sophie): June
- *Protector in a Kilt* (Ewan and Isobel): August
- *Single Dad in a Kilt* (Hamish and Afton): October

Bad Boy Bakers
Small Town Military Romance

- *Rescued By a Bad Boy* (Brax and Mia prequel)
- *Mixed Up With a Marine* (Brax and Mia)
- *Wrapped Up with a Ranger* (Holt and Cayla)
- *Stirred Up by a SEAL* (Jonah and Rachel)
- *Hung Up on the Hacker* (Cash and Hadley)

- *Caught Up with the Captain* (Grey and Rebecca)

RESCUE MY HEART SERIES
SMALL TOWN MILITARY ROMANCE

- *Baby It's Cold Outside* (Ivy and Harrison)
- *What I Like About You* (Laurel and Sebastian)
- *Bad Case of Loving You* (Paisley and Ty prequel)
- *Made For Loving You* (Paisley and Ty)

THE MISFIT INN SERIES
SMALL TOWN FAMILY ROMANCE

- *When You Got A Good Thing* (Kennedy and Xander)
- *Til There Was You* (Misty and Denver)
- *Those Sweet Words* (Pru and Flynn)
- *Stay A Little Longer* (Athena and Logan)
- *Bring It On Home* (Maggie and Porter)

MEN OF THE MISFIT INN
SMALL TOWN SOUTHERN ROMANCE

- *Let It Be Me* (Emerson and Caleb)
- *Our Kind of Love* (Abbey and Kyle)
- *Don't You Wanna Stay* (Deanna and Wyatt)
- *Until We Meet Again* (Samantha and Griffin prequel)
- *Come A Little Closer* (Samantha and Griffin)

WISHFUL ROMANCE SERIES
SMALL TOWN SOUTHERN ROMANCE

- *Once Upon A Coffee* (Avery and Dillon)
- *To Get Me To You* (Cam and Norah)
- *Know Me Well* (Liam and Riley)
- *Be Careful, It's My Heart* (Brody and Tyler)

- *Just For This Moment* (Myles and Piper)
- *Wish I Might* (Reed and Cecily)
- *Turn My World Around* (Tucker and Corinne)
- *Dance Me A Dream* (Jace and Tara)
- *See You Again* (Trey and Sandy)
- *The Christmas Fountain* (Chad and Mary Alice)
- *You Were Meant For Me* (Mitch and Tess)
- *A Lot Like Christmas* (Ryan and Hannah)
- *Dancing Away With My Heart* (Zach and Lexi)

WISHING FOR A HERO SERIES (A WISHFUL SPINOFF SERIES)
SMALL TOWN ROMANTIC SUSPENSE

- *Make You Feel My Love* (Judd and Autumn)
- *Watch Over Me* (Nash and Rowan)
- *Can't Take My Eyes Off You* (Ethan and Miranda)
- *Burn For You* (Sean and Delaney)

MEET CUTE ROMANCE
SMALL TOWN SHORT ROMANCE

- *Once Upon A Snow Day*
- *Once Upon A New Year's Eve*
- *Once Upon An Heirloom*
- *Once Upon A Coffee*
- *Once Upon A Campfire*
- *Once Upon A Rescue*

SUMMER CAMP
CONTEMPORARY ROMANCE

- *Once Upon A Campfire*
- *Second Chance Summer*

ABOUT KAIT

Kait is a Mississippi native, who often swears like a sailor, calls everyone sugar, honey, or darlin', and can wield a bless your heart like a saber or a Snuggie, depending on requirements.

You can find more information on this *USA Today* best selling and RITA ® Award-winning author and her books on her website http://kaitnolan.com.

Do you need more small town sass and spark? Sign up for <u>her newsletter</u> to hear about new releases, book deals, and exclusive content!

www.ingramcontent.com/pod-product-compliance
Lightning Source LLC
Chambersburg PA
CBHW070530100726
47907CB00004B/1057